STAKEOUT ON WILTSHIRE

Carr ducked below window level. Someone walked along the side of the house, turned right and continued toward the rear entrance. There was the sound of the sliding glass door opening.

"Police!" Bailey yelled. An explosion.

Carr ran toward the living room. There was another reverberating blast. As he entered the hallway, he saw Kelly slumped at the entrance to the living room. He was holding his chest. Carr stepped over him. Holding his revolver with both hands, he sprang into the living room.

Travis Bailey stood behind the bar aiming the shotgun at a bearded man lying in the middle of the room in a puddle of water, broken glass and flopping tropical fish. The man's left arm and half of his head were gone. The body convulsed. Pointing the weapon at the intruder, Bailey racked another round into the chamber of the shotgun . . .

Other Pinnacle Books by Gerald Petievich

MONEY MEN
ONE-SHOT DEAL

GERALD PETIEVICH

PINNACLE BOOKS

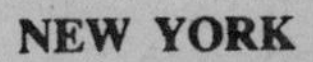

This is a work of fiction. Any similarity to persons living or dead is purely coincidental. Although there is, of course, a real Beverly Hills Police Department, I wish to make clear that no character in this book is intended to portray, in whole or in part, any member of that organization.

TO DIE IN BEVERLY HILLS

A Pinnacle Books edition, published by special arrangement with Arbor House Publishing Company.

First printing/May 1984

ISBN: 0-523-42224-5

Can. ISBN: 0-523-43214-3

Cover illustration by Paul Stinson

Printed in the United States of America

PINNACLE BOOKS, INC.
1430 Broadway
New York, New York 10018

9 8 7 6 5 4 3 2 1

For My Mother and Father

Chapter 1

THE BULLETIN board in the Detective Bureau was covered with a clear-plastic burglary occurrence chart dotted with red stickpins. Because Beverly Hills was a rich man's city, burglary was the only crime with enough weekly activity to be charted.

Detective Travis Bailey was alone in the handsomely carpeted third-floor office. Rather than the dank, coffee-stained bull pens typically found in big-city police departments, the office was spacious and clean with colorful desk partitions. Rather than brownstone tenements, the window view was of a business district made up of shops that sold ostrich leather shoes, gold toothpicks, furs. Instead of an electric fan wafting stale cigarette and cigar smoke, the bureau was equipped with a *modus operandi* computer that had been the subject of an article in a police journal, and a bank of modern-looking interview rooms furnished with two-way mirrors and upholstered chairs.

On Bailey's desk was an empty "in" basket and a message nail piercing a four-inch stack of dated telephone messages. The corners of the stack were squared and each message in the pile bore Bailey's customary red-ink check mark. He slowly opened the desk drawer to avoid disrupting the pencils and other office supplies he kept carefully arranged and took out a perfectly sharpened number-two pencil. He spent some time doodling the name Lee on a pad, then tore the sheet of paper off the pad, wadded it up and tossed it in the wastebasket.

The phone rang. He picked up the receiver. "Detectives. Bailey," he said.

"I'm at a pay phone," Emil Kreuzer said with slightly less of the German accent he affected in his nightclub hypnosis act. "We can talk."

"Was it there?" Bailey said.

"You were right," Kreuzer said. "It's there. The art gallery man has it in his back room. Lee dealt behind our backs. He fucked us. God knows, this isn't the first time. He's probably hit us for something or another on every score. I told you I never liked him. The man is a weasel, a rotten fucking weasel. He stabbed us in the back."

"You've actually seen the item?" Travis Bailey said.

"Do you think I'd tell you something like this if I wasn't sure?" Kreuzer said. "I'm telling you that the same Picasso ink drawing that I saw hanging in the man's living room last week, the same one I noted on my little diagram, is right at this very moment hanging in the back room at the art gallery. The gallery man trusts me because of all the business I bring him, so he even told me what he paid for it. Fifteen thousand. He said it's worth eighty in Europe."

"How do we know that the owner didn't rush down and peddle it five minutes after he saw that his house had been hit?" Bailey interrupted. "Everybody in this town knows how to play the collect-double-on-the-insurance game."

"You didn't let me finish," Kreuzer said impatient! "I conned the gallery man into telling me who brough. in. I told him that I had part of the action on the score. You know what he said to me? He said, 'That's between you and Lee.' We've been fucked. Let there be no doubt."

Bailey glanced at the door again. He was still alone in the office. "I don't like you to call me here," he said.

"I thought this was something you'd want to know immediately."

Bailey bit his lip as he thought about what Kreuzer had told him.

"What are you going to do?" Kreuzer asked after a moment of silence.

"I'll take care of the problem."

"I'm behind you however you decide to handle it," Kreuzer said. "I want you to know that."

Travis Bailey set the receiver down. Having pulled a tissue and a bottle of window cleaner out of a drawer, he carefully cleaned the glass covering the top of his desk. He tossed the soiled tissue into the wastebasket and returned the bottle to its proper place. He stood up and shrugged on a black-and-white houndstooth sport coat and adjusted the crotch of his custom-made trousers.

The telephone rang again.

"Detectives. Bailey."

"This is Jerome Hartmann," said a man with a mellifluous voice. "My home is on Beverly Glen Drive. I'm leaving town for a two-week vacation and I'd like to have someone from the Department stop by before I leave. I'm a little worried about leaving my home unguarded at the present time."

"Are you the Hartmann that is the bank president?" Bailey said.

There was the sound of ice tinkling in a glass. "Yes," Hartmann said, "I take it you recognize my name from the article in today's paper?"

"Yes, sir, I do," Bailey said. "I'm free this morning if you'd like to get together." Bailey used a sharpened pencil to take down Hartmann's address. He hung up the phone. There was a *Los Angeles Times* on top of a filing cabinet. He turned to the second-page article he'd scanned earlier that morning.

> Los Angeles, July 30—Assistant United States Attorney Reba Partch announced today that she plans to call Jerome Hartmann, president of the Beverly Hills Branch of the Bank of Commerce-Pacific, to testify as a witness against reputed Mafia figure Anthony Dio and three accomplices who allegedly conspired to force Hartmann to substitute counterfeit money for money held in the bank's vault.
>
> The scheme, which was aided by a bank teller supposedly enlisted by Dio, was thwarted by Hartmann when he reported the incident to U.S. Treasury Agents. At their request, he agreed to wear a recording device when he met Dio's men at a later meeting.
>
> "The government plans to show an organized crime conspiracy attempting to defraud the bank of millions of dollars by the use of extortion and counterfeiting," Partch said.

Having read the article, Bailey tossed the newspaper back on the cabinet and proceeded to the men's room. He washed his hands thoroughly with soap and water and ran a comb through his hair. Standing in front of the mirror, he fiddled his silk necktie into place and brushed off his sport coat. Knowing he looked his best, he posed his right profile. He knew that his clean features, parted dark hair and powerful jawline (which he considered to be his best feature) gave him the look of the archetypical young screen detective. Why not dress the part?

Before leaving, Bailey stuck his head in Captain Cleaver's office. Cleaver, a bald, well-fed man with a cocoa tan nourished by year-round weekend visits to his Palm Springs condominium, looked up from a copy of the *Wall Street Journal*. He arched his eyebrows.

"Heard anything?" Bailey said in a tone of deference.

Cleaver's eyes returned to the newspaper. "Delsey Piper can start in the Detective Bureau next Monday," he said without expression. "The Chief bought the undercover angle . . . says he likes the idea of having a female detective. After I walked out of his office he called up that woman on the City Council and told her it was *his* idea to bring the first woman into the Detective Bureau. His secretary told me."

"You won't be sorry, Cap," Bailey said. "With a woman working undercover we'll be able to make some heavy cases. Burglars and receivers are wise to the undercover bit, but not with a woman. I guarantee lots of stolen-property recoveries."

Cleaver turned a newspaper page. "There'd *better* be a lot of recoveries," he said without looking up. "Every officer in this department is going to be pissed off at a female with barely a year's experience in a radio car being promoted to detective. I'm not looking forward to all the moaning and bitching I'm going to have to take over this. I expect you to make sure she doesn't fall flat on her ass," he said, glancing pointedly at Bailey. "I don't need any Dickless Tracy problems."

"I'll keep her under my wing," Bailey said. "I guarantee lots of recoveries." He winked.

Cleaver grinned sardonically. "Now that you mention it, it *is* a real shame to see the insurance companies having trouble using up their stolen-property-reward funds."

The men smiled at one another. Travis Bailey turned and headed for the doorway.

"Are you balling her?" Cleaver asked.

Bailey stopped just outside his office. "No, I'm not," he lied.

As Travis Bailey climbed into his unmarked sedan in the police parking lot, a Rolls-Royce sped by at at least seventy miles per hour. Speed was a privilege of the residents of Beverly Hills. "Don't write tickets for people who live in this town," a veteran patrolman told him twelve years ago when he first reported for duty, "and call the Chief at home, even if it's in the middle of the night, before you arrest one of these rich motherfuckers. Arresting anyone in this town except a burglar is the quickest way to end up with a career in the property room. Unless you get a charge out of stacking evidence in the basement eight hours a day for the rest of your career, go along with the program."

The advice had served him well; three years in a radio car and he went straight to Detectives. He chalked up his rapid promotion to the fact that he had realized early on that the name of the game was informants. One good snitch solved burglaries that a thousand fingerprint-and-photo men could spend the rest of their lives investigating.

Bailey started the engine and drove out of the parking

lot. Almost by rote he made right turns through the glittery business district to avoid the usual traffic tie-ups. Hell, after more than ten years in the Department he could draw a map of the city blindfolded. As a matter of fact, he'd cinched his promotion to detective II by submitting a paper called "The Geography of Burglary Patterns in the City of Beverly Hills" to the easily snowable Chief of Police. In it he espoused his "funnel theory" and documented it with lots of criminology jargon and some aerial photos he'd borrowed from the Sheriff's Helicopter Unit. The theory went like this: Since the city was shaped like a funnel, with residential areas nestled against the foothills at the northern-most boundary (the rim of the funnel was the golf course), the majority of radio-car patrol services should be concentrated there rather than on the relatively burglary-free areas in the south, which formed the spout of the funnel. Or something like that.

He drove out of the business district and onto a busy thoroughfare, passing a line of medium-sized office buildings that he knew were bursting with lawyers' offices. Minutes later, he stopped at a red light that marked the city limits.

Across the street, where West Los Angeles began, was a brick building with brass letters above the front door reading Pascoe Military Academy. Centered in the square of lawn in front of the building, a bird-stained statue of a cadet saluted the boulevard. Adjoining the academy was an asphalt-covered playground surrounded by chain link fence. In the playground a group of boys wearing starched olive drab uniforms, red epaulets and garrison caps stood in military formation. A similarly costumed man with a white-sidewall haircut stood on a small platform in front of them. Bailey had attended the academy from age twelve to sixteen and knew that the man was the commandant and was probably announcing the orders of the day.

Next to the academy playground was the grounds of a pet cemetery marked by a perimeter of tall Italian cypress bushes. It was there, after taps and on weekends, that the upperclassmen initiated the younger cadets to snipe hunts, sodomy, jack-off contests and the technique of holding one's breath until one passed out; kiddie-soldier play.

Having checked for cross-traffic, he drove through the red light. After a block or so, he turned north on a street that returned him to the boundaries of The City. Slowly, he wound through wide palm-lined streets of imposing homes (realtors said there was no lot in The City valued under a million dollars) in various conservative styles. Though no two residences were identical, there were few without multicar garages, abundant flowers and greenery. Tennis courts (by unwritten law) were not visible from the street. The wide streets, sidewalks and driveways were remarkably free of stains as well as any hint of trash or other detritus.

The only vehicles parked on the street belonged to caterers and gardeners; those in service to the movie stars, kingpins, chairmans of the board, directors, producers and socialites who were residents of The City.

Finally, he reached Sunset Boulevard, turned left and drove past a bus bench. A pudgy, middle-aged blonde woman sitting on the bench reminded him of his deceased mother. Perhaps, he thought to himself, it was just her maid's uniform. Or maybe it was the uniform along with the frizzy, peroxided hair. He remembered how the vice-president-in-charge-of-production who had employed her always paid her with a studio expense check in order to beat the I.R.S. In the city, everything was a write-off.

Travis Bailey kept his eyes on the painted curb signs until he found the house he was looking for. He swerved right and followed a semicircular driveway to the front of an immaculate Tudor-style mansion. He parked, then slipped a comb from his shirt pocket and ran it through his hair before he climbed out of his car and headed for the front door. Cautiously, he used the lion's head doorknocker. A lean, middle-aged man wearing a gray blazer that matched the color of his hair opened the door. He held a drink in a slim glass.

Travis Bailey showed his badge.

"Won't you come in?" Jerome Hartmann said after the two men shook hands.

He followed Hartmann along a hallway past a darkened study and into a spacious living room decorated with abstract oil paintings and tapestries. The wall facing the rear of the house was a bank of sliding glass doors leading to a grotto-style pool. An aquarium filled the wall between the sliding glass door and the hallway. Facing it across an expanse of brown shag carpeting that matched the grotto masonry was a diminutive polished-wood bar arrangement.

Bailey took a seat on a sofa.

Hartmann sat down in an uncomfortable-looking chair. He caught himself sipping his drink and, perfunctorily, offered one to Bailey. As expected, Bailey refused. "I take it you're aware of this counterfeiting case I'm involved in," Hartmann said.

"Just what I've read in the newspapers."

"Then I'm sure you understand why I'm a little apprehensive about going away for two weeks. My help is on vacation, so no one will be here, I don't even own a dog. I'm worried about someone planting a bomb in my house while I'm gone. This probably sounds a little silly to you." He sipped his drink.

"Not at all, sir," Bailey said. "But hasn't the federal government offered you protection as a witness?"

"Yes, they have," he said, "but it's too complicated. I don't want people hanging around me all day. I'd just appreciate some special consideration by the Department while I'm gone. If you could just have one of the patrol officers stop by and check things out once or twice a day at their convenience . . ."

"No problem, Mr. Hartmann, I'll get the word out to the area car," Bailey said. "And as a matter of fact, I'll stop by myself now and then just to check things out." Bailey made a policeman's courtesy-wink.

"It'll sure help my peace of mind," Hartmann said. "Who's handling the Treasury case?"

"Agent Carr. Charles Carr."

"I've met him."

"Small world," Hartmann said without interest. He gave a banker's terse smile that meant that the meeting was over.

Bailey stood up and shook hands again with Hartmann before he left.

In the unmarked car, he wound south through familiar streets. As usual, things were quiet. Now and then a Mercedes-Benz or a Cadillac slithered out of a driveway. There was the usual number of well-attired joggers running about, a few servants carrying things in and out of homes, a caterer looking for an address.

As he drove, Travis Bailey sorted things out in his mind. As he recently lectured at a Police Management Seminar, the objective of police planning was to set priorities on problems, define challenges and make sound and permanent decisions. After cruising about for what must have been an hour, he decided to give the good news to Delsey Piper. Why not pick the most pleasant task first? Begin what was sure to be stress-causing with something stress-relieving? He reached for the radio microphone. "David Fourteen," he said in a radio voice. "Have David Niner meet me at the golf course to take a theft report."

"Roger, David Fourteen.'

By the time he arrived at their usual meeting spot, a deserted cluster of trees at the northern edge of the Beverly Hills Golf Course, Delsey Piper was already there. Her black-and-white was parked under a tree next to a high fence. Dressed in full uniform, she was perched on a front fender. Holding a little mirror, she was brushing her short blonde hair when he parked his car and climbed out.

"A theft report?" she said, amused. "What'll you think of next?"

"You start in the Detective Bureau next Monday," he told her, taking in a view of the golf course stretching below him. Here he was at the top of the city.

She squealed and jumped off the fender. Her uniform equipment rattled. "No lie?"

"No lie," he said. "Cleaver got the okay from the Chief today."

"Hooray!" she said, jumping up and down. "No more chickenshit parking tickets! No more traffic accident reports! *Ultra*bitchin'! Dynamite!" She continued to bounce up and down like a cheerleader.

Travis Bailey stared with an amused smile at her reaction. He reminded himself that she was only twenty-two years old. He grabbed her Sam Browne belt and pulled her to him. She was still giggling as their mouths met. As they kissed, he found the zippered fly on her uniform trousers and pulled it down.

"What if somebody comes up here?' she said.

"Then they'll find a policewoman getting fucked doggie style," he whispered. He unfastened her belt buckle. The belt, with its heavy equipment, dropped to the ground. He tugged on her trousers, then panties.

"You're so *gross*," she said, kicking off her trousers.

He spun her ample hips around and pushed her against the police car.

L.A.'s permanent layer of smog was hidden by darkness.

Looking through binoculars, Charles Carr stood at the window inside a dark and bare-floored apartment. He knew that the black woman standing inside the bay-windowed apartment across the courtyard couldn't see him. In his line of work, he mused, invisibility was an ideal condition. His feet certainly didn't feel invisible. They were tired to the point of numbness. The stakeout was in its tenth hour.

A fit man, Carr was dressed in a short-sleeved white shirt, off-the-rack trousers and wing-tip shoes; attire that was neither fashionable nor particularly becoming, but served the Treasury Agent's Manual of Operations requirement "to be dressed in business attire at all times while on duty except when acting in an undercover capacity." Without the weight of a gold badge, handcuffs, revolver and bullet pouch on his belt to sag his trousers, he looked like most other middle-aged men with graying temples.

In the corner of the room, Carr's partner, Jack Kelly, lay on his back on the hardwood floor. A bear-sized man with enormous ham-hock fists, he had his arms folded across his chest like a cadaver. He was snoring.

Charles Carr adjusted the binoculars to get a better view. The lanky black woman lit a marijuana cigarette and took a puff. She was dressed in a pink velour outfit two sizes too small and had a foot-high brillo pad hairdo. The woman fiddled with a stereo set. The muffled sound of rock music came from the apartment. For the next few minutes she lollygagged about the room puffing smoke, picking things up and putting them down and adjusting her frizz in a mirror over the sofa. At one point she answered her telephone and, having said a few words, hung up. Back to the mirror. More picking at her frizz.

Because of fatigue, Carr's mind wandered. He remembered being on a similar surveillance over twenty years earlier when he was a young special agent still on civil service probation status. As he'd been taught in Treasury Agent School, he had kept a surveillance log and dutifully noted everything the suspect did and the time. During the trial, he had learned that such logs were nothing more than cannon fodder for defense attorneys. "Agent Carr, your log shows a notation that the subject read the newspaper at ten fourteen P.M.," the lawyer had said. "How do you know that the suspect *read* it? Couldn't he have been just *looking* at the pictures in the paper?" From then on, he had prepared only the most concise of reports. This habit, among others, was a source of constant consternation to his superiors, few of whom he respected, either then or now.

Perhaps that was why he was still a GS-12 special agent rather than agent in charge or a squad leader, as most other agents in his peer group now were. His frequent duty transfers, rather than being part of the Treasury Enforcement Career program (the Manual of Operations used the term *career path)* resulted from his ceaseless disputes with supervisors. The agents in charge invariably handled threats of civil suits by criminal defendants and other bureaucratic headaches per the Treasury custom, by placing his name at the top of the most-eligible-for-transfer list. What the hell did he care? He was single. He had never looked at eighteen months working the streets of Miami or Detroit as a fate worse than death. The only hard part about leaving L.A. now and then was saying good-bye to his longtime girl friend, Sally Malone.

As a matter of fact, he hadn't been able to get his mind off her all day. After much musing, he had decided that the next time she brought up the subject of marriage he would not automatically shrug it off. He would not make a *commitment* (her word), he said to himself, but would try to have more of an open mind about it. God knows he was sick of restaurant food and Laundromats.

A black man carrying a briefcase approached the door of the woman's apartment. He knocked. A tall man, he wore white, skin-tight trousers and a purple long-sleeved shirt. The woman sauntered to the door and opened the peephole. She unlocked the door and let him in. Inside, the man and woman talked animatedly in front of the window.

Carr pulled a mug-shot photograph out of his back pocket. He moved to the corner of the room and pulled the penlight flashlight out of Kelly's shirt pocket. In its small beam of light Carr examined the photograph. He returned to the window. Using the binoculars again, he focused on the man's face.

"It's him," Carr said.

Kelly snored.

Carr tossed the tiny flashlight, landing it on his

partner's barrel chest. Kelly scrambled to his feet, rubbed his eyes. "What happened?" he asked in an urgent tone as he staggered to the window.

Carr adjusted the binoculars again. The black woman opened the refrigerator and removed what looked like a sack. She and the man sat down on the sofa. Because of the angle, Carr could not see what was taking place.

"She's dealing," Carr said.

Kelly snatched his suit coat of the floor and put it on. "How do you want to work it?"

"He walked in carrying a briefcase," Carr said. "It'll be loaded with fifties when he leaves. Let's grab him first."

The telephone rang. Carr reached down and picked up the receiver. "Carr," he said, keeping his eyes on the window.

"Travis Bailey here, Beverly Hills P.D. Your office gave me this number. Can you talk?"

"For a second," Carr said. He continued to watch the apartment.

"Do you have a bank president who lives in Beverly Hills that is supposed to be a major witness for you in a counterfeiting case?"

"Yes," Carr said. "His name is Hartmann."

"I have solid word that he's going to be hit. We need to talk."

"Hartmann is out of town right now," Carr said.

"I know. He's going to get hit tomorrow when he comes back. My informant is reliable."

"Can you meet me at Ling's in Chinatown in about three hours?"

"See you there," Bailey said.

Carr knelt and hung up the phone, again without taking his eyes off the window.

"Who was that?" Kelly asked.

"Bag-of-Wind Bailey from Beverly Hills."

"Only the biggest bullshitter this side of Burbank . . ."

As Kelly spoke, the door of the woman's apartment opened and the man walked out, carrying a briefcase.

The T-men exited the vacant apartment and followed the black man down the sidewalk. Hearing their footsteps, he turned to face them.

Carr held out his badge. "U.S. Treasury agents," he said. "We'd like to talk with you for a moment."

The man tossed the briefcase into the street and ran down the sidewalk. Carr and kelly chased him at full speed. The man vaulted a low fence into a backyard. In the middle of the yard the man suddenly slammed backward to the ground. The T-men grappled with him until Carr was able to snap on handcuffs.

Kelly laughed and tried to catch his breath at the same time. "Ya gotta watch out for those clotheslines in the dark, brother." The prisoner missed the joke.

Carr jogged back to the spot where the man had tossed the briefcase. It had broken open and counterfeit fifties in inch-high stacks were scattered in the street. Carr picked up the broken case and stuffed the money back inside. He carried it to the government sedan and locked it in the trunk.

Kelly brought the prisoner over to the sedan as Carr made a little wave and pointed to the black woman's apartment. Kelly gave a thumbs-up sign.

Carr trotted down the walkway toward the apartment and knocked on the door.

"Who's there?"

"It's me."

She opened the door a few inches. A look of surprise.

She tried to slam the door, but Carr had wedged his foot against it. He held his badge up to the crack. "You're under arrest for dealing counterfeit money," he said as he shoved open the door. The woman backed away, shaking her head sadly. Carr fastened handcuffs on her outstretched wrists. She seemed more resigned to the situation than frightened. "Mind if I look around for more counterfeit money?" he said.

"You got a search warrant?"

Carr took the woman by the arm and led her to the refrigerator. He opened the door and pulled out a brown paper shopping bag. It was full of couterfeit fifties.

"How'd you know that was in there?"

Carr took the bag and led the woman by the arm out to the sedan. He motioned her into the backseat next to the black man. After locking the door he climbed in next to Kelly, who started the engine.

"I thought it was heroin in the breifcase," the black man said finally. "I don't know nothin' about no funny money."

"He's the one put the funny money in my refrigerator," the woman said. "I didn't have nothing to do with it."

After depositing their prisoners at the federal lockup downtown, Carr and Kelly spent the next hour filling out forms to officially book the two.

Chapter 2

HAVING COMPLETED an hour's worth of paperwork, Carr took the elevator to the seventh floor. Kelly used the storeroom entrance to the Field Office to avoid walking past the special agent in charge, whom they hated.

In their office, a small gray room void of any personal effects or decoration except for a blown up photo of a counterfeit twenty-dollar bill hanging lopsided on the wall (it had been a government exhibit in an ancient case), they sat down at their desks. By agreement, Carr meticulously counted the counterfeit money as Kelly wrote the arrest report. They spent the next hour and a half filling out the usual plethora of standardized forms, lists and inventory sheets required to book the counterfeit money as evidence. Having completed the forms, Carr stapled them together and attached them to a fresh case file folder. Kelly dug in his pocket and pulled out a quarter. "You call," he said.

"Heads," Carr said.

Kelly flipped the coin and showed it to Carr. It was tails. "You get the honors," he said, chuckling.

Carr shook his head and sighed. He gathered up the forms and the counterfeit money.

"Try not to get in an argument with him or we'll be here all night," Kelly said as Carr left the office and headed down the hall. He stepped into Norbert Waeves's (aka No Waves) office. No Waves sat behind the desk with an oversized name plate that read Special Agent in Charge. A man younger than Carr, with bony arms and a trace of freckles across the bridge of his nose and cheekbones, No Waves wore his usual uniform of short-sleeved white shirt with pen-heavy pockets and a thin red necktie. The tie had a rifle-and-pistol pattern.

There was nothing on his desk except pipe-cleaning equipment and a stack of *Guns & Ammo* magazines.

Carr set the reports and contraband on the desk and sat down in a chair in front of the desk.

No Waves put the pipe in his mouth. He flipped through the inventories and made sucking sounds.

"I take it both of you counted the notes?" No Waves said, without looking up.

"Yes," Carr lied.

No Waves pressed an intercom button. "Kelly," he said.

"That's me," Kelly replied.

"Who counted the counterfeit money?"

"What counterfeit money?" Kelly said in a monotone enmity.

No Waves bit the pipe. "The money you and Carr seized tonight," he said.

"We both did," Kelly said.

No Waves switched off the intercom. He signed the

forms and filled out an Approval for Booking Evidence form. He pushed the forms across the desk to Carr.

Carr picked up the forms. He turned to walk out.

No Waves reached into a desk drawer. He pulled out two envelopes. "Here is your six-month evaluation," he said, handing them to Carr. "And Kelly's. Sign them and have them in the mail room by twelve hundred hours tomorrow."

Carr walked out of Waeves's office as he sat lighting his pipe. He distributed the paperwork to various "in" boxes in the office, locked the counterfeit money in the vault and picked up Kelly.

On the way to Chinatown, Kelly read aloud from his evaluation. "Special Agent Kelly has an acceptable record of properly maintaining his issued equipment and government vehicle. Though he is not a self-starter, he works his assigned cases in an acceptable manner and meets most report deadlines. I rate his investigative efforts as barely adequate. Kelly has entered himself into a number of disputes with the members of the Federal Public Defender's Office during this reporting period. I have counseled him about the importance of maintaining proper relations with other agencies, per Treasury Manual of Operations Section zero-nine-point-five-six. I frequently have to counsel Kelly to include more detail in his investigative reports. He does not accept criticism readily and has a bad attitude.

"Special Agent Kelly is eligible for transfer and is not recommended for promotion."

As Carr steered past Los Angeles Plaza, a restored city historical landmark where winos slept on benches, he pulled out his evaluation and handed it to Kelly.

Kelly tore open the envelope and read the report.

"Yours says pretty much the same thing except for the last sentence. Instead of *eligible* for transfer, he says you're *ready* for transfer." Kelly stuffed the evaluation in the envelope and handed it back to Carr.

"It's hard to believe," Kelly said, "but at retirement parties when No Waves ends up sitting alone because no one wants to sit with him, or when I see him eating lunch by himself in his office, I actually feel sorry for him. It's like he can't help being the way he is . . . but most of the time I still feel like kicking his teeth out."

"That's just the way he is," Carr said.

Kelly's face turned red. "He's nothing but a pipe-smoking, draft-dodging, headquarters-created butt-boy. Just the idea of that pencil-necked, mealymouthed, back-stabbing mama's boy evaluating me and trying to get me transferred . . ."

"Don't think about it," Carr said as he turned a corner. "He's not worth the trouble." He steered past a commercial area into old Chinatown, a maze of pagoda-style buildings with gaudy neon trim. The walkways were crowded with families of tourists milling about in a sea of souvenir shops and Chinese restaurants with anglicized names. Carr pulled the sedan into a small parking lot between Ling's bar and a tailor shop. As he climbed out of the car, the mild scent of incense, cooking steam and fried shrimp enveloped him.

An hour later, most of the twelve seats at Ling's bar were still filled. It was the usual crowd, mostly detectives and federal investigators from various agencies, all dressed in cheap suits. At the end of the bar sat a pair of puffy-eyed blondes who Carr knew were secretaries at the courthouse.

Carr and Kelly sat on their usual stools. God only

knew why the dusty place had become the favorite hangout over the years. It certainly wasn't the wall decorations: cheap oriental tapestries of swans floating on a lake, an autographed black-and-white photo of a deputy chief of the L.A. Police Department, a family photo of Ling and his three homely brothers.

Ling, a middle-aged man sporting a clip-on bow tie and granny glasses, stood by a sink at the opposite end of the the bar giving cocktail glasses his usual one-quick-dip-and-drain treatment.

"Any case Bailey touches is destined to turn to shit," Kelly said. "You can ask anybody in here . . . he never comes across with the whole story. *Never.* I'll tell you right now, the first thing he's going to say is that his informant is supersecret and the case is the biggest thing that ever came down the pike. It's his M.O. The man is a known bullshitter . . . a weasel. Working with him is like being a mushroom; he keeps you in the dark and feeds you shit." Kelly took a big drink of scotch. "It wouldn't surprise me if he had his finger in the till somewhere. He's definitely the type."

"It wouldn't surprise me either," Carr said, jiggling the ice in his emptied glass.

"And he doesn't drink," Kelly said. "Think of it. Have you ever met a man who wouldn't take a drink that could be trusted?"

Carr shook his head.

Travis Bailey moved past the inner door of hanging beads. His sport coat looked tailored and a red silk handkerchief was perfectly positioned in the lapel pocket.

Kelly slid over one stool and made room for Bailey to sit down. The men shook hands. Bailey ordered a straight soda. "I'm glad I was able to get in touch with you fellas," he said grimly as he adjusted his gold cuff links. "This thing is for *real* and I don't like to work with people I don't know." He glanced around the bar furtively. "They're going to hit the bank president at his house. The word is they're going to kill his old lady too if she's there. They don't want to leave any witnesses. The informant was very sure of that."

Carr sipped his drink. "Who let the contract?" he asked.

Bailey shrugged. "Unknown at this point, but it's definitely family. A Mafia contract all the way. No doubt about that."

"Tony Dio?" Kelly said.

"It could very well be Dio," Bailey said. "Just a supposition, but judging from where my info came from, I'd say Dio would be a very good guess."

"Where *did* the information come from?" Carr said, looking Bailey in the eye.

"My informant has proven reliable at least twenty times in the past," Bailey said. He sipped soda. "If he says something is going to happen, it happens. I've locked up loads of people behind his information. *Loads*. His word is good enough for a search warrant."

The three men were silent for a while, each mulling over what was about to go down. The blondes at the end of the bar giggled loudly about something while someone else dropped coins in the jukebox, bringing the noise back up to its earlier level. Carr waved at Ling for another round. "Hartmann was approached by one of Tony Dio's lawyers and a couple of muscle men," he said. "They tried to force him to switch three hundred grand in cash out of the vault for three hundred grand in phony twenties. Dio figured that even with a big investigation, the last person they would suspect would be the president of the bank. He offered Hartmann the choice between a trip to Forest Lawn Cemetery or a loss for which the bank was fully insured. Hartmann did the right thing and came to us. We wired him, made some tape recordings when they met again and arrested Dio's lawyer and one of his gunsels. As usual, we couldn't make a case on Dio himself. He was too well insulated."

Bailey nodded. "It all fits."

"Fits with what?" Kelly said.

"With what the informant told me," Bailey said. "It all fits."

Kelly was expressionless, sipped his drink.

Bailey glanced at his wristwatch; Carr realized it was something he did frequently.

"I've got another meeting with the informant set up for tonight," Bailey said. "I wanna make sure there are no last-minute changes."

"Have you notified Hartmann that he's on somebody's list?" Carr said.

"Finally reached him by phone an hour ago," Bailey said. "He's on vacation in Palm Springs. He said no one knows he is there. I told him to stay there until I called. He agreed. I'm planning to be inside the house when the hit man comes in to do the job . . . arrest him for attempted murder. I'd appreciate it if you fellas could help me on the stakeout. We're shorthanded."

Carr didn't answer. He lit a cigarette and blew out the smoke. "How do you know that the hit man is going to do the job at Hartmann's house?"

"My informant is right in with these people. I really can't tell you any more at this point without revealing the snitch's identity . . . but I will tell you again that the information is solid. You can bank on it. I mean *really* bank on it. I'm telling you that the hit man will make his move tomorrow." He looked at his watch again. "I've really gotta run," he said. "Should I count you gents in or out?"

"What's the hit man's name?" Kelly asked, pressing him.

Bailey eased himself off the bar stool. "That's unknown at this time," he said, turning to Carr. "I can sure use the help tomorrow . . . and I'm sure you're interested in protecting your witness."

Carr looked at Kelly. Kelly nodded. "Count us in," Carr said.

Bailey winked. "I'll give you a ring tomorrow morning. We'll go for it." He looked at his watch again and hurried out the door.

Kelly stared at the door. "I wonder what he's up to?"

"I don't know," Carr said, "but we have to go with it. Hartmann is a federal witness. Good info or bad, we have to protect him."

Because of the late hour, it took Travis Bailey less than twenty minutes to drive from Chinatown to Beverly Hills. He steered off the freeway and onto a deserted Wilshire Boulevard. As he passed a Beverly Hills City Limits sign, he stopped at a service station. He stepped into a telephone booth and dialed Lee Sheboygan's number. The phone rang seven times.

Lee Sheboygan yawned into the phone before he said hello.

"I need to meet," Bailey said.

"Now?"

"I'll see you at the same place as last time." Bailey hung up the receiver. He returned to his car and climbed in. Having cruised a few blocks, he turned into an alley that paralleled some small stores facing Wilshire Boulevard. He parked under an awning at the rear of a pizza shop that was closed for business and turned off the engine. He leaned back in the seat. Less than fifteen minutes later, Lee Sheboygan pulled up behind him in a Mercedes-Benz coupe. The diminutive man, attired in a green jump suit, climbed out of the sports car. His Greek fisherman's hat and neatly trimmed black beard gave him a Middle Eastern appearance. Sheboygan looked both ways in the alley before he climbed in next to Bailey.

"Hi, guy," Bailey said as he slid into the seat.

Sheboygan's face made its usual twitch to the left. "You woke me up."

Bailey took out a pad and pen. "When I tell you about the goodies, you'll thank me for waking you up." He drew a square on the blank paper and made *X*'s on three sides of the square. "Three entrances," he said. He drew an oval. " . . . A swimming pool in the backyard." He pointed to the *X* between the pool and the square. "Sliding glass doors. This is where you should go in."

"What kind of goodies are we talking about?" Sheboygan asked. His face went through two full twitch cycles.

"Gold Krugerrands," Bailey said smugly. "At least a hundred grand's worth and a stamp collection that is probably worth about that much. The man doesn't trust banks and keeps his goodies in a cabinet under an aquarium." He pointed to the diagram. "The aquarium is next to the sliding glass doors, across from a bar."

Sheboygan's eyes were riveted on the diagram. "I love it," he said. "What about servants?" He dug a pack of filter tips out of a pouch in his jump suit and lit up.

"No servants," Bailey said. "That's definite . . . and the owner will be in Palm Springs. This has been verified."

Sheboygan's face twitched again. "Dogs?"

"No dogs."

"Alarms?"

"I saw tape on the windows, but nothing on the sliding glass doors," Bailey said.

"Guard service?"

"I checked the records at the department," Bailey said. "There's no guard service listed."

Sheboygan twiched as he puffed smoke, then waved his hand through it. "Sounds like a piece of cake."

"Go for it, baby," Bailey said. He gave Sheboygan's beard a playful tug.

"Do you want to see the goodies afterward?"

Travis Bailey shook his head. "I trust you. Just take everything to Emil. He'll have buyers lined up."

"I don't know what Emil has told you," Sheboygan said, "but there was no fucking Picasso ink drawing inside that place I did last week. The Rolex and the furs were there. There was silver that he hadn't even told me about. I got it all and took it straight to him. He looked at me like I was an asshole or something. 'Where's the Picasso?' he says, like I got it in the trunk of my car or something. He accused me of holding out and I don't like it. As far as I'm concerned he's nothing but a goddamn punk . . . a red-assed punk. I swear to God there was no Picasso anywhere in that house. I went through every room."

"I trust you," Bailey said with a tone of confidence, "and don't let Emil Kreuzer get to you. He's just a little money-hungry. After you turn the goodies to cash, give me one ring at my apartment and we'll meet. Make sure you bring me small bills. It looks funny for a cop to carry hundreds." He smiled.

Sheboygan grinned. "You ain't a cop," he said.

"You're just a crazy low-class motherfucker who carries a badge."

"You didn't talk to me like that when I caught you red-handed peddling silverware," Bailey said. "You used to talk real nice to Detective Bailey. You used to say yes, sir, and no, sir."

Sheboygan twitched. "Now I say three bags full, sir."

Both men chuckled.

It was 2:00 A.M. The freeway was almost empty.

It took Carr less than twenty minutes to get from Ling's to his Santa Monica apartment.

He trudged up the steps, unlocked the door and headed for the refrigerator. Inside, a milk carton, a head of lettuce that he knew had been there for ages and one pickle left in a jar. He ate the pickle and tossed everything else in a trash can. His stomach growled. He dismissed the thought of going for a hamburger and staggered wearily into the bedroom. Having tossed his clothes in a pile, he crawled into the unmade bed and closed his eyes.

The telephone rang. Carr grabbed it off the nightstand.

"I'm sorry if I woke you up," Sally said. "I really am. But I can't sleep. I want to come over."

Carr ran a hand through his hair. "Right now?"

"You have someone else there, don't you?"

"No," Carr said.

"If you do, please tell me and I'll just hang up. It's that Korean cocktail waitress, isn't it? . . . I'm sorry. It's none of my business . . ."

"There's no one here," Carr said.

"I'm sorry I called. I really am. I hope you won't have trouble going back to sleep." The phone clicked.

Carr hung up and fell back onto the pillow.

A short time later the doorbell rang. Carr awakened, but didn't move. It rang again. He crawled out of bed and stumbled to the door.

"It's me," Sally said, hearing him move across the living room floor.

He opened the door. Sally was dressed in a jogging suit. Her auburn hair was pulled back and he could tell that, despite the hour, she had put makeup on. He smelled something perfumy as she walked past him into the bedroom. He followed and got back into bed.

She stood at the window. "I suppose now that I've made a fool out of myself and come over here in the middle of the night you're just going to go back to sleep and leave me standing here," she said wistfully. Carr didn't say anything. Sally waited a few minutes before she moved closer to the bed. "You don't care enough even to talk to me for a few minutes."

He grabbed her arm and pulled her into the bed. They kissed. His hands tore at her clothing. They made love for what must have been an hour. Afterward Sally lay next to him, rubbing her hand lightly across the hair of his chest.

"You live as if there's no future," Sally said softly. "You don't save money. You hate to make plans. I have to force you to buy new clothes. You're driving the same car you had when I met you nine years ago. You could probably get a loan, but you won't buy property. You might as well be a corporal living out of a duffel bag. Your television didn't work almost all of last year. Are you aware of that? Are you aware that it took you a year to have your television fixed?"

"I don't like television."

"That's not the point, Sally said. "The point is that you're living as if there's no tomorrow. Our relationship is an endless succession of one-night stands." With this, Sally rolled away from him. "I've never tried to change you," she said after a while. "Not that I wouldn't have liked to, it's just that you're probably the most stubborn and unchangeable person I've ever met. It's because you've been in an all-male environment since you were seventeen years old . . . the army, Korea, your career with the Treasury Department . . . you're in a paramilitary organization. Are you aware of that?"

"I guess you're right," Carr muttered. His eyelids were heavy. In the darkness, he felt Sally stir. She rested her head on his shoulder.

"I love you," she said in an almost inaudible whisper.

"I love you too," he said. Sleepily, he wrapped his arms around her. He thought of their first date years before. Sitting at a table in a restaurant Carr couldn't afford, they had treated each other with deference.

"It's as if our whole relationship is *déjà vu*," she said.

Her skin was soft and he could feel the outline of her breasts against him. In the darkness, he thought she wiped her eyes. He considered asking her if she was crying, but didn't.

When Carr woke up the next morning Sally was gone. He daydreamed about walking along the beach with her, and their frequent Sunday-afternoon routine of dinner at her place. She always cooked too much. Finally he forced himself out of bed.

In the bathroom, he realized he'd forgotten to buy shaving cream again, so he shaved with bar soap. Having showered and dressed (thank God he had one clean white shirt left), he went into the kitchen.

He boiled water and poured it into a cup. Dug through the cupboard and found the instant coffee container.

There was less than a teaspoon in the jar. Regardless, he emptied the jar's contents into the boiling water. He mixed the water with a spoon; it turned barely brown. Having forgotten his search for something to eat the night before, he went to the refrigerator and saw that he was out of milk for the coffee. "Damn," he said out loud. He slammed the door shut. Fed up, he tossed the semicoffee in the sink and rinsed out the cup, tore off a piece of brown paper bag. With a broken pencil he found in a drawer he wrote a shopping list.

Having checked the stove, he returned to the bedroom and slipped a holster and bullet pouch on his belt. He shoved his revolver into the holster and shrugged on a suit coat on his way out the door.

As he reached the freeway, he realized that he'd left the shopping list on the sink.

Travis Bailey, carrying a pump shotgun on his shoulder in duck-hunter fashion, led Carr and Kelly, who carried a black lunch pail, through the two-story Beverly Hills home. Carr figured that the living room alone was as big as his entire apartment. In it, pastel sofas had been picked to match the abstract art originals that covered the walls (or vice versa?). In the corner, an enormous aquarium built into the wall. It was equipped with fluorescent rocks and multicolored lights. In front of the facing wall, a bar with an inlaid-tile counter top.

Bailey spoke as if he were in a library. "Kelly, you've got the front door. Carr, you cover the bedroom window and the side of the house. I'll handle the rear. I've got a little stool so I can sit below counter level behind the bar . . . 'areas of responsibility,' so to speak. Agreed?"

The T-men nodded. Bailey stepped behind the bar next to the sliding glass door.

Carr and Kelly sauntered down the long hallway. Kelly took his post at the front door. "I don't like the whole operation," he whispered.

"Neither do I," Carr said.

Kelly pulled off his suit coat and hung it on a coatrack next to the front door. He adjusted the volume of the Treasury radio which was clipped to his belt, pinned his gold Treasury badge to his shirt pocket and rolled up his sleeves.

"We're here now," Carr said. "Might as well wait and see what happens."

"It all counts towards retirement," Kelly said. He unsnapped the latches on his lunch pail. It was filled with sandwiches. He offered one to Carr. "Help yourself. Meat loaf with lots of onion and green chiles. My favorite."

"Thanks anyway," Carr said. He strolled into the bedroom and sat down in a chair in the corner of the room. He checked his revolver and shoved it back in the holster. During the next two hours, Carr heard Kelly open and close his lunch pail three times.

The doorbell rang.

Carr jumped out of his chair and pulled his gun. He heard the sound of footsteps outside.

"He's heading for the rear," Kelly whispered from down the hall.

Carr ducked below window level. Someone walked along the side of the house, turned right and continued toward the rear entrance. There was the sound of the sliding glass door opening.

"Police!" Bailey yelled. An explosion.

Carr ran toward the living room. There was another

reverberating blast. As he entered the hallway, he saw Kelly slumped at the entrance to the living room. He was holding his chest. Carr stepped over him. Holding his revolver with both hands, he sprang into the living room.

Travis Bailey stood behind the bar aiming the shotgun at a bearded man lying in the middle of the room in a puddle of water, broken glass and flopping tropical fish. The man's left arm and half of his head were gone. The body convulsed. Pointing the weapon at the intruder, Bailey racked another round into the chamber of the shotgun.

Carr ran across the room. He snatched the shotgun out of the cop's hands. He flicked the safety on and tossed the weapon on the sofa. "He's dead," Carr said angrily.

He ran back to Kelly. The Irishman had pushed himself up so that his back rested against the wall. His left hand clutched his bloody chest. In his right he held his .38, barrel pointed toward the living room. His eyes were wide, his jaw set.

Carr dropped to his knees. Gently, he extricated the gun from Kelly's grasp. "He's dead," Carr said. "Everything's okay." He tore the Handie-Talkie radio off Kelly's belt and pressed the transmit button. "Stakeout Foxtrot Four. Shots fired. Agent down. Gimme an ambulance!"

An excited voice said, "Ten-four, Foxtrot." The radio beeped loudly three times.

Carr tossed the radio down. He grabbed Kelly's shirt with both hands and ripped it open. Using a penknife, he sliced Kelly's bloody undershirt up the middle. There were three holes on the left side of the chest. One made a sucking sound. Kelly coughed and gagged. He spit blood. Carr glanced around. Kelly's lunch pail. He tore it open and ripped the clear plastic wrap off a sandwich. He placed the material directly over the sucking wound. On top of it, he pressed a handkerchief.

Kelly gulped air. He coughed more blood. "Charlie," he said, his voice no louder than a whisper.

"Shut up, goddammit," Carr said.

"Tell Rose I love her," Kelly gasped. "Take care of my boys." Then his eyes rolled back in his head.

Without releasing pressure on the wound, Carr unfastened Kelly's belt. He yanked it off.

Bailey, breathing hard, knelt next to Carr. "Jesus," he said, "he musta caught some of the spray."

Violently Carr shoved Bailey out of his way. Bailey fell backward. Carr fastened the belt around Kelly's chest in order to seal the wound. Carr put his ear to Kelly's nose. He was still breathing. "I'm not gonna wait," Carr said determinedly. He lifted Kelly's arm and placed it over his shoulder. "Help me," he said, looking at Bailey.

"But the ambulance . . ." Bailey said dumbly, struggling to his feet.

"No time . . ." Carr snapped. "Help me carry him to the car."

Bailey stood frozen.

"Now!"

Bailey hurried to lift Kelly's other arm. Half trotting, they carried him to Carr's sedan. Carr arranged him on his side in the backseat with the wound down. "Call Cedars of Lebanon," Carr said as he started the engine. "Tell 'em I'm coming in with a cop . . . a sucking chest wound. I want them to meet me outside." He sped off. As Carr rounded corners like a sports car driver, the Treasury radio operator barked instructions to various agents.

The trip to the hospital took less than five minutes.

Attendants were waiting outside as Carr arrived. They swung open the rear doors of the sedan and lifted Jack Kelly onto a hospital cart. Carr climbed out of the sedan and followed the wheeled cart through the emergency entrance and down a corridor. In a trauma room, Kelly was immediately surrounded by a team of nurses and doctors. Someone asked Carr to leave the room.

As he stepped out into the corridor, his mind flashed to the scene of a field hospital in Korea. He remembered the smell and taste of carbide being overwhelmed by the powerful scent of rubbing alcohol. Soldiers, some of whom were dead, were carried about on stretchers. Charles Carr rubbed his eyes for a moment before he headed for a telephone.

It was midnight.

Carr sat on a sofa in the hospital visitor's room with Rose Kelly, a red-haired woman who wore her hair in a long braid. The lines of her dress were plain and she wore a cardigan sweater. She sat with her hands folded, staring at the wall. During the entire day, she had neither shed tears, sobbed nor sought refuge. Her demeanor was as usual—demure, polite, composed. Other than her constant wringing of hands and an occasional quiver of her chin, she had shown no signs of breaking down. Hours earlier she had kissed her husband on the forehead, and as a young priest had administered the last rites, she had knelt next to the bed and prayed. Before the priest left, she thanked him effusively, as if he had done a favor rather than perform a duty. She told him that Jack's brother was a priest in Chicago.

A middle-aged doctor in a green operating smock came in through the swinging door. A heavy man, he had wiry black hair, an aquiline nose and thick glasses. Rose Kelly started at his sudden appearance. Carr jumped up.

"Your husband is going to live," he said. "He's sleeping, but you can go in and see him for a minute." Rose rushed out of the room.

Carr shook hands with the doctor. "Thanks, Doc," Carr said, blinking back tears.

"He may or may not be able to return to the job," the doctor said, "it's too early to tell." He made a little nod and exited the room. A second later he stuck his head back in the door. He smiled. "Next time you plug up a sucking chest wound with sandwich wrap, scrape the onion off it first." He winked and left.

Carr went into Kelly's room. Rose stood by the bed holding her husband's hand. His face was ashen and there were tubes entering his mouth and nose. He tried to speak. Carr leaned closer. He put his ear to Kelly's lips.

"It was a setup," Kelly whispered.

"I think you're right, partner," Carr said. "Try to get some rest. We'll talk later." Kelly licked his lips. He closed his eyes. Carr tiptoed out of the room. Rose followed a few minutes later. He offered her a ride home and she accepted.

Rose Kelly sat in the passenger seat clutching her purse and staring out the windshield at nothing in particular. Her demeanor reminded Carr of other victims he'd seen: the blank gaze of the wounded, the robbed, the deceived.

"The first time I saw Jack I fell in love with him," she said. "He was watching a counterfeiter that lived across the street from the school. He used my classroom every night after class for a week. He would come with a camera on a tripod. I could tell he was single because he used to bring hamburgers in a bag and his white shirts needed ironing. I found myself making excuses to stay after class and talk with him. One night I brought a nice meal to the classroom and we had sort of a picnic. Jack is such a gentleman. After the surveillance was over, he sent me a real nice thank-you note. I was very touched. I prayed that he would call me and he did. At the hospital today I prayed to the Virgin Mary that Jack's life would be spared." Her voice cracked. "God answered my prayer again." Rose Kelly put a hand over her mouth to muffle her sobs.

Carr tried to think of something to say, but couldn't. He felt tears, but managed to blink them back.

As Carr maneuvered the sedan through the empty streets of West Los Angeles and onto the freeway toward Orange County, Rose Kelly continued to sob quietly. Finally they arrived. Before getting out she wiped her eyes, blew her nose and thanked Carr three or four times for the ride home.

Chapter 3

IT WAS early morning and Carr had a hangover. The office intercom buzzed and a secretary told Carr the agent in charge wanted to speak with him. Carr got up from his desk and headed down the hallway. As he rounded the corner into an anteroom in front of No Waves's office, a young black woman wearing a summer dress sat behind a typewriter. She held up a sheet of paper as he approached. It read HIS RECORDER IS ON! She crumpled the note and tossed it in the wastebasket.

Carr winked at her and continued into the office.

No Waves sat behind his desk thumbing through Carr's report on the Beverly Hills stakeout. Pipe-cleaning equipment was scattered about the desk.

Waeves did not acknowledge Carr's presence, but continued reading the report. Carr was accustomed to this behavior. In April, Waeves had spent a week at his desk reading a book entitled *How to Intimidate and Succeed*.

Waeves licked a thumb and turned to the last page of

the report. He made a little note in the margin, then looked up. "I don't see any need for this interview to be recorded, do you?" He dug his meerschaum into a plastic tobacco pouch.

Carr shrugged and sat down.

"Have you had any feedback from Mr. Hartmann?" No Waves said.

"About what?"

"About the damage to his home. Even though the Beverly Hills detective did the shooting, the government could be held liable for the shotgun damage to his walls and aquarium. I understand he had a lot of very valuable tropical fish in there."

Carr blinked back anger. He took a deep breath. "No feedback."

"All we need is another damage claim against the government," Waeves said sarcastically. He held up the report. "Your report says that you and Kelly met with Bailey in Chinatown when he first informed you of the possible hit on Hartmann. Was any liquor consumed at this meeting? I'm asking this strictly off the record. I mean that."

"No."

"I take it you were in a bar?"

Carr nodded.

"And you didn't order even one drink?"

"That's right."

"Why?"

"Because I was on the wagon."

"And Jack Kelly?"

"He's on the wagon too."

Waeves blew into his pipe.

"From your diagram, it appears that you were in the

bedroom when the shooting took place," Waeves said. "Who made the assignment?"

"Bailey did. He seemed to know the layout of the house. It was just a matter of covering the three entrances. The assignments seemed okay to me. We had things covered."

"I'm asking this totally off the record, but were you sleeping in the bedroom when the shooting occurred? Your answer will be kept just between you and me."

"No."

"Then what were you doing?"

"I was in the bedroom covering my position," Carr said. "I was waiting for someone to break into the house."

"You're saying that you were in a nice comfortable bedroom with a king-sized bed literally for hours and you didn't even *think* about lying down on the bed and taking a little rest?"

"Come to think of it, you're right . . ."

Waeves smiled.

"I did think about it once . . ." Carr said, ". . . but I didn't do it."

"Just asking. As you well know, it's my responsibility as the special agent in charge to ask questions when accidents happen." A smoke signal billowed from his pipe. "Nothing personal, you understand."

"Bailey fired a shotgun," Carr said. "Some of the pellets hit Jack. That's what happened."

Waeves ignored the remark. "This Leon Sheboygan . . . we probably should check into his background. Tony Dio could be behind this."

"Good idea," Carr said to the wall.

"It was a hot day. And I'm sure Hartmann's house was

sweltering. You fellas probably had a couple of beers to cool off in there, right? I know I would've."

"No, we didn't."

Waeves fiddled with his pipe. He took some puffs.

"I haven't had a chance to get over and see Jack," Waeves said. "How's he doing?"

Carr stood up. "Is there anything else?"

Waeves licked the stem of his pipe. "Not at the moment."

Carr turned and walked out of the room.

Travis Bailey's condominium was furnished modern: chrome hanging lamps, a dining table with a glass top, unconventional sofa and chairs upholstered in purple leather. On the wall behind the television hung a four-foot-square oil painting of a bolt and nut on a barren desert. Bailey, who had decorated the place himself, lay back on the sofa with his feet in Delsey Piper's lap. They wore matching blue terry-cloth bathrobes and nothing else.

Delsey Piper turned the pages of a newspaper. "Here it is," she said excitedly. "Officer Shoots Hired Killer. An alleged underworld hit man was killed yesterday in a shootout with Beverly Hills Police Detective Travis C. Bailey. Police sources report that the suspect, who was not identified, entered the Beverly Hills home of Terence J. Hartmann, president of the Southern California-based Bank of Commerce-Pacific. Hartmann was in Palm Springs at the time, attending a bank conference. Acting on a tip that Hartmann might be the target of an attack, Detective Bailey, with the assistance of two U.S. Treasury agents of the L.A. Field Office, initiated a stakeout of the Hartmann residence. In the early afternoon, an armed man gained entry to the palatial home by forcing entry through a back door. When confronted by

Detective Bailey, the suspect drew his weapon. In the ensuing shoot-out, the thirty-six-year-old Bailey fired two rounds from a shotgun. The suspect was killed and U.S. Treasury Agent John A. Kelly was wounded. Kelly was rushed to Cedars of Lebanon Hospital, where he underwent emergency surgery for wounds to the chest. He remains in critical condition. Police sources report that the incident at Hartmann's home may be related to the fact that he is a potential witness in a federal trial now under way against reputed Mafia figure Anthony Dio. Dio has been charged with engineering a bank extortion plot involving the use of counterfeit U.S. securities." Delsey Piper giggled. "It's like a movie!"

Bailey smiled. He grabbed the phone receiver off the coffee table and dialed.

"City Desk, Sanders," the man answered.

"This is Travis Bailey, Beverly Hills P.D. I've got some more on the shoot-out for you. The suspect has been identified. I thought you might want to know."

"Got a name?"

"Leon Sheboygan," Bailey said. "Spelled like the city. He's thirty-four years old. A local hit man for the Dio mob . . . but don't quote me on that. Keep it deep background."

"Sure. What sort of a weapon was he carrying?"

"A thirty-two automatic. All the hit men use 'em these days."

"How many shots were fired?"

"It all happened so fast I don't really know. Things were pretty hot and heavy . . . I guess I was just a little better shot." He winked at Delsey.

"Have you been involved in other shoot-outs?" the reporter asked.

"Yes, but I've always been able to come out on top."

"Keep up the good work."

"I'm just glad I was able to save Mr. Hartmann's life," Bailey said in a serious tone. The phone clicked.

"Reporters used to call my father all the time," Delsey said. "When I was a kid, paparazzi would be waiting outside restaurants. Once they took a picture of us coming out of Perino's. A few days later there was an article in a movie magazine asking whether the young blonde seen with Rex Piper was going to be his sixth wife." She giggled. "That was at the time when my father was really big . . . right after he made *Sundown Morning*. He took me with him to Italy on location. I met some kids and we spent the whole summer smoking hash and taking trains around Europe. When we got back to the States the movie really hit. There were fans hanging around in front of our house all day. I used to flip 'em the bird out the window. Once this thirteen-year-old named daddy in a paternity suit. He told me he didn't do it but one of my girl friends had seen him with her at the Pro-Celebrity golf tournament. Our maid told me about her too. She used to tell me everything if I would give her a free day off when my father was out of town." She sighed and caught her breath. "Daddy finally settled out of court. He hired a private detective to handle the negotiations. Everyone in Hollywood knows my father as a real cockhound. Once when I came home from boarding school he had these two Puerto Rican women in his bedroom . . ." She laughed. "It was really *gross*."

Bailey left the sofa and strolled into the bedroom. He opened a dresser drawer and removed two marijuana cigarettes from a small wooden box. As he headed back toward the sofa, Delsey picked up where she had left off.

"The day my father's house was burglarized and you came over to investigate was the same day he accepted his first role in a dinner-theater musical. It was a blow to his ego. He said he couldn't get work in Hollywood because he fired his agent for cheating him on a contract and his agent's brother was a producer and between the two of them they destroyed his career . . ."

He tossed her a marijuana cigarette. She caught it.

"But I think the real reason was that my father is just getting old," she said.

He lit a match and offered it to her. She leaned toward him and fired the cigarette. He lit his, and with a puff, felt a wave of relaxation. Bailey leaned back on the sofa and propped his legs up on the table. Delsey's voice seemed to emanate from far away.

"When you asked me if I wanted to be a police officer I thought you were crazy. But my father thought it was a great idea. I know I would have never been accepted on the Department if my father hadn't lived next door to the mayor. They're old friends from when they worked together on *The Enchanted Castle*."

"Don't forget that every cop on the Department *knows* that the mayor was your hook," Travis Bailey said.

"Fuck 'em if they can't take a joke," she said with a giggle. She cupped her hands around the roach and took a couple of deep drags. She held the smoke in her mouth, then let it crawl out. "I can't wait till tomorrow. My first day as a detective . . ."

Bailey puffed. "Go for it, baby."

Charles Carr wandered around Jerome Hartmann's living room. The carpet was stained with the still-damp mixture of water and blood. In addition to the buckshot holes in the wall next to the hallway door, there was shattered glass and dried-up aquarium fish everywhere.

In the middle of the mess, white tape outlined where the burglar's body had ended up.

Hartmann stood next to the sliding glass doors. He was dressed in tennis togs, which failed to hide his slack stomach muscles. He shook his head sadly. "I had no idea when those hoods approached me that it would end up in something like this. It's like a bad dream," he said. "I can't tell you how grateful I am to Agent Kelly. I hope you will let me know if there is anything I can do for him or his family. I really mean that."

Carr nodded. His eyes followed the reverse path of the bullet holes, from the wall to the bar. He stepped gingerly on the wet rug toward the hallway door where Kelly had been hit. Another tape mark.

"I guess I took a vacation at just the right time," Hartmann said, shaking his head in disbelief.

Carr returned to the living room. He checked the lock on the sliding glass door. Having pulled out pad and pen, he made notes.

There was the sound of vehicles pulling into the driveway and car doors closing.

TV cameramen and photographers followed Travis Bailey in through the sliding doors. He winked at Carr. "The Chief wants a little coverage," he said. Flashbulbs popped. The newsmen jostled for position. Bailey pointed at the bullet holes. More photographs.

While this was going on, Carr drew a diagram of the room and the location of the evidence on his note pad. Having completed the sketch, he strolled out the glass door into the backyard. Hartmann followed. "I'm a member of the Beverly Hills Police and Fire Commission," he said. "I intend to thank Detective Bailey publicly at the next meeting. It's a good feeling to know that one's police department is on the ball."

Carr nodded approvingly. "Did you tell anyone about your trip to Palm Springs?"

"Certainly not," Hartmann said. "I followed your instructions and didn't tell a soul. Not a soul . . . with the exception of the Beverly Hills Police Department. I phoned them and gave Detective Bailey a brief rundown before I left. I was worried about someone putting a bomb in my house while I was gone. Certainly you don't consider that a breach of confidence on my part?"

Carr shook his head. "Of course not." The photographers shuffled out of the house and piled into station wagons, then drove off.

Travis Bailey sauntered over to Carr. He shook his head mournfully. "I really feel bad about Jack. It was just one of those things . . . a cross-fire situation."

"These things happen," Carr said ruefully.

"I hope Jack has no hard feelings."

"He doesn't. And as a matter of fact, he asked me to tell you that."

"I'm glad," Bailey said. He patted Carr on the shoulder.

Carr avoided the urge to cringe and, instead, smiled at the detective.

"By the way," Bailey said, "what brings you back here?" He spoke as if he were doing nothing more than making conversation.

"I'm doing a diagram of the scene. My agent in charge loves lots of paperwork."

"Why don't you just copy my reports? Save yourself some time."

"Good idea. By the way, the powers that be want me to interview your informant. Do you see any problem with that?"

"None whatsoever," Bailey said. "If I knew where to

find him . . . He split town right after the shooting. I'm afraid that he might be gone for good."

Carr shrugged. "I guess that was to be expected."

Bailey glanced at his wristwatch. "Gotta run. Press conference at the police station in ten minutes." He waved as he rushed down the driveway.

The Beverly Hills apartment complex was shielded from Wilshire Boulevard traffic noise by a high wall and replanted palm trees. Though it was a weekday, suntanned men and women (most of whom seemed to be fighting midriff bulge) roamed and lounged around a swimming pool and a couple of tennis courts. Carr figured the rents would be three or four times what he paid for his Santa Monica one-bedroom.

Carr approached a ground-floor apartment with a Manager sign on the door. He knocked. An attractive, fortyish woman wearing a turquoise lounging outfit with matching scarf answered the door. He held out his badge. "Federal officer," he said. "Are you the manager?"

"Yes."

"Which apartment is Leon Sheboygan's, Miss . . ."

"Kennedy. Amanda Kennedy. Mr. Sheboygan lives in apartment nineteen," she said haughtily. "What seems to be the problem?"

"Mr. Sheboygan is dead."

The woman's jaw dropped. "My God," she said, covering her mouth with her hand, "what happened?"

"He had an accident. I need to look inside the apartment. I'd appreciate it if you'd let me in. You may accompany me if you wish."

"There was a Beverly Hills detective here last night. He asked to look in the apartment too, but didn't say a word about Lee being . . ." The woman gulped. "I just thought that he was in some sort of trouble."

"Did the detective go in the apartment?"

"No. I wouldn't let him in. And I'm not going to let you in either. I don't think it's legal to hand over someone's apartment key. In fact, I called an attorney last night and he told me not to let any policeman in any apartment no matter what they said."

"I take it you understand that Mr. Sheboygan is *deceased,*" Carr said. "That he is *dead* and will not be paying any more rent?"

The woman adjusted her scarf. "I don't see where that makes any difference one way or the other."

Carr closed his eyes for a moment, then opened them. "Did Mr. Sheboygan live alone?"

"He had a roommate. I don't know his name. He moved out a couple of weeks ago." She paused for a moment. "What kind of accident was it?"

"A gun accident. I really do need to look through his apartment. As I said, you can accompany me inside to see that nothing is disturbed."

"This is Beverly Hills, officer. Apartment managers in this city don't just hand apartment keys over to police types. If something turned up missing from the apartment I'd be responsible."

Carr made his best kindness-to-animals expression. "Ma'am, I am a federal law enforcement officer. All I want to do is look around in a dead man's apartment for a few minutes. I'm not a burglar."

The woman folded her arms across her chest. "Just how do I know that?"

Carr dug an identification card bearing his photograph and signature out of his pocket. He handed it to her. She glanced at it and handed it back. "Anyone can get a card like that these days."

Carr shrugged. "You're certainly within your rights to say no. Thank you for your time."

"You're quite welcome," the woman said.

As Carr turned to leave he heard the door shut firmly behind him.

Chapter 4

CARR STOOD outside the woman's apartment for a moment. He looked around. None of the sunbathers around the pool seemed to notice him. A brass number 19 was affixed to an apartment on the second floor facing the pool. Carr left using the front entrance. To his left was a driveway, which he followed to a rear parking lot.

Using steps that were out of the line of sight from the manager's apartment, he trotted to the second-floor balcony. Staying close to the wall, he walked to apartment 19. Though he expected no answer, he rang the doorbell of the apartment and waited awhile. He tried the lock. It was secure. Having fished a credit card out of a wallet that Sally had given him for his birthday, he took another look around. He was still invisible to the tenants. Deftly, he probed the credit card between the door and jamb. The lock clicked. He opened the door and went inside. Having closed the door behind him, he flicked on a wall switch.

The living room was decorated with expensive modern furniture that Carr guessed came along with the apartment. There was an enormous oak wall unit stacked with stereo equipment, and on a driftwood coffee table were some locksmithing trade journals and a book entitled *The Dos and Don'ts of Burglar Alarms*. Carr picked up one of the magazines. The address label had Sheboygan's name and address.

In the bedroom, Carr saw that the king-sized bed was unmade. Shelves on the wall were filled with items reflecting a typical California life-style—tennis rackets, sports car hats, a jogging suit. The closet was bursting with clothes bearing Beverly Hills men's store labels. There were lots of pairs of shoes, mostly handmade with English labels.

In the dresser drawers, Carr found stacks of silk shirts. Under one of the stacks was a zebra-skin shoulder holster. In the corner of the same drawer was an inch-high stack of color snapshots. The photograph on top was of Leon Sheboygan, wearing nothing but a flat cap, posed on the edge of his bed with a naked brunette. The smiling pair held up champagne glasses. The small-breasted woman looked fortyish and had a tattoo of a butterfly on her shoulder. Other shots showed her engaged in various sex acts with Sheboygan. In one photograph Sheboygan used the neck of a champagne bottle as a dildo while the woman drank from a champagne goblet.

Other photos depicted a naked man who looked to be Sheboygan's age, only with gray-streaked hair, mounting a freckled, bored-looking redhead with abdominal stretch marks. At the bottom of the stack was a color photograph of a naked Amanda Kennedy sitting cross-legged on the bed littered with jewelry as Sheboygan, who wore only a T-shirt, knelt behind her. As she gave the finger to the camera, the smiling and red-eyed

Sheboygan appeared to be affixing the clasp of a necklace with an expensive-looking, star-shaped gold medallion around her neck.

Carr shoved the photographs in the pocket of his suit coat.

On top of the dresser, among laundry receipts and other pocket litter, was a black-and-white photograph of Sheboygan and the man with the gray-streaked hair sitting in a bar at a table covered with cocktail glasses, cigarette packages. A matchbook was visible leaning against an ashtray, though the painting on it was indecipherable. Sitting between them was a young blonde woman with extremely short hair and the brunette. He shoved the photograph in his pocket with the others.

In the kitchen drawer next to a wall phone, Carr found a scrap of paper covered with scribbled phone numbers. He stuffed it in his pocket. Having returned to the front door, he peeked out of the peephole. The lady manager exited her apartment and headed up the steps and down the balcony toward him. He flicked off the lights and held his breath. The woman strode past the door and knocked on an apartment door farther down. Someone answered the door. The woman asked to borrow something. A man's falsetto vice offered her a glass of Chablis (which he pronounced "Shabliss"). She accepted and stepped into the apartment. The door closed.

A few minutes later, Carr opened the door quietly and crept out the way he came in.

Sitting at his desk, Carr leafed through a copy of Sheboygan's multipage arrest record, which he'd picked up from the Sheriff's Department Records Bureau on his way back to his office. The list of arrests, beginning when he was a teenager, reflected that Sheboygan (real name Leon Adolph Sheboygan III) had been arrested for the first time when he was sixteen years old. The yellowed and dog-eared burglary report for the arrest recounted, in police language, that he had been caught trying to pawn a set of golf clubs stolen from his next door neighbor's house. A juvenile-court judge named Pregerson had sentenced him to a year in a county road camp.

Carr noted that with the passage of time, there was more time between arrests and fewer convictions. Also, Sheboygan's residence address, as listed on the face sheet of each arrest form, moved inexorably west from a trailer court in San Bernardino to apartments in Alhambra, Pasadena, Glendale, West Los Angeles and, finally, Beverly Hills. As the rent got higher, so did the lawyer's fees. The names in the fill-in box on the arrest report labeled *Attorney Representing:* were changed from names Carr recognized as the ex-public defender's, with offices near the county courthouse, to those with offices in Beverly Hills. The arrest package read like that of thousand of other crooks Carr had reviewed through the years. A biography of learning from experience.

Carr's final note was that there were no arrests in Beverly Hills. He tossed the file in a drawer and pulled the scrap of paper he'd taken from Sheboygan's apartment from his coat pocket. He picked up the phone and dialed the first number. The phone rang.

"Go," mumbled a man with a deep voice who sounded as if he might have just woken up.

"This is Charlie," Carr said. "I'm trying to get in touch with Lee Sheboygan. Do you know where I can find him?"

The man yawned. "You can probably find him at the cemetery," he said. "He got wasted by the cops."

"No shit."

"They caught him inside a house . . . which Charlie is this?"

"Charlie Carr. I need to get in touch with Lee's ex-roommate. Do you know where I can find him?"

"I never met any of his friends . . . *who* the fuck is this?"

"Thanks anyway," Carr said and hung up. He dialed another number.

A woman answered.

"This is Charlie. Did you hear about what happened to Lee?"

"You mean little Lee with the beard?"

"Right. He got killed in a shoot-out with the cops in Beverly Hills."

"Goddamn."

"I'm trying to find the guy he used to live with."

"Lee had some of my records and tapes. How am I going to get my records? They're in his apartment. How did you get my phone number?"

"I found it in Lee's apartment."

"Oh," she said.

"What is Lee's ex-roommate's name?"

"Have no idea," she said. "I met Lee at a party in Malibu. We dated once and he never called me again. Damn. How am I going to get my records?"

"Do you know *any* of his friends?"

"No, I don't," she said. "Would you get my records for me?"

Carr hung up the receiver and made a note of the numbers he'd called.

* * *

At the Los Angeles Police Headquarters building, Carr took the elevator to the third floor and followed the hallway to a door marked Homicide. The room was filled with detectives scattered at desks, most of whom were talking on the telephone. Higgins sat at a desk in the corner of the room. Except for his blond crew cut, he looked pretty much like the rest of the murder dicks; neither young, underweight nor particularly well dressed. Carr strolled to Higgins's desk, where, come to think of it, he had sat since Carr met him. It had been close to twenty years ago.

"How's Jack?" Higgins said.

"Doing as well as can be expected." Carr sat down.

"I heard it was a ricochet."

Carr shrugged. "I'm not sure. I was in another room when it went down. All Bailey remembers is seeing the suspect pull a gun. He doesn't remember how Jack was hit or even how many rounds he fired from the shotgun. You know how those things go."

Higgins nodded. "What were the positions?"

Carr pulled out a ballpoint pen. He drew a rough diagram of Jerome Hartmann's house on a pad of paper. He described where he, Bailey and Kelly were before the shooting. He drew an arrow to show the direction of fire.

Higgins rubbed his chin as he perused the diagram. He shook his head. "I guess anything can happen once the trigger is pulled," he said.

"I'm still trying to piece everything together. That's why I stopped by. I'd like to have you take a look at the reports and tell me what you think. You're the ballistics expert." Carr handed him the stack of reports.

Higgins looked Carr directly in the eye for a moment. "Sure," he said, "I'll check 'em out for you."

"There's something else," Carr said. He pulled out

the photograph of Sheboygan and friends sitting around a cocktail table and handed it to Higgins. "There's a matchbook on the table. I need a blowup of it."

"No problem," Higgins said.

"I'd like to keep this just between you and me."

"Got it."

Carr nodded, got up and left.

It was almost 1:00 P.M. and Travis Bailey was alone in the police department's underground parking area. He strolled toward a row of vehicles with grease-penciled notes that read "Hold for Evidence" or "Impound" on their windshields. Lee Sheboygan's Mercedes-Benz was parked at the end of the row next to a Cadillac covered with fingerprint dust.

Bailey approached the passenger door of the car. With some difficulty, he tore the red evidence tape off the lock, inserted a key and opened it. To avoid soiling his sport coat, he took it off, folded it carefully and set it in the backseat.

He snatched an impound sheet off the dashboard. The section marked Comments read: "Owner was suspect/DOA after burg stakeout/Tow to police lot & hold as evidence per Det II Bailey." He set the sheet back on the dashboard. In the glove compartment he found an address book, credit card receipts, matchbooks, a bank-book and some telephone bills. Having scooped out the contents of the cubbyhole onto the floorboard, he searched thoroughly under the seats. He pulled out a sports car magazine, a pamphlet printed by a burglar alarm company and a thick wallet. In the wallet was a stack of credit cards, all bearing Sheboygan's name, a tiny address book (Bailey found his own initials and the Detective Bureau phone number scribbled on the first page), business cards of locksmiths, jewelers, antique dealers, owners of West Side art galleries, Hollywood massage parlors that Bailey knew were whorehouses and three hundred dollars in twenties and fifties.

Travis Bailey removed the cash and stuffed it in his trouser pocket. Having dropped the rest of the items in the pile, he proceeded to the trunk. He unlocked it gently and lifted the lid. Inside was an open metal box and a duffel bag. The metal box was filled with pry bars, key blanks, lockpicks, ratchets of various sizes and other burglar tools. Scattered among the well-used instruments were five or six Polaroid photographs of two-story homes. He removed them and closed the toolbox. Next to the toolbox was a small zippered bag containing a jogging suit and a pair of running shoes. He examined the pockets of the suit carefully and recovered a pawn shop receipt for a diamond ring and a laundry ticket. He shoved these items, along with the photographs from the toolbox, into the duffel bag. After thoroughly searching the rest of the trunk, he removed the toolbox and the duffel bag and set them on the cement floor. He slammed the trunk lid shut.

Kneeling down, he filled the duffel bag with everything from the glove compartment, including the wallet and its contents.

Carrying the bag and the toolbox, he walked across the garage to a smelly room filled with trash receptacles. He shoved the duffel bag deep into a brimming trash can. Using the stairs rather than the elevator, he proceeded to his office. Before he had a chance to wash his hands, Captain Cleaver stopped by his desk. Bailey noticed that he was wearing a monogrammed shirt.

"Find anything in the car?"

Travis Bailey shook his head. "Just burglar tools," he said as he opened the box and displayed its contents.

"No address books? Nothin' else?"

Bailey shook his head. "The man traveled light."

"Typical hit man."

The phone buzzed. Bailey picked up the receiver. It was for Cleaver.

"Yes, sir," Cleaver said. "Where did it occur? Okay, sir." As Cleaver stood with the receiver an inch or so from his ear, Bailey could hear the sound of a voice coming from the receiver. "Yes, sir," he said finally. "I'll certainly do my best. I'll try to take care of it." He set the receiver down.

"Superman's brother got arrested last night at a pajama party. Superman wants it fixed. He says *Screen Confidential* magazine hired some private eyes to check out the party because lots of movie people were there. They stiffed a robbery-in-progress call into the complaint board to see what would happen. When the patrol officers went in the front door everybody ran out of the back. Superman's brother got pinched for possession of nose candy. He had an ounce in the pocket of his robe. The guy who plays the Black Knight on TV got away. He jumped over the back fence. The private dicks took pictures of everyone."

"They all ran because of a little cocaine in the place?"

Cleaver shook his head. "It was a pajama party for *men*. The host was some big-time agent. The house was full of hairdressers, hired teenage butt-boys, leather freaks . . . a can of worms. I bet I'll have twenty phone calls from high-power attorneys before the day is over."

"I don't really see what else I can do on this

Sheboygan thing," Bailey said, changing the subject. "His tracks were covered."

Cleaver had a preoccupied look. "Close it out," he said offhandedly. "Let the Feds do the follow-up. They've got the resources. We've got other things to worry about besides a hit man who fucked up and walked into a trap." He left quickly and headed back to his office.

Having booked the burglar tools in the evidence room, Travis Bailey washed his hands. He left the office and took lunch alone in a health food restaurant a few blocks away. After a meal of bamboo shoots, shredded carrot salad and guava juice, he strolled past shops that specialized in men's clothing with Italian brand names, gourmet cheeses and furs. Having browsed for a while in a small shop featuring electronic solitaire chessboards, he returned to the Detective Bureau and completed the rest of his reports.

The restaurant had seen its day, but Carr figured it still served some of the best downtown fare. He stepped in the front door of the place and looked around. It was furnished with marred wooden tables and cane-backed chairs. On the walls were photographs of long-forgotten football teams and the floor was covered with sawdust. Bow-tied waiters wearing aprons and long-sleeved white shirts took their time serving a luncheon horde made up mostly of courthouse employees, detectives and downtown business types.

Higgins waved from a table in the corner. Spotting him, Carr made his way over to the table and sat down. Sheboygan's autopsy report was under a plate of French bread slices. Higgins said hello as he slapped a butter pat onto bread. A florid-faced waiter with thick glasses came to the table. Carr and Higgins ordered without using a menu.

"What d'ya think?" Carr asked after the waiter had left.

Higgins touched the autopsy report. "Very interesting reading," Higgins said with his mouth full. He dabbed more butter on the bread.

"Something was wrong," Carr said. "I was there and something was wrong."

"In the past few years I've heard rumbles that *Bailey* is wrong."

"I've heard the talk too. Sometimes info like that comes from people with grudges. Double-crossing stoolies love to put out that kind of crap."

The waiter returned to the table, set down plates of cole slaw and rushed away.

"Sheboygan had a defensive wound on his right hand," Higgins said. "Shotgun pellets in the palm and out the back of the hand and into the sternum. I've seen this type of wound on victims who are shot in family fights. Daddy or mommy comes out of the bedroom with a gun. It's as if the victim is saying 'Please don't shoot me,' right before they become Swiss cheese."

"Maybe it was his gun hand," Carr said. "Sheboygan had a gun."

"Maybe, but if that's the case, why didn't he pull the trigger? That's the natural human reaction. The gun hadn't been fired. Here's an ex-con sneaking into a house to do a number on somebody. He has a gun *in his hand* and doesn't do anything with it?" He shrugged. "Of course anything is possible."

"Maybe Bailey just fired before Sheboygan did."

"Maybe. Then again, why did the thirty-two end up lying in front of the bar instead of frozen in a death grip in his hand? That's what usually happens. Or if the gun was blown out of his hand, why did it end up lying in front of the bar instead of being blown backward, the same direction Sheboygan's body was?"

Carr swallowed a few bites. "Unless it was a throw-down gun," he said, wiping his mouth with a napkin.

Higgins stopped eating. "You and I have been around for a long time, Charlie. We both know what that means. It means that a cop is going to go to jail or be lucky enough to just lose his job and pension. I don't like Bailey. He's one of those slick types that always end up in a jam of one kind or the other. In fact, just *talking* to him gives me the creeps. I feel like washing my hands in alcohol afterwards. But I'm also telling you right now that if Bailey legitimately caught Sheboygan breaking into the house, I personally don't give a rat's ass if he wasted the son-of-a-bitch. I truly don't care if he killed the man in cold blood. Sheboygan had been in prison for half of his life. He made his living by breaking into people's homes and stealing their property. He knew the chance he was taking. If Bailey was dumb enough to carry around a throw-down gun and use it because he got scared after the shooting when he realized that Sheboygan was unarmed, that's his business. Slick people do slick things. But the last thing in the world I would want to do is get involved in trying to screw a fellow cop, even an asshole like Bailey, for making a mistake in a split-second judgment. I've been to too many autopsies of people killed by burglars—old ladies, housewives with kids, people who had never harmed anyone—to worry about how a career burglar got his ticket punched."

Carr and Higgins ate silently for a while.

"What if I told you I thought Sheboygan getting killed

had nothing to do with either a burglary or a murder contract?" Carr said.

"Then I would ask you just what in the hell *are* you trying to say?"

"I think Bailey committed premeditated murder and didn't care if he had to shoot my partner to get it done. I think he used Jack and me as a cover."

The waiter brought plates filled with short ribs, mashed potatoes and string beans. Carr picked up knife and fork. Higgins stared at the plate for a moment. "What are you gonna do about it?" Higgins asked him.

"I'm going to find out what's going on. And if it wasn't just an accident, I'm going to pull the plug on Bailey. I'm going to sink him."

"You're talking about a blue-clue caper," Higgins said. "You're talking about going against another cop. It could get real sticky."

The men ate their meals in silence. After finishing they both ordered coffee. Casually, they discussed the latest Los Angeles City Council attempt to cut the police budget and whether the Dodgers would come out of their slump. Finally their small talk, as well as their coffee, was finished. The two men stood up and Higgins picked up the autopsy report. "I'll need to do some more work on this," he said.

On the way out of the restaurant, Carr gave him a slap on the back.

The next morning Carr returned to Amanda Kennedy's apartment. He knocked on the door. After first peeking at him through the window, she opened it. She was dressed in designer jeans, high heels and a peasant blouse. She wore a necklace with a star-shaped medallion that looked like the one Sheboygan had been fastening around her neck in the snapshot. He wondered if the diamonds on the star points were genuine.

"The answer is still no," she said. "I'm not going to let you look in the apartment. I spoke with an attorney again and he told me you have absolutely no right to go in there."

Carr smiled humbly. "I didn't come for that. I'd just like to ask you a couple of questions. May I step in for a moment?"

She stared at him as if he were a trash-picker. "Questions about what?"

"About Mr. Sheboygan."

"I'm busy right now."

"Sheboygan was shot during the course of a burglary. It's important that I talk with you about him."

"I really don't see what that has to do with me," she said as she folded her arms over the medallion.

"It'll just take a minute."

"No. I choose *not* to be interviewed. I have a right not to be interviewed if I so choose. Now please go away and don't bother me again." She shut the door in Carr's face.

Carr fished in his pocket for the bedroom photograph of her with Sheboygan. He found it, then rang the doorbell for a long time. As Amanda Kennedy angrily swung open the door he held up the photograph. She looked at it and blushed. Carr shoved the photo back in his coat pocket.

Amanda Kennedy turned and sauntered back into the living room, where she sat down on the sofa. The television was tuned to a soap opera. Following her inside, Carr closed the door softly and sat next to her on the sofa. He could see that she lived alone; the room was very feminine: women's magazines, pastel lamps, an arrangement of dried flowers.

Amanda Kennedy lit a cigarette. "Where did you get that photograph?" she said to the television screen.

"It was found in Sheboygan's car."

"Where was his car?"

"I didn't come here to *answer* questions," Carr said. "Just *ask* them."

Amanda Kennedy's face was expressionless. A soap opera couple embraced.

"When did you first meet Leon Sheboygan?" Carr asked patiently.

"I'm the resident manager here. I met him when he moved in. It was about six months ago. He filled in an application. The application was approved and he moved in."

"What kind of a person was he?"

"He never talked about himself," she said in a tone of disgust. "I think he was in the jewelry business. That's all I really know about him. We had a brief . . . affair . . . we really never got to know one another."

"May I take a look at his rental application?"

"I don't have it anymore," she said. The man and woman on television alternated between sighing and making emotional statements.

"Who were Sheboygan's friends?"

"Various people."

"What are the names of the various people?"

"I don't remember."

Carr reached into his coat pocket and pulled out the bedroom photograph of the man with the gray-streaked hair. He held it out to her. She glanced at it and back to the TV. "Do you know this man and woman?" he asked.

"That's Lee's friend. He moved out a few weeks ago. The woman is someone he . . . uh . . . dated."

"What's her name?"

The TV lovers hugged and kissed. More sighs. The male opened a cardboard door and walked out of the house.

"I don't remember," she said.

"Is there anything you *do* recall about Sheboygan or his associates?"

She looked at him and shook her head. "I want that photograph. You have no right to keep it."

"I'm very interested in Sheboygan and what you know about him," Carr said. "If you could see your way to being more cooperative, it might save a lot of problems that could develop for you later. As I'm sure you've read in the newspaper, Sheboygan was killed breaking into the home of a federal witness. Unless the matter can be cleared up, it could drag on and on."

"Are you through?"

Carr pulled out the bedroom photograph and handed it to her. She tore it up and crumbled the pieces in her hand. He stood up and walked to the door, opened it and left quietly.

From Amanda Kennedy's apartment, Charles Carr drove directly to the Los Angeles Police Department's downtown headquarters. He parked his sedan in an underground garage and took an elevator to the sixth floor. There, he wound through some corridors to a small office. The door of the office read Pawn Shop Detail.

Six hours later he was still there, sitting at a desk in the corner of the room reading three-ring binders full of pawn shop circulars. The binders he had finished reviewing sat stacked around him on the desk and the floor. He had decided not to replace them in the metal filing cabinets until he had completed them all. God forbid he should get mixed up and waste an hour or more reviewing one of the boring volumes for the second time. Turning page after page of mimeographed sheets bearing rough sketches of stolen pendants, rings, silverware, wristwatches and medallions had given him a headache after only an hour or so.

By three hours his back and butt, as well as his head, ached. Somehow, he developed a second wind. Later, the second wind went away.

Finally, he felt like his entire body had fallen asleep and only his brain was working. The room was hot and he had an urge for a cold beer. He turned another page. A sketch of a star-shaped medallion did not jump out.

It just sat there staring at him.

The detective responsible for the sketch had drawn little arrows pointing to three points on the star. The notation read: "*inlaid diamonds on these points only, victim says they are ¼ carat.*" Below the drawing and the notation was a printed caption: "*Medallion stolen during West L.A. residential burglary.* See Crime Report L4921368/Victim: Morganthau, Adam." Carr closed his eyes and pictured the medallion Amanda Kennedy had been wearing . . . It had to be the same one.

Carr snapped the binder release and removed the page from the folder. He carried the page to a copying machine in the corner of the room. Having made a copy, he replaced the page in the binder. It took him almost a half hour to refile the binders.

On his way downstairs to Higgins's office, he stopped at a bank of food vending machines, where he bought a stale candy bar, which he ate in two bites, and a fresh pack of cigarettes.

* * *

Early the next morning Carr waited in a dingy visiting room at the L.A. County Women's Jail. He lit another cigarette and realized that the pack was almost empty. A bearded young man who looked like an attorney and a fat black woman sat at one of the long tables. They were separated by a face-high clear-plastic partition. Because of the early hour, they were the only ones in the room. In a ceiling corner, a closed-circuit TV camera scanned back and forth.

There was the sound of a hydraulic lock snapping open. A large steel door in the corner of the room slid slowly into the wall. Amanda Kennedy, dressed in a county-issued blue denim sack dress, walked through the doorway. She stopped and stared at Carr for a moment, then came forward and sat down on the other side of the table.

"I hope I didn't keep you from getting breakfast," Carr said.

"Oatmeal mush," she said. "Oatmeal mush makes me sick." She had neither makeup nor any form of expression on her face. "I didn't know that medallion was stolen."

Carr lit another cigarette. He held the pack above the partition. She shook her head as if he had offered poison.

"You're the one who told the police I had the medallion," she said. "They wouldn't tell me who told them, but I know it was you. You told them to put me in jail. I was up all night being processed. I don't feel well. Although I'm sure this will come as a shock to a person like you, I've been in jail only once in my whole life. I was at a friend's apartment one night. He was an airline pilot and these narcs broke down the door. They said my friend was a heroin smuggler. I hadn't done anything, but they arrested me anyway. Every time I'd try to tell them that I was just visiting, they'd tell me to shut up. I spent three days in jail and I hadn't done anything . . . May I ask you a question?"

Carr nodded.

"If someone gives you a gift and that gift turns out to be stolen, is the person who accepts the gift guilty of possession of stolen property?"

"It depends."

She sat back. "I want to see a lawyer."

"Why waste the money? I can give you the same advice he'll give you and without a retainer fee: *Don't talk. Don't say a word to the cops, no matter what they promise you*. There, I just saved you a thousand bucks."

Amanda Kennedy began to pick at her face, then self-consciously stopped herself. "I don't want to go to jail for something I didn't do."

Carr looked nonchalant. "I just stopped by to ask you a few questions."

"And if I don't answer them I'm going to be prosecuted, isn't that right?"

Carr stared at her for a moment.

Amanda Kennedy picked at her face furiously. She folded and unfolded her arms. More picking. "I don't believe in talking about people," she said finally. "It's against my principles."

"Mine too," Carr said. He wondered if he was playing it too hard.

"What if I told you that Lee gave me the medallion? He's dead. What good is information about someone who's dead?"

Deliberately, he reached into his coat pocket and removed the photograph of the man and woman cavorting in Sheboygan's bedroom. He held it up to her. She stared at it without expression. "Who are these people?"

"Friends of Lee's."

"What are their *names?*"

"I'm not going to tell you."

Carr stood up. Casually, he removed his sport coat. He hung it on the back of the chair and sat down again.

"I have a brief relationship with a man who lives in one of the apartments I manage," she said. "He gives me a medallion as a gift for my birthday. The next thing I know he's dead and I'm in jail being treated like an animal. Is that fair?"

"What is the man's name?"

"You had them arrest me in order to force me to answer your questions," she said, her voice rising. "Some people would call that coercion. Coercion is against the law."

"If you're innocent, why not just answer my questions and stop changing the subject?"

"It's the principle of the thing. I have principles."

They stared at each other for a while.

"Would it violate your principles if I found the information written on a scrap of paper in that wastebasket?" He pointed to a metal trash receptacle next to the door.

She made a quizzical expression.

"The information would be anonymous. I just found it on a scrap of paper in a trash can. That way no one is informing on anyone."

Face picking.

"What would you put in your report?"

"My report would reflect exactly that," Carr said, "that I found the information in a trash basket at the County Jail."

"What's going to happen to me?"

"The detectives want you prosecuted," he said. "A

valuable medallion was stolen in a burglary. It was around your neck. Under the law, you are a receiver of stolen property. I think they can make the case stick. You might end up doing a little time for it. Just a guess."

"And if I answer your questions?"

"Then the charges might be dismissed."

Nothing was said for a while. Carr pulled a ballpoint pen and a note pad out of his inside pocket. He passed them over to her, stood up, put on his coat and left the room. He walked briskly down a tiled corridor and entered an office. Higgins sat straddling a chair in front of a small television screen. On the screen, Amanda Kennedy picked at her face as she stared at the paper and pen.

"She's thinking about it," Higgins said. "If she'd been around a little more, she'd know that the D.A. would never file a receiving case on her. Hell, it's hard enough to get them to file a case when you catch a burglar red-handed inside someone's house."

Amanda Kennedy reached for the pen. She pulled her hand back, glanced at the trash basket.

"Come on, sweet meat," Higgins said. He slid his chair closer to the television.

Amanda Kennedy seemed to be sniffling. She wiped her eyes. "The waterworks," Higgins said. "This is a very good sign. A very good sign."

Amanda Kennedy pulled a handkerchief from the pocket of her prison smock. She blew her nose and put the handkerchief away. Having done this, she picked up the pen and wrote something on the piece of paper.

Higgins clapped. Carr took a deep breath. Amanda Kennedy stood up and went to the door. The lock snapped and the door slid open. She crumpled the paper into a ball and tossed it in the trash can on her way out.

Carr and Higgins hurried back to the room. The trash can was empty except for the note. He picked it up and unfolded it. The note read:

> His nickname is Bones and he is a bartender. That's all I know. The redhead is Shirley. She's a cocktail waitress. I think they work in the same place.

"Gee thanks," Higgins said. "A nickname."

"I guess it's better than nothing," Carr replied.

Chapter 5

IT WAS the middle of the day and the tall palms that lined Coventry Circle Avenue swayed gently west. The sky was uncommonly azure—the heraldic, smogless Southern California blue of tourist postcards and movie sets.

Emil Kreuzer steered his Mercedes-Benz sedan off Coventry Circle Avenue and into a semicircle driveway leading to a two-story home. The juniper bushes guarding the spotless driveway were shaped into perfect globes and the manicured expanse of lawn was money green. He parked the sedan in front of the house and climbed out. Having put on a suit coat, he straightened his necktie, then headed toward the mansion's main entrance. At the door, he used a door knocker that was a brass *W*.

A frail, middle-aged woman with slack jowls answered the door. Her hair was pulled back at the temples and she wore an abundance of rouge that seemed to match the color of her dress, and a string of pearls.

"Good morning, Mrs. Wallace," Kreuzer said using

his German accent. He noticed brown age-spots on her forehead, even under the layer of makeup.

She motioned him in. "I'm glad you didn't come early. My husband just left to go on location. He'll be in Spain directing a Western. He wanted me to go, but I hate hotel rooms and not being able to say what I want in my own language."

Kreuzer stepped in and she closed the door. He followed her through a hallway decorated with impressionist art into the living room. Was the watercolor nearest the door a Degas?

"Arthur is so *anti-everything,*" she said. "If I would have told him I had retained you for hypnotherapy he would have come unglued. My husband is from the old school I'm afraid. To him, hypnosis is equated with voodoo."

"This is understandable," Kreuzer said sympathetically.

The living room was a striking combination of pink satin, glass and oil paintings of flowers in vases. The floor was covered by an immaculate sea of white shag carpeting. Mrs. Wallace sat down on a sofa, while Kreuzer chose a chair. "I detect an accent," she said. "Is it German?"

Kreuzer nodded. "I received my doctorate at the University of Berlin." He recognized an oil painting on the wall behind her as a Gauguin.

"I've heard so much about you from my friends at the club. Both Ivy and Harriet told me they haven't had an urge for a cigarette since their first session with you. My doctor has been literally *begging* me to stop smoking." She picked up a gold cigarette case off the coffee table. It was thin and her initials were inlaid in rows of tiny diamonds. "This is a birthday present from my husband.

It holds ten cigarettes and it has a time lock. It can be opened only every hour and a half. It was supposed to limit me to ten cigarettes a day, but I can't help cheating. I've tried millions of times to quit and nothing has worked." She folded her arms.

"At the end of our session you will feel pleasant, more relaxed than you have in a long, long time, and you will no longer have the desire to smoke cigarettes," Kreuzer said. His tone was authoritative.

"I have a couple of questions."

"Of course. Everyone has questions about hypnosis. It's only natural."

"I know that you appear in the nightclub acts. I've heard that in your stage act, audience volunteers sometimes are made to act foolish . . ."

"You will do nothing under hypnosis that you wouldn't do in the waking state," Kreuzer said in a reassuring manner. "And I promise not to suggest any stage behavior to you. I am here to simply cure you of your smoking habit. I consider you my patient and you should trust me as you would any doctor."

"What happens if I go into a trance and don't wake up? Could I get stuck asleep?"

"That question is the one I'm most frequently asked," Kreuzer said patiently. He folded his hands. "The answer is that no one has *ever* been stuck in hypnosis. The state of hypnosis is nothing more than a state of deep relaxation. It's similar to the way you feel at night just before you fall asleep. It is a healthy, grafitying experience that can help one to control one's bad habits."

Mrs. Wallace set the cigarette case down on the table. She rubbed her hands on her dress. "I have the urge for a cigarette right this very minute."

Kreuzer gave her a fatherly smile. "Are you ready to relax and lose your desire to smoke?"

She nodded.

"You may find it easier to relax if you lie down on the sofa," Kreuzer said, "or you may sit up if you'd like. This is your choice."

She lay back on the sofa, adjusted a decorative pillow under her head, then straightened her dress to cover her knees.

Kreuzer slid a glass ball pendulum from his pocket. He hung it slightly above her eye level. "Focus on the pendulum. You will find that as you do your eyes will become tired and want to close . . . more and more tired . . . more and more difficult to keep them open . . ." He repeated the phrases over and over again. In a minute she closed her eyes. "Now you can feel the tension being released from the bottoms of your feet and a deep feeling of relaxation moving slowly along the muscles in your legs . . . now your arms are starting to feel heavy and so comfortable . . . and the muscles in your neck . . . so, so relaxed . . . relaxed and comfortable and more pleasant than you have felt in a long, long time."

After a half hour of such patter Kreuzer noticed the deep abdominal breathing, the sure sign of a trance. "You are becoming more and more relaxed with each and every breath that you take." He stood up and strolled quietly around the room. He took a small notebook out of his back pocket and sketched a diagram of the living room.

Walking on his tiptoes, he crept up the stairs and into the master bedroom. He sketched another diagram. Back down the stairs. He thoroughly examined the paintings in the hallway, then returned to the living room. Mrs.

Wallace swallowed. Kreuzer put the notebook and pen away. She was still breathing deeply. Because of the position of her head, a face-lift scar above her ear was evident.

"More and more relaxed with each and every breath that you take," Kreuzer said softly. "We are reaching the end of our pleasant period of relaxation. When you awake, the smell of cigarette smoke will remind you of the disagreeable smell of a hospital. You will be strongly repulsed and disgusted by the smell of cigarette smoke and you will find any contact with cigarettes to be an unpleasant experience. To you, cigarette smoke will be as acrid as the fumes of disinfectant on a contaminated hospital floor. In a moment I will snap my fingers three times. At the third snap you will come awake feeling relaxed and rested, as if you had a full night's sleep, but you will not consciously remember the suggestions I have made to you about cigarette smoke." Emil Kreuzer snapped his fingers three times.

Mrs. Wallace stirred. She opened her eyes.

"How do you feel?" he asked.

"I feel rested." Mrs. Wallace rubbed her eyes.

Kreuzer picked up the cigarette case. "I'm afraid you won't be needing this anymore," he said as she sat up.

Kreuzer took off his eyeglasses and cleaned them on his necktie before he stood up to leave. "You were a very good patient. A fine, fine patient." Kreuzer handed the cigarette case to her. She stared at it for a moment, then set it back on the table. Kreuzer pulled a pack of cigarettes out of his shirt pocket. He offered them to her.

Mrs. Wallace stared at the pack. She said, "No, thank you."

"I want you to hold the pack to your nose and inhale."

The woman obeyed. She coughed and dropped the cigarettes on the floor.

"They smell awful!" she said with features contorted.

"You have been a very good patient. I'll come back and see you in two weeks to check on your progress." He patted her hands.

Mrs. Wallace gave him a check for four hundred dollars and he left. Outside, he started the Mercedes-Benz and followed the wide Beverly Hills streets to the freeway toward downtown Los Angeles. He glanced at his wristwatch. Unless there was heavy traffic or an accident tie-up, he would have just enough time to make it to his monthly appointment with his parole officer.

Emil Kreuzer parked the Mercedes-Benz in a parking lot next door to the Federal Building and made his way to the ninth floor. He entered the double doors of the Federal Parole Office and gave his name to a young black woman wearing designer jeans and a leotard top. She motioned him to one of the musty sofas lining the walls of the waiting area. The men and women sitting on the sofas had the familiar, more-than-bored expression that was the mark of those who shared the prison experience: the zombie face of those who shuffled in line to take a shower, had their feet fall asleep during dreary, chickenshit counseling sessions, read the same magazine for the fourth or fifth time and listened to the same smelly cons cud-chew the same bullshit stories over and over and over again month after boring month.

Emil Kreuzer took a seat on a sofa next to a lanky black man wearing a flat cap. The man stared at him for a moment. "Remember me?" he said. "I was in D Wing. You got released before I did."

Kreuzer looked at the man disdainfully. He shook his head.

"You're Mr. Hocus Pocus," the black man said.

Kreuzer flashed a cold smile. He leaned back and rested his head against the wall. Having closed his eyes, he took deep breaths until he sank deeply into restful relaxation. As usual when he practiced self-hypnosis, time seemed to fly. His name was called and he sat up. The black man was gone. Kreuzer stood up and wandered through an open doorway and down a hallway to his parole officer's office. Oddly, as he stepped into the messy office, he realized that although he had visited him monthly for five months, he had forgotten the man's name.

The parole officer, a prematurely bald, sunburned man who could not have been over thirty years old, held a Dictaphone to his lips. ". . . and I have found that the parolee's ego needs exceed her social abilities in effective terms as relates to her probable adjustment to family, general societal and job pressures . . ." He clicked off the machine and set the microphone on a cradle. He looked at Kreuzer as if he had walked in the office with a paper bag over his head.

"I'm Emil Kreuzer." *And I can't remember your name either, fuckface.*

The parole officer nodded. He swiveled around in his chair and sorted through a stack of files. He found a file and turned around to the desk. Having licked his thumb, he flipped through pages.

"Are you still employed?" the parole officer said without looking up from the file.

"Yes, sir."

The parole officer opened his desk drawer. He pulled

out the usual memo pad printed with little boxes. He filled one of the boxes with a check mark. "Where?"

"The same place. The Magic Carpet nightclub."

The parole officer made another check mark. "And during the last month have you been arrested?"

"No."

"Have you associated with any persons known to you to be convicted felons?"

"No."

"Have you used any dangerous drugs?"

"No."

The parole officer made another check mark. He looked up. "Not even marijuana?"

"Sir, I don't need to get high on marijuana. Since I've been out of prison, I've been high on life." *You bald-headed blob of shit.*

The parole officer scribbled something on the memo pad. He paper-clipped it to the front of the file and tossed the file in an "out" box. He pressed an intercom button. "Send in the next one," he said. As he picked up the Dictaphone and began to speak, Emil Kreuzer stood up and left the office.

On the way to his West Hollywood apartment, Kreuzer drove slowly along Sunset Boulevard. Though it was early in the day, the usual assortment of street hustlers, whores (they all seemed to be wearing straight skirts slit up the side), bun boys (tight jeans, tennis shoes and tropical shirts) and black pimps (outrageous hats and shoes) paraded about in front of the gaudy motels along the boulevard that once catered to star-struck tourists. Young hitchhikers of both sexes lined the curbs on both sides of the street like human ornaments. Everyone was waiting to meet strangers.

A teenage girl wearing a loose-fitting blouse and white

shorts stood next to a bus bench with her thumb out. She had a small canvas knapsack on her back. Her sandy hair was naturally curly and her features were attractive. Kreuzer thought she looked like a high school cheerleader. He made a right turn and drove around the block. He pulled up to the bus bench and the teenager approached the car. He could see that she had freckles. "I'm going to Malibu," she said.

"I'm going right past there." Kreuzer leaned over and unlocked the passenger door. She shrugged off her knapsack and climbed in the front seat.

"I'm Dr. Kreuzer," he said. "What's your name?"

"Charlene." She stared out the window. "What kind of a doctor are you?"

"A medical doctor. I specialize in the practice of psychiatry."

"I bet you meet some really weird people."

"As a matter of fact, I work mostly with young people."

"Are they all crazy?" she said, showing mild interest.

"Just kids with problems. Most of them have run away from home and have second doubts about it. They're glad to be out from under the pressures they had at home, but on the other hand they are unhappy with the usual hassles of life on the street." He glanced at her. There was no visible reaction.

Charlene stared at the road.

"What's in Malibu?" Kreuzer asked.

"A job. This guy I met told me there was a coffee shop opening up. They need waitresses."

"May I ask how old you are?"

"Fifteen and a half."

They passed a movie theater. On the marquee was a

color blowup of a long-haired movie star hugging a chimpanzee.

Charlene pointed at the theater. "I saw that movie," she said. "It was really neat. This guy trains these monkeys to be spies and they parachute into Russia. This one monkey was riding around on a dog. I really laughed."

"I love animals," he said. "I have horses and dogs at my ranch in Santa Barbara. I go there every weekend."

"I love horses, too," Charlene said. "At home I had a scrapbook with pictures of horses. And when I was fourteen, I worked in a stable. My uncle got me the job . . . Can I turn on the radio?"

"Certainly."

As Charlene fiddled with the dials, he tried to look down her blouse. She tuned into a station with screaming rock music. Her hands tapped her smooth thighs to the beat.

"Have you ever worked as a waitress before?" he asked.

Charlene shook her head. "No, but this girl I met said that you can make a lot of money in tips."

"Do you have a Malibu work permit?"

She turned toward him with a puzzled look. "What's that?"

"Malibu is an environmental impact area. No one can be hired without a special work permit. As I understand it, there's a four-month waiting period for permits. I'm afraid you're not going to have much luck finding work in Malibu."

"Shit."

"Are you still interested in horses?" he said in an offhand manner.

She nodded.

"I have an opening for a horse groomer at my ranch. "You're certainly welcome to fill out an application if you'd like."

"Gee, that'd be great."

"I live nearby. We can stop and you can fill out an application."

"How do I know you're really a doctor?"

He pulled a phony business card out of his shirt pocket and handed it to her. "It pays to be cautious. That's exactly what I tell all my young patients. It's better to be safe than sorry."

Nothing was said for a while. They passed a restaurant that featured transvestite waiters.

She examined the card again and looked him over. "Okay," she said finally. Charlene fiddled with the radio as he swung onto a side street and headed north toward the Hollywood Hills.

Emil Kreuzer's apartment was furnished handsomely with a black L-shaped sofa and matching reclining chairs. The prints on the wall above a modern-looking fireplace were of sad-eyed children. They were mounted on either side of a phony Univeristy of Berlin diploma. Charlene stared at the diploma for a moment, then wandered to the bay window. The view was of the Hollywood business district. Finally she strolled to the sofa and sat down.

Kreuzer picked up a small box off the coffee table. He opened the lid and offered Charlene a marijuana cigarette. She hesitated. "Doctors use it too," he said. "It's harmless. I even allow my patients to use it." She took one of the neatly rolled cigarettes, which he lit with a lighter.

"This is like a movie star's house," Charlene said.

"It used to be owned by John Wayne."

"Jeez."

"You've had problems with your family, haven't you?" Kreuzer asked in a fatherly tone.

"How did you know that?"

"I'm a doctor. I get paid to recognize these things."

Using her hands to cup smoke, she took a powerful drag on the cigarette. She blew out smoke. "My father is an asshole, that's why I ran away."

"It helps to talk about it."

"I went to the beach with two of my girl friends and when I got home late he called me a whore and grounded me for a month. I just couldn't stand it anymore."

"And your mother?"

"She left two years ago. She wrote me once." Another marijuana puff.

Kreuzer stood up, went to the kitchen and brought back a glass of water. Having set the glass on the coffee table in front of Charlene, he handed her a small white pill. "I want you to take this," he said. "It will help you to express your thoughts and resolve some of your problems."

She stared at the pill for a moment.

"I am a doctor, Charlene. There is nothing to worry about. Go ahead and take the pill. It will make you feel more pleasant and comfortable than you have in a long, long time; pleasant, secure and relaxed."

Charlene took the pill, puffed more marijuana.

A few minutes later she leaned back. Her eyes shut. She mumbled something about her mother. Emil Kreuzer took the burning roach out of her hand and dropped it into an ashtray. "Can you hear me, Charlene?" he said. She didn't answer. He quickly straddled her on the sofa. Having unbuttoned her blouse, he massaged and licked her firm breasts. His hands rushed to her panties. Because of the fastener and the fact they were at least one size too small, it took him longer than usual to pull them off.

It was 1:00 A.M.

Travis Bailey parked in front of a store whose display window was full of mannequins wearing mink and sable coats. He climbed out of the car and trotted across the street to a door with a three-foor-tall eye painted over it. Above the eye, polished brass letters spelled:

The Magic Carpet
Dr. Emil Kreuzer—One Night Only

He nodded at the valet parking attendant standing in front and went in.

Inside, a well-dressed crowd sitting at cocktail tables stared at a small stage.

Emil Kreuzer stood in the middle of the stage holding a microphone. In mellifluous tones he reeled off hypnotic patter to a dark-haired young woman sitting in a chair. Because of the stage light his tuxedo and powder blue dress shirt appeared to have a fluorescent tinge. Suddenly he grabbed the woman's arm and raised it in the air. "Stiff!" he commanded. "Your arm is *stiff!* As stiff and *rigid* as a *steel bar!*" He took his hand away and the woman's arm remained pointing straight up in the air. "Now as you try to move your arm, you will find that you are unable to do so. The harder you try to move it, the more *stiff* and *rigid* your arm becomes." The woman tried to move her arm but couldn't. The crowd murmured. Someone in the rear of the room spilled a drink and said, "Damn."

Kreuzer touched the woman's arm again. "At the count of three your arm will return to normal and fall pleasantly and comfortably into your lap," he said. He counted to three and the arm dropped. The crowd applauded heartily. He snapped his fingers and the woman opened her eyes. He shook hands with her. She returned to her front-row table. The applause continued as Kreuzer bowed from right to left. The curtain dropped and the show was over.

Travis Bailey found his way behind the stage into a small office. He sat down at a desk covered with wholesale liquor receipts.

Minutes later, Kreuzer plodded into the office. He locked the door. Having removed his tuxedo jacket, he hung it over a chair, then pulled off his bow tie. "What the fuck happened?" he said through gritted teeth. "I've been biting my nails for three days."

"It was an accident," Bailey said without expression. "He got in my way."

"Any feedback?"

Bailey bit his lip for a moment. "Carr was nosing around Hartmann's place but I think he was just filling in details for his reports. I'm not worried."

Emil Kreuzer pulled off his shirt and undershirt and tossed them on the floor. He got a towel out of a desk drawer and wiped his sweaty chest and arms. "You'll have to watch out for Carr. He's a snake. He'll creep up on you when you least expect it. He's mean and he won't give up. When he put me in the joint years ago I never knew what hit me. He just pulled the rug out."

"It was your idea to call him in on the stakeout," Bailey said. "I told you I wanted to do it alone."

"Calling him in was . . . all things considered . . . without question, the best thing to do," Kreuzer said, gesturing. "With the Feds involved, no one will ever question what went down. With the owner of the house being a federal witness in Tony Dio's bank scam case, the incident will wash as a contract hit that went sour. There will be a grand jury investigation and they'll subpoena Tony Dio and every other wop in the San Fernando Valley. They'll take the Fifth. The grand jury will adjourn and that's that. I'm telling you the whole thing will *wash*. And you'll have a plausible reason for refusing to reveal who your informant is. You're just trying to protect him from the *Mafia*."

"They'll still ask."

Kreuzer took off his trousers, which he arranged carefully on a hanger. He scooped the tuxedo coat off the chair and brushed it off with the back of his hand. Having hung the evening attire on a wall hook, he pulled on a pair of plaid pants. Because of his blubbery midsection, he could barely pull up the zipper.

"I'm sure you didn't call me just to Monday-morning-quarterback," Bailey said.

Kreuzer pulled on a bright orange shirt. He pointed to a small notebook on the desk. Bailey picked it up. The notations on the first page read:

Wallace
Phone: 242-9168
1402 Coventry Circle Avenue

On the next page was a rough diagram of a house with the entrances marked with *X*'s.

"There is a set of silver in the dining room that is worth at least ten grand," Kreuzer said. "The oriental vase in the living room looks like the real thing. I want the art hanging in the hallway. One is a Degas. Unless you have the time, forget the oils in the living room. They're more trouble than they're worth. There's got to be jewelry too. I saw alarm tape on the front window only." He pulled a comb out of his pocket and ran it straight back through his oily straight hair. He blew into the comb and put it back in his pocket. "There are no private patrol stickers on the windows."

Travis Bailey ripped the page out of the notebook. He stuffed it in his shirt pocket. "I finally got Delsey in."

"Congratulations," Kreuzer said perfunctorily. "I hope she works out. I really do."

Travis Bailey stood up to leave.

"In general, I'm very pleased with the way things are going," Kreuzer said. "There will be little obstacles from time to time, but I'm sure you agree that, overall, things are going well. I don't believe in being greedy. I really don't. There is enough sugar for everyone. I've always said that. There's more than enough sugar here in Sugarland."

"The town's been good to me," Bailey said. They exchanged smiles. Bailey opened the door, then looked both ways before he headed for his police car.

Chapter 6

IT WAS almost 2:00 A.M.

The wide and sterile streets of downtown Beverly Hills were all but deserted. Travis Bailey steered his police car off Rodeo Drive and onto a parking lot filled with Mercedes-Benzes, Cadillacs, expensive sports cars and a few limousines. He parked, locked the car and headed toward a two-story building adjoining the lot. He entered by a glass door. Inside a carpeted, theater-style lobby, a muscle-bound, sandy-haired young man wearing a tuxedo stood in front of a pair of ten-foot-high doors inscribed with blue velvet letters that read:

The Blue Peach
A Private Club

Standing behind ropes and stanchions on the other side of the lobby was a group of teenagers who hung out there on the nights the club was open: movie star groupies.

"Good evening, Mr. Bailey," the bouncer said. He opened the door. As Bailey entered the place, a Eurasian woman wearing satin culottes and a sable stole brushed past him on her way out. She was on the arm of a seven-foot black basketball star who, as Bailey recalled from a recent article in *Variety,* had just signed with Twentieth Century-Fox to do the lead in a musical on the Watts riots. The groupies squealed as the door closed behind him.

Bailey stopped for a moment to allow his eyes to adjust to the darkness. It was the regular Blue Peach scene of garishly dressed men and women lounging on sofas that, because of the ceiling lights and the effects of the dark shag carpeting, appeared as fluorescent rafts on a black sea. To the left, a long bar extended the length of the wall. Its mirrors winked reflections of colored lights. At the opposite end of the room was a dimly lit stage backdropped with a blue velvet curtain.

Travis Bailey found his way to the end of the bar and climbed onto one of the few empty stools. The crowd was made up of men and women dressed similarly; jeans tight enough to make crotches bulge, open-collar shirts and blouses with gold chains, and boots—expensive ones made of snake or shark or lizard. The man and woman sitting next to him, with their twin blonde hairdos, could have been mistaken for sisters. They spoke to one another with great urgency and used lots of hand gestures; cocaine language.

"It was absolutely, incredibly, wonderful," the woman said in a New York accent. "I've never seen anything in my life that was so great, so . . . powerful, so emotional. It makes tears come to my eyes just thinking about it. I loved every minute of it. Damn, it was fantastic, terrific . . ."

"I just can't begin to tell you how much I agree with you," interrupted her male companion. "I completely agree with every word . . . I mean *every* single fucking word you have just said. Jesus, it was a beautiful movie . . ." Both of them tapped their fingers on the bar frantically.

Bobby Chagra, an athletic-looking man of Bailey's age, stood at the opposite end of the bar drying cocktail glasses. He wore a blue Hawaiian-style shirt and white form-fitting trousers that glowed in the dark. He acknowledged Bailey and headed toward him. He pinched a bar napkin and set it in front of Bailey. "What can I get you, sir?" he said as if they had never met.

Bailey ordered a drink. Chagra scooped ice into a glass. He poured, then set the drink in front of Bailey.

"So, what's new in here?" Bailey said.

Chagra glanced at the couple sitting next to Bailey, who continued to rattle intensely to one another. "There's a lady lawyer at the end of the bar that likes to take it in the ass," he said. "She'll even tell you that if you ask her . . . Interested?"

Travis Bailey shook his head. "No dirt roads for me," he said with a smile.

"You should have seen this young bitch that cruised in here last night. She sat down right where you are and starts talking about how she loves coke. She was a healthy-looking bitch, a jogger type with a great rack . . . a couple of real pointers. And I'm not talking about a bra with rubber nipples. I'm talking about a pair of honest-to-Christ pointed nips that must have weighed as much as silver dollars." He cupped his hands at chest level. "I'm talking about *radar,* man. Plus the bitch had a nice ass; small waist, nice ass. I blew a little smoke on her, introduced her to a few of the studio people who hang in here. Like I can see she's buying my act. Before closing time I hit on her and she goes for the 'horn-a-little-coke-at-my-place' act. The only problem is I don't have any fucking cocaine! She follows me over to my pad. She wants a spoon right off. I asked her to wait, that I'm into balling *naturally.* I promised her I'd drag out my stash as soon as we got it on. 'Fair enough,' she says. Then she bends over, undoes her four-hooker and tosses the rest of her clothes. She musta read one of those sex manuals. You should see her act. She was really getting *into* it. Afterward we're lying there in the bed. The bitch is sweating. She has come all over her and she says, 'Where's the cocaine?' I told the dumb bitch to get the fuck out of my apartment. You should have seen the look on her face!"

They laughed.

"Bitches like her are in here every night," Chagra said. "They all claim to have a script that's going to sell *next week*. Either that or they've just had an argument with their boyfriend and she walked out and left him in Palm Springs or La Paz. I let 'em tell their little sob story, then I ball 'em at closing time."

A red-haired cocktail waitress wearing a see-through blouse flitted up to the bar station. "Hello, Travis," she said in her best slinky tone. She called off the names of drinks. Chagra prepared them quickly and set them on her serving tray. "You're sure talkative tonight," she said to Bailey. He ignored her as she hefted her tray and headed toward the lounge area.

"There's a Jewish guy at the end of the bar who's got the broad sitting next to him convinced that he's a Cherokee Indian," Chagra said, laughing.

"We need to talk," Bailey said.

"I know we do."

"Get someone to fill in for you." Bailey climbed off the bar stool and wandered into the men's room. The carpeted and mirrored room smelled of lilac deodorant. It was vacant. He turned on the faucet and washed his hands. A minute later Chagra pushed open the door. He joined Bailey at the sinks. He had a worried look.

"I wish you would have told me you were going to do it," Chagra said. "It was chickenshit that you didn't tell me."

"Tell you what, Bones?"

"Lee screwed up and if somebody screws me I don't give a shit what happens to him," Bones said. "Lee had it coming. You and I always split even with him and he turned around and fucked us right in the ass. Things were going perfect and he ruined everything by shaving off the top. I told you when I first brought him in that I wasn't one hundred percent sure of the motherfucker . . . but that he *seemed* okay. I had no way of knowing."

"He *was* okay . . ." Bailey said, "until he got greedy." His smile was sarcastic.

"I told Emil that Lee sold that Picasso behind our backs. I had a right to know if you were going to do anything radical. You should have told me."

Travis Bailey dried his hands. He slipped a comb out of his back pocket and ran it through his hair a few times. "You've made your point," he said to the mirror. He put the comb away. Having slipped the note with the Coventry Circle address from his pocket, he handed it to Chagra.

Chagra unfolded the note. His lips moved as he read it.

"Questions?" Bailey said.

"Dogs?"

"Emil says no dogs."

"Is he *sure* there are no dogs? It seems like everyone who lives on Coventry Circle has dogs."

Bailey shrugged. "Emil said there are no dogs to worry about."

"Is there a safe?"

"He didn't see one when he cased the place," Bailey said, again speaking to the mirror. "But if you see one, I'd say it would definitely be worth spending some time on. Why rush and miss a prize?"

The men's room door opened. Bailey and Chagra busied themselves at the sink. A frizzy-haired man in his twenties wearing a red jump suit and European-frame eyeglasses staggered in the door and approached a urinal.

Bailey followed Chagra out the door. In the dark alcove outside the rest room he grabbed Chagra by the arm. "Do you remember the address?"

"Fourteen-oh-two Coventry Circle."

Travis Bailey pulled the note bearing the address from Chagra's shirt pocket. He tore the note into pieces and tossed them into a stand-up ashtray. "Go for it," he said, and walked away. As he passed through the lounge area on his way to the front door, the stage lights came on. A tall black woman wearing a skin-tight black leather outfit strutted onto the stage. The combo behind her started playing. She straddled the microphone and shrieked unintelligible lyrics.

The ceiling lights pulsated.

Charles Carr sat at his desk in the Field Office. The notepaper scribbled with phone numbers that he'd found in Leon Sheboygan's apartment was in front of him. He lit a cigarette and set it in an ashtray. He dialed a number. It was not in service. He drew a line through it.

He dialed another. A man with a whiskey voice said, "Hello."

"This is Charlie," Carr said. "Did you hear about Leon?"

"Leon who?"

"Leon Sheboygan."

"What about him?" the man said. He yawned Indian-yell style.

"He got wasted by the cops."

"No lie?"

"No lie. They blew him up inside a house in Beverly Hills."

The man yawned again. "That is some real heavy shit, man. Wow."

"I'm trying to get in touch with Bones to let him know," Carr said. ". . . any ideas where I can reach him?"

"You tried Manny?"

"Not yet."

"He should know," the man said.

"I lost his phone number."

"Where'd you say we met?"

"At the party."

"Yeah, I think I remember. What'd ya say your name was?"

"Charlie."

"Okay," the man mumbled. He read off a number.

Carr wrote it down, then hung up the receiver for a moment. He dialed. A woman answered. Carr asked for Manny.

"Manny's not here," she said. "Who is calling?"

"Charlie. I'm trying to find Bones. It's important."

"Bones hasn't been around here in a couple of weeks," she said. ". . . Charlie who?"

"Lee's friend."

"Lee's dead."

"That's why I'm trying to find Bones."

"I think Manny is supposed to see him this week."

"Where?"

"Fuck if I know."

Carr said thanks and hung up. Carr dialed another number. A woman answered.

"I'm trying to find Lee," Carr said. "Is he there?"

A silence. "God . . ." she said in an anguished tone, "haven't you heard?"

"About what?"

"Lee is . . . uh . . . dead. Sorry for saying it over the phone like that."

"Jeez," Carr said. "How did it happen?"

"The pigs shot him. He was doing a place and they were waiting inside. I couldn't sleep all night after I heard."

"Does Bones know?"

"Who's Bones?"

"His roommate. The guy with the gray hair."

"Oh, him. I've only met him once."

"Any ideas where I can reach him?"

"By the way, who is this?" the woman's tone changed abruptly.

"Charlie," Carr said. "Lee and I did some time together."

"Oh. Lee probably mentioned your name and I just don't remember. I'm really superbad with names. Really superbad."

"Do you have a number for Bones?"

"No . . . he was living with Lee up until a couple of weeks ago. I think they had an argument about something. Bones was supposed to have moved up to Malibu."

"Where can I find him?"

"I think he's still working at the . . . Say, just how did you get my telephone number?"

"Lee left an address book over at my place. He mentioned your name once."

"Even so, I don't think I should give any more information out over the phone," the woman said. "For all I know you could be a cop or something."

The phone clicked.

Carr set the receiver down on the cradle. There was one number left. Carr dialed. A man's voice answered, "Beverly Hills Police Department." Carr hung up.

It was late and he couldn't decide whether he was more hungry or tired. On his way to the Federal Building parking lot he toyed with the idea of heading straight for his apartment and getting a good night's sleep. Having climbed in his sedan, it seemed to drive itself to Chinatown. In a restaurant that was getting ready to close, he ordered an oversized plate of diced chicken with peanuts, a bowl of steamed rice and a pot of tea. He paid his bill and headed for his car. He climbed in and looked at his wristwatch. It was 1:00 A.M. After he rubbed his eyes for a while he started the engine.

He drove to Cedars of Lebanon Hospital and took the elevator to the fourth floor. He found his way to Jack Kelly's room and tiptoed in. Kelly still had tubes attached to his nose and arms. He breathed deeply. Carr thought his face looked yellowish in the dim light. He stood next to the bed for a long while. There were sounds in the hallway until a Filipino nurse pushed her way in the door. She was carrying a small tray. "He's not supposed to have visitors," she said as she approached the bed, "especially at this hour." She wiped Kelly's upper arm with alcohol-soaked cotton and gave him an injection.

Carr tiptoed out of the room.

Travis Bailey's unmarked police car was parked in the circular driveway in front of the Wallace residence.

Inside, he sat on the sofa in the white-carpeted living room with a clipboard on his lap. As Mrs. Wallace spoke, he filled in the spaces on a burglar report form.

"My gold lighter is gone too," she said gloomily. "I had left it on the bedroom dresser when I left for the theater. Just the thought of some strange person, some burglar, having been in my bedroom gives me goose bumps. My husband is on location and I phoned him and begged him to come back. I know I won't be able to sleep a wink in this house from now on without him here."

Bailey printed "gold cigarette case" under the section of the burglary report marked Property Taken. "What is your estimate of the value of the cigarette case?" he said.

"It had a diamond inlay," she said as she wrung her hands. "My husband gave it to me for my birthday. I know it cost at least three thousand dollars . . . Of course, diamonds have appreciated a great deal during the last year."

"Would six thousand be a fair estimate?"

"I'm sure it's worth at least that much," Mrs. Wallace said without looking him in the eye.

"I hope you have insurance. You've suffered quite a loss."

"California Life and Casualty," she said. ". . . Thank God the burglars didn't steal my abstracts." She pointed to them. They were painted by my sister . . .

in fact, she was the one who always said it was better to look at the brighter side of life. She said that out of all bad things comes something good. I've always believed that too."

Bailey read off the list of stolen items. He asked her if there was anything else. She said no. He handed her the clipboard and asked her to sign the burglary report. She signed the report and handed it back to him.

"Do you think there is any chance at all that you will be able to catch the burglar?" she said. "To get my things back?"

Travis Bailey shoved his pen into his shirt pocket. He looked the woman in the eye. "I'm going to do my very best to apprehend the person who committed this crime, Mrs. Wallace. You can count on that." He stood up.

"What will the burglar *do* with my things?"

"With luck, he'll try to pawn some of the items," Bailey said. "I capture a lot of burglars by checking the pawn books. But I must be candid and tell you that burglars are often able to dispose of their stolen property without being detected. I can't guarantee that the crime will be solved. The only thing I can tell you is that I'll be working very hard to find out who did it. You have my word on that."

Mrs. Wallace shook her head. "I can't believe this has happened to me . . . that an intruder has actually been inside this house."

"Is there anyone you suspect?"

Mrs. Wallace looked toward the door leading to the kitchen. "The maid has been acting a little strange lately," she whispered. "She told me that her father is ill in Mexico." She touched her fingertips to her cheeks. "Do servants act strangely before they steal things?"

Bailey nodded. "This is very common. And sometimes help that has been employed the longest are the ones that should be watched the closest."

A look of dismay crossed the woman's face. She stood up and followed Bailey to the door. He opened it. "I wish I could be more optimistic," Bailey said, "but unfortunately crime is on the increase in this city."

"I feel so *violated,*" Mrs. Wallace said, her voice trailing behind him as he left.

Chapter 7

AS WITH a lot of insurance companies in L.A., California Life and Casualty's main office was situated in a high-rise building on Wilshire Boulevard.

Travis Bailey stepped off an elevator into a reception area with wall-to-wall orange shag carpeting and brush-flick oil paintings with lots of brown and black. The receptionist, a ginger-haired woman wearing a summer dress that showed off acne scars on her back and chest, gave him a nod of recognition. She pressed a button. The door lock behind her buzzed open. Travis Bailey went through, heading down a hallway to Mark Davidson's office.

Davidson, a thinnish man in his late thirties, was on the phone. He motioned Bailey to a chair. Davidson's moustache and muttonchop sideburns were carefully trimmed and his teeth were crooked; extraordinarily white, but crooked. He hung up the phone. "And what, pray tell, doth thee bringest me this fine day?" Davidson asked. He smiled and Bailey thought of the talking horse on television: all teeth.

"I bring gold." Bailey smiled back as he handed Davidson a copy of the burglary report. "The gold of one of your insurees, a Frau Gertrude Wallace of Coventry Circle Road in our fair city. It seems that someone broke into the old lady's castle and stole all of her jewelry. I have an informant that's been offered the load. I thought you might be interested in the recovery."

Mark Davidson glanced at the report. "Lots of jewelry." He pressed an intercom button and gave Wallace's name, then asked for the file. "When are we going to be able to get together for lunch?" Davidson said. "Every time I call your office they tell me you're out in the field."

"Been busy as hell lately. The burglars have been working overtime."

"I read about the shooting."

"It was a close call, but it's all part of the job. What's new with you?"

"I've been jogging six miles a day. I'm at the point now where I can't wait to get out and start jogging as soon as I get home from the office. If I miss a day I actually feel *guilty* about it. I don't sleep well without the exercise. You should try it. Jogging is the greatest tension reliever in the world. A few months ago I was a bundle of nerves. Now I could care less. I just let things sort of *happen*. I've come to the realization that no one knows what I want better than *me*. And jogging is something I do for me. When I'm jogging, it's *my* time, *my* day, *my* body."

"I get my exercise by fucking," Bailey said.

Mark Davidson horse-smiled at the remark. "I've even got my wife into the jogging program. We get up early in the morning and get in some miles. At first she hated it, but now she's into it as much as I am. We run in a six-mile race every Sunday. We don't have arguments anymore because we're too tired. The feeling one gets during jogging is hard to explain. It's like the whole world begins and ends in your own body. You breathe and sweat and put one foot in front of another and nothing else matters. Your mind is clear. The experience is almost sexual." Horse smile.

The receptionist brought the file to Mark Davidson and left. He sat quietly reading it for a while. "Mrs. Wallace is a smart lady. She has every piece of jewelry listed in her policy. It looks like we're on the hook for all of it."

"I have an informant . . ."

"You *always* have an informant," Davidson interrupted, but his tone was good-natured.

"My informant says he can recover everything that was stolen in the Wallace burglary. He's been approached by some people who are trying to fence the jewelry. They're asking a lot of money for it. These people are professional burglars. They know what the stuff is worth. The thing we have going for us is that most of the items are custom-made. Any pawn shop would recognize them as hot. Therefore, my man has been approached. They want him to smuggle the jewelry to Paris or London and get rid of it there."

Mark Davidson perused the burglary report. He tapped the keys on a pocket calculator for a while, then jotted some figures. "The insured value is forty-six thousand. This is what we'll have to pay Mrs. Wallace to settle her claim."

"That's a lot of bucks," Travis Bailey said offhandedly.

"But they're not my bucks. And the sweet thing about working for an insurance company is that if we pay out a little more this year, we just raise the rates next year and make up for it. Can your informant recover *all* of the items listed in the burglary report?"

Bailey nodded. "Everything except the cigarette case. Apparently the burglar already sold it."

"If your man can recover everything else we'll be willing to pay him three thousand dollars," Davidson said.

"He'll have to front more money than that just to show good faith. To get his hands on the jewelry, he'll have to put up six thousand. That's the minimum they'll take as a deposit. The plan the informant has worked out goes like this: He puts up the six grand as security. The burglar gives him the jewelry. He gives the jewelry to us. A couple of days later, he calls the burglar and tells him that he got stopped by Customs in London and they seized the jewelry. If they don't believe him, I furnish the informant with a phony Customs seizure form that he can show as evidence that the jewelry was taken away from him. That way my informant is able to recover the goodies for us without compromising his position. The informant wants a four-thousand-dollar reward for himself. The operation will cost you ten grand total, but considering that your company could end up forking out forty-six thou', I'd say it seems like a fairly good deal."

Mark Davidson opened a desk drawer, pulled out a pair of blue running shoes. He set them on the desk. "Runner's World says these are the best running shoes made. I just bought them this morning and I can't wait to try them out." He stared at the shoes, then at Bailey. He showed his teeth. "Is there any way we can do it for less than ten thousand?"

"Nope."

"Then ten it is. See, I'm easy. Do you want the money the same way as last time?"

Bailey nodded. "Small bills. The informant insists on small bills."

Mark Davidson broke into nervous laughter. "For all I know your informant may have burglarized the woman's house himself."

"The informant is not your average churchgoer," Bailey said, "but he isn't a burglar. He's just one of those people who seems to be in the right place at the right time to get in on these things. I've known him for years. Shall we say he's *well placed?*"

Travis Bailey stood up to leave.

"You really should try jogging. Once you get into it it's all you think of. It's a real *trip*."

"I'll have to try it sometime," Bailey said on his way out the door.

Mark Davidson threaded laces in the new shoes for a while. His phone rang.

"Is Bailey gone?"

"Yes, sir."

"What is this one going to cost us?"

"He wanted twenty thousand, sir, but I talked him down to ten. I finally had to put my foot down. It's a forty-six-thousand-dollar claim, so, all in all, I think we did rather well. It was a difficult negotiating session."

"Good job, Mark."

"Thank you, sir."

Charles Carr tiptoed into the hospital room. The curtains were drawn and the sunlight that crept through gave the one-bed cubicle a dusky haze. Carr wondered about the smell; the odor of every hospital he had ever been in. Was it rubbing alcohol? He stepped to the side of Jack Kelly's bed. Kelly's breathing was labored. His barrel chest was pasted with a thick bandage. Carr touched Kelly's arm. He opened his eyes. He licked his lips. "Charlie," he said in a weak voice.

"Do you have pain?"

"Hurts like hell. It was like getting hit right square in the chest with a sledgehammer."

"Do you feel like talking?"

Kelly licked his lips again, opened and closed his eyes a few times. "When I was a kid I was playing catch on the front lawn with my brother. *Burn 'em in* we used to call it. Throw a hardball as hard as you can at one another. I got hit in the chest and it knocked me out. That's what flashed through my mind when I got hit. I was on the front lawn and my mother was holding me in her arms. She held a wet towel on my forehead. My brother was crying because he thought he'd killed me. My mother ran out of the house to help me because I couldn't breathe. While they were operating on me, I dreamed that I was riding on the roof of an ambulance made of glass. It was going a hundred miles an hour. I was lying on my stomach on the roof and I watched what was happening inside. I saw myself lying on the gurney inside and the paramedics were working on me. *Jack Kelly is dying,* I said to myself. Just as if Jack Kelly was a stranger. *Jack Kelly is taking a ride in a glass ambulance and he's dying. He's checking out of this world.* But it was as if everything was okay. I didn't feel pain right then. I had this urge to say good-bye to everyone, but that if I didn't get to, someone would take care of it for me and everything would somehow be all right. Jack Kelly rolled a deuce. He was being driven out of the world inside a see-through ambulance and everything was okay."

"Can you remember what happened before the shooting started?"

"I heard Bailey holler, 'Police,' so I figured he had the suspect roscoed. I stepped into the living room to back him up. That's when I got it . . . like getting hit in the ribs with a ten-man battering ram."

"What did you *see* when you stepped into the living room, Jack?" Carr said quietly. He noticed yellow antiseptic stains around Kelly's chest bandage. The hair on his chest had been shaved.

"I sort of slid around the corner with my gun out. The suspect was in the middle of the room with his back to me. He was wearing a leather jacket. Bailey must have let him walk all the way to the middle of the room before he drew down on him. When I stepped into the room from the hallway I was right in the line of fire."

"What was the suspect doing with his hands?"

Kelly closed his eyes in thought. "His hands weren't at his sides." He hesitated. "They weren't above his head either."

"Could he have been holding a gun?"

Kelly thought for a moment before answering. "No, his back was straight. He wasn't crouching. He wasn't standing the way someone holding a piece does. In fact, I got the impression that he was controlled, that he was afraid, rather than that he was going to fight. That's when the shit hit the fan. It was a damn setup. That no-good son-of-a-bitch Bailey used us as stooges. The caper didn't make sense from the get-go. Like how would Bailey know exactly *when* a hit was going to be made?"

"There was a chrome thirty-two found lying in front of the bar," Carr said. "Bailey had himself covered."

"Did the suspect live?"

Carr shook his head. "Bailey blasted him again when

he was on the deck. He was pronounced dead at the scene."

"Who was he?"

"He had a long record as a cat burglar, lots of joint time. I have just one more question and then you can get some sleep. Was anything else *said* in the living room? You told me Bailey yelled, 'Police,' but was anything said before or after that?"

Kelly's face contorted in thought. "I don't think so."

"I'll stop by tomorrow."

Jack Kelly nodded his head slightly. He winked.

Carr quietly left the room. The pale green hallway was bustling with doctors and nurses dodging gurneys and strolling in and out of rooms. At the end of the corridor, Carr passed a nurses' station. A black nurse's aide behind a counter said something into an intercom, then looked up at him as he passed. "Mr. Carr?"

"That's me," Carr said. Behind the woman on a desk was a portable television. Nurses on the TV screen talked in a hospitial corridor.

"Mr. Kelly wants you to come back to the room."

Carr retraced his steps to Jack Kelly's bed.

"Someone said, 'No,'" Kelly said.

"Whatsat?"

"In the living room at Hartmann's house . . . I'm not sure who said it, but I heard someone say the word *no*. No, like a statement. It was said after Bailey said, 'Police.'"

"Did Bailey say it?"

Jack Kelly closed his eyes for a moment. He opened them. "I'm not even absolutely sure that's what I heard. I'm pretty sure though. Damn. My mind isn't working full speed yet. I guess they've been giving me lots of shots."

Carr patted Kelly on the arm. "Get some rest." He left the room and followed corridors to the hospital's main entrance, passed through a set of revolving glass doors into bright sunlight. The blacktop parking lot shimmered with heat. He played out the shooting a couple of times on the way to his sedan, trying to make the pieces fit.

The L.A. County Sheriff's Department Records Bureau took up an entire floor in the Hall of Justice, a pre-World War II brownstone building with a pillared lobby that invariably smelled of cigar smoke.

Charles Carr peeked around eight-foot-high filing shelves looking for Della Trane. He found her sitting at a desk in the corner. He thought she looked about as sexy as a woman dressed in a khaki short-sleeved blouse and green uniform skirt could look. Her back was straight as she worked computer keys. As always, her gold deputy's badge was pinned, about two inches lower than regulation, on the very point of her left breast. "Strutting her stuff," as she called it. Della would be Della.

She stopped tapping keys as he approached. "Hello, stranger," she greeted him.

Carr had almost forgotten her well-formed nose and mouth, the flawless, though perhaps slightly flushed, complexion. Only the hint of midriff bulge gave any real hint that she was over forty. Years ago she had been the topic of more than one police-bull-pen conversation.

"How do you like it here?" he asked.

"Anywhere is better than eight hours a day in the women's jail. I got to the point where I was waking up in the morning depressed as hell. The thought of pulling my shift gave me a headache. Anyway you cut it, it's eight a day in jail."

"I haven't seen you around any of the spots lately."

"I stop for a drink now and then," she said as she reached for her purse. She found a pack of cigarettes, lit up and blew out smoke. "Have you missed me? I love it here," she said without giving him a chance to answer. "I'm getting the salary of a deputy sheriff to sit here at this computer rather than shagging prisoners, driving around in a radio car waiting to get my neck broken or flexing my ass on a street corner to set up johns for the vice detectives. Hell, I just spent four weeks in a computer school. I actually *liked* it . . . By the way, I was sorry to hear about your partner."

"One of those things," Carr said. "Do you have time to run a nickname through your computer for me?"

"What's in it for me?" she smiled.

"Drinks?"

"Keep going."

"Dinner?"

"You're on. What's the nickname?"

"Bones. A male white about forty years old. He has gray-streaked hair and may have a record for burglary."

"Do you know how many people have the nickname Bones?" she asked smugly.

Carr nodded. "I have a photo I can compare with the mug shots." He pulled the nude photograph of Bones from his shirt pocket and showed it to her.

Della Trane curled her lower lip as she examined the photograph. "I've seen better."

Carr returned the photograph to his pocket.

Della Trane's fingers tapped keys. The nickname appeared on the computer screen. In a moment, the following message flashed onto the screen:

407 records match criteria

She tapped the printout button and the teleprinter raced as it printed the names of arrestees nicknamed Bones. "What you see is what you get," she said, squirming to point her breasts. "I mean the printout of course." Della Trane laughed with cigarette smoke in her mouth.

Six hours later Charles Carr still sat at a long wooden table in the musty-smelling Records Bureau. Next to him was a wheeled cart full of manila arrest folders. Who would believe that there were literally *boxes* of file packages on criminals nicknamed Bones?

He opened another manila folder, flipped pages until he found the mug shot envelope and opened it. Oddly, the prisoner, a man with greasy hair and beard, was smiling. Carr compared the mug shot to the photograph of the man in Sheboygan's bedroom. They weren't the same. He replaced the mug shot in the envelope and tossed the file back onto the cart. He stood up and stretched. His mind wandered back to the time he and Jack Kelly had sorted through hundreds of photos of red-haired men in order to identify a murder. Was it three or four years ago?

Carr sat down and dug into another file. A mug shot, which was stapled to a booking form, was of a man with gray-streaked hair. He wore an open-collared shirt. Carr held the bedroom photograph up to the mug shot. It was the same man. Carr sorted through a stack of hand-printed arrest reports in the file. They showed that Robert Chagra aka Bones had been arrested nine times during the past twelve years. Six arrests were for conspiracy to commit burglary, three for illegal gambling (the arrests took place at private homes during the course of crap games). A note by one sheriff's detective in the file read as follows:

Forward copy of this arrest report to Organized Crime Intelligence Division: Chagra hangs with heavy hoods in Hollywood/Beverly Hills. He is a dice hustler, a mechanic. Games are usually set up by someone else. Conventioneers or other suckers are invited to a game usually at a private home. Chagra is brought in with loaded dice, suckers are allowed to win a little, then fleeced. He takes a piece of the action. When there is no game in town, he acts as a middle man between burglars and Beverly Hills types who want their homes burglarized to collect the insurance. For a fee, he gives back the swag after the burglary and the victim collects the insurance claim. Sometimes he just sets up burg's. He doesn't do them himself, but farms out the address and steers the stolen property to his own fencing channels. For a while, he worked as a chauffeur for movie actor Rex Piper, who reportedly bought lots of stolen jewelry from him.

Carr copied Chagra's address off the bottom of the form. On his way out, he stopped by Della's desk.

"Ready for some more files?"

Carr shook his head. He handed her the mug shot of Bobby Chagra. "This is our boy."

She looked at the photograph and handed it back.

"Thanks for all the help," he said, stuffing the photo in his pocket.

She turned back to the computer screen. Her fingers moved on the keys. "I'll be ready at eight. Do you remember how to get to my house?"

"Of course," he said. *Was it Highland Park or South Pasadena?*

"Be there or be square," Della Trane said in a Mickey Mouse voice. Her lips made a kiss movement.

Carr stopped at a pay phone in the downstairs lobby. He dropped a dime and dialed.

"Judge Malcolm's courtroom," Sally Malone answered.

"Hi."

"It's Friday afternoon," she said. "You're going to tell me that something came up at work and we're not going to be able to go out tonight, right?"

"How did you know?"

"Because I've known you for nine years of Friday nights. I had reservations for us at a real nice place too. I may just go anyway."

"I'm sorry, Sal. I'll stop over tomorrow and we'll make some plans. Maybe we can drive up to Santa Barbara for the day. How does that sound?"

"Unless you call me tomorrow morning and tell me that you're on a stakeout somewhere and you can't get away. Does that sound familiar?"

"What can I say?" Carr said, humbly.

"You could say that you miss me."

"I miss you."

"Sometimes I hate you. I really mean that." She hung up.

Back at the Field Office, Carr searched a telephone directory for Della Trane's address. It wasn't listed. He flipped through his address book, though he knew it wasn't there. Having completed this ritual, he opened his wallet and pulled out a stack of business cards, matchbook covers and other scribbled-on miscellanea. On his second tour through the material (on the way he tossed out four or five cards with names and numbers written on them he couldn't match with faces) he found a Ling's bar matchbook cover with Della Trane's name and address written on the reverse. It *was* Highland Park and not Pasadena. He breathed a sigh of relief.

No Waves stepped quietly into the office. "Cleaning out your wallet on government time?" His hands fiddled nervously in his pockets.

Carr ignored him. He dropped the matchbook cover in his shirt pocket and stuffed the wallet full again.

"Yoo-hoo."

Carr looked up, expressionless.

"Have you come up with anything on the Tony Dio angle? I say he's still the best suspect. Hiring a hit man to kill a federal witness is right down his alley. I smell La Cosa Nostra in this thing from top to bottom. It reminds me of when I worked in the New York Field Office."

Carr nodded. He knew that Waeves had been in charge of the Treasury vehicle fleet in New York.

"I want you to check the airports and see what you can put together," Waeves said, using his best intimidation voice.

"The airport?"

"Dio probably flew his hit man in the day before," Waeves said. "That's the way it's done." His hands worked feverishly in his pockets. Change rattled loudly. "So I want you to check with the airlines and see if this fellow Sheboygan flew in from out of town. I have a hunch. And you'd better get together with . . . uh . . . what's his name?"

"Hartmann."

"Right. Hartmann. To cover our asses, so to speak, we probably should offer him—"

"I've already offered him witness protection," Carr interrupted. "He declined."

"Do we have that in writing?"

"Have what in writing?"

"We ought to have his refusal to accept protection in writing," Waeves said with his mouth formed into a sardonic smile. "This will be CYA for us if anything happens to him. *Cover your ass* is the name of the game in any case involving organized crime. Once when I was working in New York we had a case that—"

"No problem," Carr said. *You'll forget you asked in a day or two.* "Is there anything else?"

No Waves cleared his throat. He gave the change in his pockets a healthy jingle, then pulled a pipe out of his shirt pocket. He shoved it in the side of his mouth. "Be sure and use an OC suffix."

Carr furrowed his brow.

"On your report number," Waeves said. "Add the letters OC to the end. OC stands for 'organized crime'. This came out in the revised Manual of Operations." Waeves rattled change with both hands. Pipe jutting, he sauntered back down the hallway.

Chapter 8

THE RUSH-HOUR traffic had just ended. Charles Carr steered through the Mulholland Pass past signs for a high-priced hilltop condominium development constructed on what he knew was the site of an abandoned public dump. There was a warm breeze; Mojave Desert air wafting, at its own speed, across L.A.'s landscape of ranch-style homes, fast-food stands, parking lots and gas stations on its way to the ocean.

Della Trane sat beside him. She wore a low-cut black dress with an open back that revealed a deep and even tan. Her perfume mingled with the summer air rushing in the wind-wings, as did the smell of alcohol on her breath. Earlier, when he picked her up at her tiny two-bedroom place in Highland Park, he could tell immediately that she'd been drinking.

So far, the conversation had been small talk about police acquaintances: rumors of promotion and demotion.

"No more shoptalk," she said finally.

"That's a deal."

"Do you remember the first time you met me?"

"Sure."

"I doubt that. But *I* remember. It was in Chinatown. I was with a group of friends. We'd just come from a retirement party and we were gassed. We needed another drink like we needed a hole in the head. You were sitting at the bar with your partner. You know why I liked you? Because you could carry on a decent conversation and you weren't crazy. Most of the men I meet are crazy. I mean that. Either married and on the make or just plain crazy. It seems like the men I meet are either one-night-stand artists, or I end up sitting there all night trying to make conversation while they stare at my tits. I mean how would you like it if I sat here staring at your crotch?" She leaned over and mocked a groin stare.

Carr laughed. "I see what you mean."

"I didn't really think you'd call me. Men always take numbers and never call. Isn't that right?"

Carr shrugged.

"I've been married four times," Della Trane said, ". . . all policemen. One is a captain now, one is a sergeant, one was killed in a shoot-out and one retired on a disability. He was a beeroholic. Not an *alcoholic;* a *beeroholic*. He used to drink a six-pack of those large cans of beer on his way home from the station house. For him it was just a warmup. He gained lots of weight and finally took the cure, but by then things were finished between the two of us." She stared out the window for a moment. "Where are you taking me? I hope it's not straight back to your apartment. When I go out with a cop, nothing surprises me."

"Trust me," Carr said jovially. He swung the sedan onto a transition road that led to the Santa Monica Freeway.

A few minutes later Carr turned off the freeway at Pacific Coast Highway and wound along some narrow streets to the strand. Having parked in a lot near the decrepit Santa Monica Pier, he helped Della Trane out of the car. She held his hand tightly as they wandered toward a small building. Over the bay window facing the ocean hung a sign that read Prince Nikola of Serbia—Yugoslav Food.

Carr opened the front door and they stepped into a restaurant that consisted of ten or so tables with checkered tablecloths and a tiny wine bar. On the walls were black-and-white framed photographs of a shaved-head, muscle-bound wrestler in aggressive poses. In the photos, his midsection was adorned with a metal-studded championship belt. The only hair above his chest was bushy Slavic eyebrows.

The crowd in the place was a potpourri of Muscle Beach types, young people who looked like college students and a few red-cheeked Yugoslavs that looked enough like Prince Nikola of Serbia to be relatives.

"I used to see him on TV," Della said.

Prince Nikola of Serbia strode from the kitchen carrying bottles of red wine. He wore a form-fitting T-shirt and butcher-style apron. His eyebrows were sprinkled with gray, and he looked heavier than in the championship photos. "Charlie, long time no see!" He flung an arm around Carr's shoulder, almost throwing him off balance.

Carr introduced Della Trane.

"Welcome to Nick's, beautiful lady." He dragged them through a swinging door into a spotless kitchen. "Look who comes to see us!" Nick said. A woman with hefty arms and shoulders turned from a stove. She had strong features and wore her hair braided and pinned closely to her head. Wiping her hands on a kitchen towel, she rushed to Carr. After bussing him on the cheek, she scolded him for not visiting more often.

Nick hustled them back into the restaurant, seating them in a corner booth that Carr knew was reserved for family. He rushed about setting the table with plates of French bread, green onions, garlicky black olives. "I'm so sorry about Jack," he said as he uncorked a bottle of wine. He shook his head as he filled wineglasses, then rushed off to the kitchen.

Della Trane took a big drink of the wine and set the glass down, licking her lips. "My first husband was Nick's size. He was a motor cop. We had a big wedding in the Police Academy rock garden. Chief Parker himself came." She took another sip. "It seems like such a long time ago," she said, wistfully. Having taken another healthy sip or two, she excused herself to the ladies' room.

Nick of Serbia came to the table with an appetizer plate of goat cheese and crackers. Carr asked him to sit down. He slipped Bobby Chagra's mug shot out of his shirt pocket and handed it to him.

The wrestler stared at the photograph. He snapped his fingers. "Beverly Hills Athletic Club," he said. "When I work there as a gym instructor, he work in bar. He used to work nights. This is six years ago, maybe seven. He worked there for just a little while. His nickname is Bones. I can't remember his real name."

"What kind of a guy is he?" Carr said.

"Sunnabitch is no good. He's a garbage can. I tell you truth."

"What's he into?"

"He used to set up crap games at the club. All the big shots would play in the locker room on Friday nights

. . . big money . . . hundred-dollar bills. Judges, doctors, movie stars, they all used to play. Once I see Frank Sinatra in the game. He stayed for just a few minutes, then leaves. I ask him why he didn't play longer. He say to me, 'Nick, you ever seen the magician pull rabbit out of a hat?' That's when I first knew something was wrong. The big shots played every week. They'd lose five, maybe ten thousand without batting eye. Finally, somebody figured out that the game was fixed. It was a big scandal. Grand jury investigation, stories in the newspaper. Big-shot movie producer lost hundred grand in one night and called the cops. Bones got fired."

"Any friends?"

Nick of Serbia shook his head. "He always had lots girl friends, though. He always talk about how he fucks them, you know . . . she did this to me, I did that to her. It's all he talks about. He's like a little boy. He was always trying to fuck the daughters of movie stars. He met them at the Bel Air parties catered by the club. Once the sunnabitch asked me if I wanted to help him steal one of the Rolls-Royces parked outside. He is a garbage can . . . a big damn phony like everybody else in Beverly Hills. The people who really have money aren't that bad. It's the rest of the goldbricks, the ones who use ten towels to dry off. They all want special treatment. I tell you truth: the peanut seller at the Olympic Auditorium, where I wrestle, makes more in tips in one night than I made in five years I worked in Beverly Hills. I tell you truth." Nick laughed uproariously. "Now *I'm* big shot. When customer give me shit, I put 'em in hammerlock and toss their ass out front door." Another burst of laughter. "I break their damn neck with the

Boston Crab!" With catlike speed, he interlaced fingers and leaned back. His biceps flexed.

Carr chuckled.

"This Bones," Nick said, "what did he do?"

"I just need to ask him some questions," Carr said. "Is Bones the kind of person who'll answer questions?"

Nick of Serbia shook his head. "I would say no," he said. "When the cops came to the club to ask about the dice game, he told them to go to hell."

"If you hear anything about what Bones has been up to recently, I'd appreciate a call," Car said.

"I check around for you." Nick excused himself as more customers came in the door.

Della returned to the table and immediately hoisted her wineglass. "Here's to ya," she said, and tossed back half a glass. Carr noticed that she had reapplied makeup. She dabbed her lips with a napkin, leaving a lipstick stain. "My third husband loved wrestling," she said, gazing at one of the wrestling photos on the wall. "He knew it was phony, but he loved it anyway. Isn't that crazy?"

Carr nodded. "I haven't seen you at Ling's lately," he said, trying to change the subject.

She sipped again. "Too much shoptalk in there. After my last divorce, I used to go to a lot of the cop hangouts, but everyone I met seemed to know one of my ex-husbands. So I started hitting the places in West L.A. I met nothing but creeps with gold chains and open-collared shirts. All they could talk about was skiing or buying property. I stopped going out all together. Finally, when I couldn't stand it anymore, I started going out with this divorced guy who lives across the street from me. He turned out to be a real butt. He's one of those people who keeps a budget. He actually makes a note of every dime he spends. If he buys a pack of cigarettes he actually makes a note of it on a little calendar in his kitchen. I think he's a neurotic." Della picked up the wine bottle and filled her glass close to the rim. "Oops." Hefting the glass with both hands, she drank off a half inch or so.

Nick brought a steaming platter of fried fish, bowls of boiled potatoes, string beans and salad. Carr ate heartily as Della pushed food around her plate and finished the bottle of wine. By the end of the meal her lips were purple. "I just love this place," she said. After dessert, Carr went through the ritual of trying to pay for the meal while Nick threatened to crush him with a bear hug if he left money on the table. Finally the men shook hands and Della took Carr's arm on the way out the door. Once in the sedan she slid next to him, kissing him on the cheek.

"Would you mind too much if we took a drive along the coast? I haven't done that in years?" Her words were slurred and the wine had flushed her cheeks. Somehow, the color in her face made her look younger.

"Sure," Carr said. Carr found his way through some side street to Pacific Coast Highway. He turned north and they drove for a while without saying anything. The air was comfortably cool and there was the sound of waves breaking along the rocks.

"Funny," Della said. "I'm willing to make commitments in a split second, and you wouldn't commit yourselt to someone at the risk of the death penalty. You've never been married, have you?"

Carr shook his head.

"I guess that's just the way it is between men and women."

"Men and women are at war these days. It's a game of who can rip off who first."

Della nodded in agreement.

In Malibu, they passed a restaurant whose exterior was covered with synthetically weathered wood and decorative anchors. A coiled rope over the door spelled The Galley.

"Let's stop in there for a drink," Della said. "Please."

"I don't think you need any more to drink."

"Don't be an old klutz," she whispered in his ear.

Inside, the floors and walls were bare planks. There were lots of cheap oil paintings of sailing ships and a few diver's masks lamps for decoration. Because of the hour, there were empty tables next to the windows. A young man wearing a sea captain's cap seated them. Della ordered a rusty nail with double scotch. Carr asked for coffee. Outside, in the ocean's blackness, a silhouette of what looked like a cruise ship moved slowly along the coastline beyond a well-lighted offshore oil rig whose metal structures had been camouflaged with painted partitions in an attempt to make it look like a tiny, palm-treed island.

"It almost looks real," Della said.

"The ship or the oil derrick?"

She slapped his hand playfully.

"No matter what it looks like," Carr said, "it's still an oil derrick . . . an oil derrick built right smack in the middle of the ocean view so somebody could make a buck."

The waiter brought drinks. "Pretend it's not there," she said, taking a couple of sips.

Impulsively she put her hand in his. "Thanks for not being crazy. All the men I've been out with lately seem crazy."

A few minutes later the maître d' walked by them

leading three women to a table. One of the women was Sally Malone. She stopped and stared at Carr for a moment, her lips quivering. She said something to her friends, then turned and quickly headed toward the door.

Carr excused himself from the table and followed Sally out the door. Jogging a few steps, he caught up with her in the parking lot as she fumbled for car keys. He grabbed her by the arm.

"Don't touch me," she said as if he were a leper.

He turned her toward him. Her eyes were closed tightly in anger. "You humiliated me in front of my friends," she said through gritted teeth. "I told them that you had broken our date tonight because you were working."

"I'm sorry," he said. "I mean that, Sally. I'm very sorry."

She pulled away from him and unlocked the door of her sports car. Having swung the door open, she climbed in. As she started the engine, he saw tears on her cheeks. She slammed the car into gear and raced out of the lot onto the highway.

Carr rubbed his temples for a moment, then returned to the table. Della Trane had finished her rusty rail. She stared out the window as she fiddled with a swizzle stick. "She may never forgive you," she said to the window. "I know I wouldn't."

Carr gestured to a cocktail waitress, who took his order for a round of double scotches. The waitress made frequent trips to the table until closing time. Della Trane told and retold her marriage stories.

On the trip back to her apartment she fell asleep on Carr's shoulder. When they arrived, he nudged her awake and helped her up some steps to her front door. He helped her find keys and unlock the door. Pulling him inside, she threw her arms around him. They kissed until Carr pulled his lips away from hers. "You drink too much," he said.

She pushed him away. "You cops should talk. If it hadn't been for cops I would never have started drinking in the first place." She covered her face with her hands and cried. Carr put his arms around her again. "I really like you," she said, crying. "Now you'll probably never ask me out again."

"I will."

"Promise?" She looked up at him, tears welled in her eyes.

"Promise." He touched her cheek with the back of his hand and walked out the door. Carr drove the speed limit along a deserted Pacific Coast Highway toward Santa Monica, keeping on the alert for Highway Patrol vehicles. He knew a drunk-driving incident would give No Waves enough ammo to have him transferred again. Finally, he reached Santa Monica. On the way to his apartment, he passed by the street Sally Malone lived on. Her car was parked in front of her apartment complex. He made a couple of turns around the block as he considered her possible reaction if he stopped. "The hell with it," he said out loud, and continued the few blocks to his apartment. He parked the sedan in a carport, locked it and made his way up the steps to his apartment.

After fumbling with the key, he unlocked the front door and went in, flicking on the light. The place looked as it always did: neither messy, spotless nor particularly lived in. The brown leather sofa and recliner chair (Sally hated both) showed few signs of wear. On a bookcase the stacks of outdated criminology and police journals, as well as the James Jones and Graham Greene novels, needed dusting. The Miró prints on the wall were a

Christmas gift from Sally. She always said the place looked like a motel room. Carr flopped down on the sofa. Hell, he thought, he might as well live in a motel room.

After staring at the blank screen for a while, he stood up and staggered to the television. He flicked it on and switched channels; cowboys shooting from horses, cops shooting from behind the doors of police cars, used-car commercials.

He turned off the set.

In the kitchen, he checked the refrigerator. There was nothing on the shelves but eggs and wilted lettuce. He slammed the door shut. He yanked a bottle of scotch from the cupboard and a glass from the dish drainer, poured a stiff drink. He sipped and felt acidy booze-warmth roll slowly down his throat and into his empty stomach. For some reason, he thought of Jack Kelly's home, where he had Sunday dinner once a month or so: there were always catcher's mitts and bicycles scattered about . . . and a kitchen that always smelled delicious.

He poured the scotch into the sink.

In the bedroom, he picked up the telephone receiver and dialed Sally Malone's number except for the last digit. Hesitating, he dropped the receiver back in the cradle. On his way out the front door, he lit a cigarette. Having staggered down the steps to his sedan, he realized that he had left his car keys in the apartment. Without hesitation, he headed toward Sally's place on foot. As he trudged along the dark, narrow streets crowded with apartments and double-parked cars, a foggy mist dampened his face and hair. Chilled, he picked up his pace.

By the time he reached the door to her apartment he was slightly out of breath. He knocked softly. There was no answer. He knocked louder. There were footsteps inside.

"Who's there?" Sally said.

"I want to talk for a minute."

"There's nothing to talk about." Her tone was angry. He heard her walk away from the door.

Carr knocked again. He waited, knocked again. Finally, he slammed his fist against the door a few times. Sally's footsteps. "Please go away," she said, pleading.

"Open the goddamn door or I'll kick it in."

He heard her fasten the chain latch and a dead-bolt lock.

Carr leaned close to the door.

"I'm sick and tired of being alone," he said. "I've never cared about anyone except you, and the last thing in the world I ever wanted to do was to hurt your feelings, or to embarrass you. I love you and I . . ." he swallowed ". . . want to marry you."

"Are you drunk?"

"Yes," he said.

The chain latch was unfastened. The dead bolt snapped. Sally opened the door. She wore a robe over her nightgown. "Did you mean that?"

Carr nodded.

She came into his arms. "I've waited for years to hear you say that," Sally whispered. They kissed. "Please tell me you really mean it."

"I mean it."

"Let's leave right now," she said. "We can go to Las Vegas."

"Right now?"

"Why not?" she said, kissing him again. "I think I've waited long enough."

Chapter 9

DURING THE five-hour trip through the dessert, Carr and Sally discussed particular matters diplomatically. Gingerly they came to agreement on the following issues: One, that he would break his lease and move into her apartment (her rent was cheaper and the place was larger); two, that Carr's furniture, which Sally hated, would be donated to the Salvation Army; three, that they would keep both cars. Carr was surprised that he found himself discussing such topics with relative ease.

By the time they reached the outskirts of Las Vegas, it was sunrise, the only quiet period in its entire twenty-four-hour day. Nevertheless, the bank of casino neon that lined both sides of the highway still flashed, glimmered and burst intermittently into inanimate forms: silver slippers, gold nuggets, jacks and queens. Because of the early hour, the usually congested Vegas strip was void of traffic jams and, except for a few tired-looking tourists still wandering in and out of casinos, was generally deserted.

A pink neon sign planted close to the roadway read

Cupid's Heart Marriage Chapel—Open 24 Hours. A neon cupid fired an arrow to the right. Carr turned into a parking lot between casinos. Ahead of them, almost directly underneath an enormous silver dollar balanced on a forty-foot pole, was a diminutive wood-frame cottage. A picket fence surrounding the structure was built with a flat base, so it could balance on the parking lot asphalt. In the bay window of the cottage, accented by pink lights, was a large, heart-shaped bouquet of artificial roses. Like Friday-afternoon customers at a bank, couples waited in line at the door.

Carr steered the sedan behind the building and parked. Sally squeezed his arm affectionately. He climbed out and approached a service window at the rear of the chapel. A fat woman wearing a white, frilly dress handed him some printed forms and a pen attached to a string. He filled in the forms and handed them back. He paid a fee and the woman rang up the transaction on a cash register. She handed him a receipt. Without explanation, she pointed around the side of the building. He returned to the sedan.

Having completed a fresh application of makeup, Sally stepped out of the car. They joined the line waiting at the front door of the chapel. The sound of a recorded wedding march came from inside. A young couple standing in front of them in line introduced themselves. They were dressed in matching shorts and T-shirts bearing the slogan I Found It. Without encouragement, the young woman shared the fact that they had been living together for six months. Carr forced a smile. He noticed a well-dressed, elderly couple directly in front of the chapel door. They were obviously drunk, holding one another up. The wedding march ended. A minute later the door opened and a man wearing a cowboy hat and polyester suit walked out holding hands with a Mexican woman who looked older than he. The drunk couple stepped inside the chapel and closed the door behind them. The wedding march began again.

Carr noticed that Sally's head was down.

"Is everything okay?" he said.

She nodded without looking up.

"Sally?" Gently he touched her chin. She looked up. There were tears in her eyes.

"Please tell me what's wrong."

"I don't want to get married here," she whispered. "Not like this. It's so . . . impersonal . . . and that dumb wedding march record. I love you and I want to be your wife but I just don't want to remember this as the place I got married."

"Of course not." Carr put an arm around her shoulder and walked her back to the sedan.

Sliding in next to Carr, she hugged him. "You'll lose the marriage fee," she said.

"Better than losing it at the crap table, I guess." He started the engine.

After stopping for gas, Carr headed onto the highway toward Los Angeles. Oddly, though he hadn't slept all night, he wasn't sleepy. During the trip back, Sally spoke eagerly of trips they could take together, using their combined incomes to purchase a condominium, and how well he would get along with her sister and brother-in-law who lived in Nebraska.

By the time they reached Santa Monica Carr's eyelids were heavy, and though he wasn't sure if it was just the result of fatigue, he had second doubts about the whole thing.

* * *

As Amanda Kennedy, wearing a denim prison smock, stepped into the visitor's room from a door marked Inmates Only, Travis Bailey realized that he had never seen her before. An hour earlier, she had called his office from a pay phone at the Women's Jail and told him she wanted to speak with him about a confidential matter. On the way to the jail he wondered whether she was the wife or girl friend of someone whom he had arrested. Why would she ask for him by name? He certainly hadn't recognized her voice.

There was no one else in the visitor's room except a young priest quietly counseling a woman with a large purple birthmark on her forehead; Amanda Kennedy walked directly to him.

"Mr. Bailey?" she said.

He nodded and she sat down. "Have we met before?"

"I'm a friend . . . or perhaps I should say I *was* a friend of Lee Sheboygan."

Travis Bailey felt his stomach tighten. He had the urge to curl his toes. "I see."

"Well?"

"Well what?" he said after pausing for a moment.

"Do you know who I'm talking about?"

"Yes," he said. "Now what do you want?"

"I want out of here."

"I'm sure there are lots of ladies in here who'd like to get out. So what else is new?"

"I shouldn't have to explain anything to you. You know very well what I'm talking about. You know very well." She crossed her arms across her chest.

Travis Bailey shrugged, stood up to leave. *What is this woman up to?*

"I think you'd better sit down again," she said matter-of-factly. "Lee told me about everything. Everything about you and him and Bones."

Suddenly, Bailey's knees felt weak. He sat down again. Without any attempt at subtlety, he stared at Amanda Kennedy's chest for signs of a hidden microphone.

Having lowered her voice to a whisper, she said, "I know about the burglaries you set up for Lee. He told me about everything one night when he was high. We were just sitting around my apartment horning a few spoons of coke and he just came out with it. At first I didn't believe it. But I do now."

Bailey glanced around the room. The priest and the birthmarked woman were praying. He knew that if he was being set up, Kennedy would have to be wearing a listening device. Since he had picked the spot to sit, he knew there was little chance the table was bugged. He stared at the woman and said nothing.

Amanda Kennedy rested her elbows on the table. She leaned forward. "The Feds have already been here to talk with me. They wanted to know who Lee's friends were. I gave them just enough to make it look like I was cooperating. Nothing they couldn't find out on their own . . . but I'll spill the beans if I have to in order to get out of here. I mean that. I'll do whatever I have to to get out of this place. I'm not staying in jail for anyone. I mean that. I'm not staying in this fucking place for anyone."

Without making it obvious, Travis Bailey took a deep breath. "What are you in for?" he said.

Amanda Kennedy removed a package of chewing gum from the one and only pocket on her denim smock. She unwrapped a stick as if it were something valuable. "I'm in here because I was just sitting in my apartment just sort of kicking back the other day, and this Fed knocks on my door. He asked me some questions about Lee, so I just shined him on. I mean, like why should I answer any questions? I didn't do anything wrong. So the Fed leaves. The next thing I know these two burglary detectives are pushing their way in my door with a search warrant. They turned my apartment inside out and arrested me for possession of a necklace with a pendant that Lee had given me. They put handcuffs on me and booked me in here . . . and you'll never guess who comes to visit me after I'm booked in. The same Fed who came to my apartment asking about Lee Sheboygan." She shoved the gum in her mouth and chewed.

"What was his name?"

"Carr."

"What did you tell him?"

"Don't worry," she said. "I didn't tell him anything he couldn't have found out on his own." She folded her arms and chewed gum rapidly for a moment. "I'm not like the other people in here. I used to be married to one of the biggest scriptwriters in town. He wrote the original script for *The Volkswagen That Could Fly*. So don't think I'm going to sit in here and vegetate waiting to go to trial. My bond is five thousand dollars and if you know what's good for you and for Bones, you'll get me out of here. If you don't, I'm going to blow the lid off your little game. I'll tell the Feds everything I know. It's as simple as that." She held the unfolded gum wrapper to her mouth and pushed the chewing gum into it with her tongue. Having packaged the moist gum carefully, she shoved it back in her pocket. "If you don't chew the gum too long, you don't get the calories," she explained.

"How do I know you aren't trying to frame me?" Bailey said. "Sometimes people have been known to wear hidden microphones. They try to get policemen to say things in order to frame them."

"Look, dammit," she said angrily, "*I'm* the one who's been framed. I'm the one who's sitting in a stinking cell. If you don't get me out of there, and I mean quick, then you will be in trouble. I mean that."

Travis Bailey reached into a coat pocket. He pulled out a pad and pen. He printed, "*I'll have you out by tomorrow morning. Be careful of what you say in this room—bugs?*" on the pad. As he held a finger to his lips he showed Amanda Kennedy what he had written.

Amanda Kennedy stood up. "Don't forget." She turned and walked toward the steel door.

Travis Bailey drove down a winding road from the Women's Jail past rows of pink and green stucco dwellings whose walls and fences were covered with spray-can graffiti. Though he had the car's air conditioner on at maximum, his hands were so wet with perspiration he could hardly hold on to the steering wheel. At a stoplight at the bottom of a hill, he wiped his palms on his trousers. Doing this, he remembered stealing cash from the wallet of a businessman whom he had arrested for drunk driving. His fear of getting caught had reached the point of nausea. It had been easier the second time.

He turned right on Eastern Avenue and drove a block to a taco stand. He pulled over, parked and walked deliberately to a telephone booth. He stepped into the booth and closed the door. He stared at the receiver for what must have been a long time as his mind wandered to unrelated incidents in his life: the death of an aunt who had always offered him refuge from his stepfather's unreasonable punishments, the childhood experience of being lost in a department store, the visit to an alcoholic doctor who falsely diagnosed ulcers to keep him out of the military draft, his teenage ex-wife pushing him off her as he was in the act of orgasm, the recurring nightmare of lying on a beach on which the sand becomes increasingly hot until finally his back and legs burst in flames.

As he dropped a dime in the coin slot he became aware that the booth was sweltering. He dialed Bones Chagra's home number. The freeway sounds, the sound of metal whizzing through air, seemed to get louder.

Chagra answered.

"We need to get together," Bailey said.

"Can it wait? I have two studio bitches coming over to do a tag team on me before I go to work. It's taken me two nights of bullshit to talk 'em into it."

"I need to see you right now."

"You wanna come over?"

"No," Bailey said. "I'll meet you at the pastry shop."

"I hope it's important enough to give up two pieces of ass."

Travis Bailey hung up the phone.

The pastry shop sandwiched between exclusive shops on Rodeo Drive was crowded as usual. In a dining room adjoining a spotless bakery with glass display counters filled with tortes, cream pies and other ultrarich baked goods, groups of women wearing the latest styles sat at bistro tables in groups of two and three. They buzzed amiably (but loudly enough to be heard by others) about clothing, the chefs at Ma Maison and L'Orangerie and European vacations. The walls were decorated with nostalgia prints of old bakeries and bakery trucks.

Travis Bailey sat alone at a table in the corner,

glancing impatiently at his wristwatch. Finally Bones Chagra hurried in the front door. He wore an Italian-cut sport coat and white loafers. Spotting Bailey, he made his way through the bakery to his table. As he sat down, he gave the crowd a glance of disdain. "I hate this place," Chagra said. "Why do you always want to meet here?"

"Because no one I know comes in here." He lifted a cup and sipped *café au lait*. "Who is Amanda Kennedy?"

"The bitch who managed the apartment house where Lee lived; fair jugs, good ass. Lee had her over all the time. He thought she had class. He loved anything with class. We did a ménage with her a few times. She likes to take it both ways at once. She would blow Lee while I fucked her up the—"

"What does she know?" Bailey said abruptly.

Chagra gave him a puzzled look.

"I said what does she *know?*"

"Nothing," Chagra said. "She was just a punch. Once we did switches with her and one of the cocktail waitresses from the Blue Peach." He smiled.

"She's in jail right now, and she tells me she knows all about our game. She knows about you and me and Lee and says if I don't get her out of jail she'll sing a song."

Chagra's jaw dropped. "How? . . ."

"She said that Lee got high one night and told her the whole story; laid it all out for her. She got pinched with some jewelry: a necklace with a pendant."

An expression of agony spread across Bones Chagra's face. He rubbed his temples, then set his hands, palms down, on the table. "Lee did give her a necklace. I told him I didn't like the idea and he just laughed. The necklace came out of a house I did."

"Where was the house?"

"It wasn't in Beverly Hills. It was a block or two over the boundary into L.A.," Chagra said. He closed his eyes. "Damn."

A young, long-nosed woman wearing a Dolly Madison-style dress and hat served oversized pieces of cream cheese pie to a pair of middle-aged fat women sitting at the table next to them. One of the women remarked on the size of the serving and said she would never be able to eat all of it. She dug in with her fork and took an enormous bite.

Chagra looked pale. "I've been down the road three times. I'm a fucking three-time loser. Another jolt means ten years for me. I can't do ten years. There's no way I could handle that kind of a jolt. I'd rather take my chances at being a fugitive for the rest of my life. Fuck it." He bit his lip. "I don't like this place. I hate places like this."

"Ten years is a treat compared with a trip to the gas chamber," Bailey said. "If she sings I could be put together on Lee's murder. She could tie me right to him with a motive. Even if I beat the rap it would be the end for me. I'd lose my job."

"Exactly what *does* she know?" Chagra said.

"I didn't want to go into detail with her sitting in the visitor's room at the jail," Bailey said sarcastically. "We definitely need to find out. We need to find out real soon."

"What the hell are we gonna do?"

"Find a bail bondsman that you trust. Have him post bail for her. Be waiting outside the gate when she's released. Be nice to her. Play a tune for her. And find out exactly what she knows. We've got to know what kind of damage she could do to us. Call me at home when you find out."

The women at the next table continued to eat and chat loudly. They dabbed their lips with sterile cloth napkins.

Travis Bailey motioned to the waitress. She came to the table. He paid the bill and left her a sizable tip. "You first," he said with a nod toward the door.

"Huh?"

"You leave first."

Chagra nodded, stood up to leave.

"Go for it," Travis Bailey said offhandedly. Chagra left. The women at the next table continued to eat, chat loudly and dab their mouths with napkins as Bailey sat deep in thought. He rubbed his temples and felt what he believed to be an increase in his heart rate. Finally he pushed his chair back and stood up. He left the restaurant and strolled casually past trendy shops toward his police car. At the corner, he window-shopped at a store with a window display featuring a mannequin couple attired in thick canary yellow vests standing in front of an enormous human silhouette target decorated with bullet holes. A sign leaning next to one of the mannequins read The Latest in Men's and Women's Bulletproof Sportswear. He crossed the street and climbed in his car.

Back at the Detective Bureau, he opened a file drawer next to a telex machine and rummaged through the day's stack of crime Teletypes. In the middle of the stack he found a homicide Teletype that read as follows:

To: All L.A. area Vice and Homicide details
Fm: Santa Barbara Sheriff's Dept.
Re: 187 PC Victim *Waters, Jackie (no middle name)*
Fem. cauc. 34 yrs, 5′4″, 110, possible prostitute.

Female corpse found in bushes off Highway 1 near El Capitan Beach had pocket litter and trick book with L.A. area phone numbers. Only I.D. found on body is expired Calif. Driver's License. No suspects. Cause of death appears to be bullet wound to rear skull. Request you check with vice details re: possible L.A. area associates.

He shoved the stack of Teletypes back in the drawer and left the office. He walked down the street to a drugstore and bought a package of chewing gum.

Outside the drugstore, he stepped into a telephone booth, fished a dime out of his pocket and dialed. He unwrapped two sticks of the gum and, after a few chews, used his index finger to position the gum between his teeth and upper lip.

A man answered, "FBI."

"I know who set up the attempted murder on the bank president in Beverly Hills," Bailey said. "The one who is a witness in the counterfeiting case."

"May I send a special agent out to meet with you, sir?"

"No," Bailey said. "I don't want to get involved. The guy who wanted the bank president killed is Tony Dio. He's a loan shark. He hired a guy named Leon Sheboygan to kill the bank president. It was a contract thing. Dio provided the gun. It was a thirty-two."

"I'm familiar with the name, sir," the FBI agent said. "May I ask where you got the information?"

"Look, I said I don't want to get involved," Bailey said angrily. "But I'll tell you this much, just so you won't think I've made up the whole story. I'm dating a girl that just broke up with Dio. She was living with him and overheard Dio lay the whole thing out to Sheboygan.

She was in another room at Dio's house when Dio laid the contract on this Lee. She heard the whole thing. Dio told him that the bank guy was leaving town for a vacation and that he had to hurry up and do the job. Is this call being taped?"

"No, sir," the FBI man said. "You have my word on that. We'd like to interview the lady who gave you the information. If you'll give me her name I'll guarantee that your name will never be mentioned. We could question her on a routine basis."

"I don't want to get involved," Bailey said. "I'm a married man and I've got too much to lose."

"You have my personal assurance that we will never reveal you as the source of information."

Bailey waited before speaking.

"Sir? Sir? Are you still there?"

"Her name is Jackie Waters."

"How old is she?"

"She's about thirty-five," Bailey said. "I'm not going to answer any more questions. I've probably said too much already."

"Can you give me her address?"

"She left town," Bailey said. "A couple of days ago she told me she thought Dio was acting strangely . . . as if he didn't trust her. He ended up slapping her around. She was scared to death and left town. She told me she thought Dio had let a contract on her. She was so scared she couldn't eat."

"Is she employed?"

"I guess you could say that."

"How did she earn a living?"

"She was a call girl," Bailey said. "Tony Dio got her started."

"Where do you think she is now?"

"She said something about Santa Barbara," Bailey said in his best sincerity tone. "I'm worried. She hasn't called and I think something has happened to her. I think I've said enough."

"Sir, it would be a real help if we could get together in person just for a few minutes—"

"I don't want to get involved," Bailey said, and hung up.

Though it was only 7:00 A.M., the California sun could already be felt on the back of one's neck. Carr, in an early-morning hangover haze, pulled into the parking lot of the coffee shop near the Field Office. Dreadful fare, but it was convenient and there was always room in the parking lot. He staggered inside.

Because he considered it a hangover cure, Carr ordered the "Lumberjack Special" from a waitress with a beehive hairdo who he hoped would not want to talk about her son who was serving a year in the county jail. A stocky, broad-featured woman who lacked any hint of poise, she scribbled his breakfast order on a pad. Having completed the order, she slipped the stub of pencil under rubber bands on her wrist. "You look like you could use a shot of whiskey in your coffee," she said, putting her hands on her hips.

"I'll never drink again," Carr muttered.

"Sure," she said on her way to the kitchen.

Carr sipped ice water. It hurt his teeth.

The waitress returned carrying a newspaper, which she set on the table before sitting down across from him. "This guy I'm going out with told me that my boy should have never pled guilty. He said that if he would have asked for a jury trial, the District Attorney would have made a plea-bargain and he would have gotten straight probation. He only had half an ounce in his car when he was arrested. Do you think he's right?"

"They don't call it plea bargaining anymore," Carr said. "It's called case settlement."

"Which means that you plead guilty to something that maybe you didn't even do in order to get less time in jail, right?"

"Right." Carr noticed No Waves walking toward him from the take-out counter. He carried coffee in a Styrofoam cup with a plastic lid.

The waitress glanced. "He's your boss, isn't he?" she whispered.

Carr nodded.

"He never leaves tips," she said as she slid out of the booth and headed toward another table.

No Waves smirked. "You look like you might have had a few too many last night," he said.

Without looking up Carr opened the newspaper.

"Got a call at home last night from the FBI," Waeves said. "They're confirmed that Tony Dio hired Sheboygan for the hit."

"Who told 'em that?" Carr said, keeping his eyes on the newspaper.

"An informant. Everything he told them has checked out, including info about a hooker whose body was found in Santa Barbara. The informant knew all about it. She was killed because she knew about the Sheboygan thing. She overhead Dio lay the contract on him to kill Hartmann. FBI is opening a case on it from the organized-crime angle. You'd better get over there today and see what they've got."

Carr nodded without looking up from the newspaper.

"Like maybe right after you finish breakfast."

Carr glanced at him. "Sure."

No Waves turned and sauntered out the front door.

The waitress returned to the table carrying a plate of eggs and hash browns. "He's kind of an asshole, isn't he?" she whispered, setting the food in front of him.

"He is the king of assholes."

The woman giggled and hurried back to her duties.

After breakfast, Carr drove to L.A. Police Department Headquarters. He met Higgins in his office and they took the elevator to the basement. At a large coffee pot they filled paper cups. They wound through a corridor and into a dingy photo lab strewn with empty boxes. The odor of coffee from the cups they carried mixed with that of photographic chemicals.

Taped to an easel in the corner of the room was a blown up color photograph of Sheboygan, Chagra and a woman sitting in what appeared to be a nightclub. The wall behind them was covered in red velvet and to their right was what looked like the edge of a stage curtain. Higgins, standing next to him, pointed to a crumpled matchbook cover on the cocktail table in the oversized photo.

Carr sipped coffee, leaned close to the blowup. Because of the photographic technique used, details on the photograph were fuzzy. The letters *Carp* were on the visible portion of the matchbook cover.

"Carp," Higgins said. "Mean anything to you?"

"The type of fish that swims in the lake at MacArthur Park."

"Carp . . . carp . . ." Higgins said, ruminating. "Maybe the matchbook was just a stray. Sometimes people carry things around with them for months. We're going to need more than four letters on a matchbook cover in order to develop some background on these people. And background is what we're definitely going to need to be able to prove motive on Bailey."

Carr turned away from the photograph and lit a cigarette. It tasted awful. He took another sip of the stale coffee. "Maybe we should stir things up a little," he said.

"What do you have in mind?"

Carr stepped to a desk covered with empty film boxes, picked up the phone and dialed. A woman answered, "Beverly Hills Police Department."

"Detective Bailey, please."

Higgins had a puzzled look.

"Bailey speaking."

"Charlie Carr here. If you're not busy this morning, I thought I'd stop by."

Chapter 10

CARR WALKED up some stairs and entered the well-furnished Beverly Hills Detective Bureau. Travis Bailey stood gazing out the window. A young blonde woman sat at a desk near him. She was on the phone. Two other detectives in short-sleeved shirts worked on reports on the opposite side of the room. "Hi," Carr said.

Startled, Bailey turned toward him. "Just daydreaming," he said quickly. He motioned Carr to a seat in front of a desk. Both men sat down as the blonde woman hung up the phone.

Bailey introduced Delsey Piper. "My new partner." Carr shook hands with the woman.

"How is Jack doing?"

"Just fine," Carr said. "Just fine. He should be out of the hospital in a week or two."

"Glad to hear it. What brings you out here to the land of the fur coats and end cuts?" He leaned back in his chair comfortably.

"I'm still checking into the Tony Dio angle. He still

looks like the best suspect to be behind Sheboygan. But I'm running into dead ends. I can't seem to tie Sheboygan into the Tony Dio mob. As a matter of fact, as far as I can determine, Sheboygan was just a cat burglar plain and simple. And for the life of me I can't figure why a cat burglar would pick up a contract on a federal witness."

"Maybe he owed someone a favor," Bailey said. His hands hugged the back of his neck.

Carr stared at the detective. Nothing was said. Bailey unfolded his hands, sat up. Delsey Piper fidgeted. She glanced at both men.

Bailey cleared his throat. "Maybe Sheboygan is listed in an organized-crime file somewhere in town. Have you checked?"

"Checked every file in town," Carr said. "L.A.P.D., Sheriff's Intelligence, District Attorney's Bureau of Investigation, all the federal agencies. I came up with a zero. Nobody lists him with any OC connections."

"You know how incomplete police files are. There's lot going on out there that no one knows about."

Carr looked out the window. The Goodyear blimp floated in front of a fluffy cloud. "That's for sure," he said, staring at Bailey. "There's always a sleeper or two in town. Somebody's secret little game just waiting to make the headlines."

Bailey nodded.

"Did Hartmann tell you he was leaving town?"

Bailey gave a puzzled look.

"Before the shooting . . ." Carr said, "Hartmann told me he spoke with you."

"As a matter of fact he did. He wanted to let the Department know his house would be vacant for a few days. A routine thing . . ."

"Oh."

The phone rang and Delsey Piper answered it in a subdued voice. Carr studied her for a moment, lit a cigarette and blew out smoke. "I'm going to need to talk with your informant," he said, turning to Bailey.

Bailey swallowed. "He's moved out of town."

"I'm willing to travel."

Bailey cleared his throat again. "And even if he was still in town, I'm not sure I could let you talk to him. A confidential informant doesn't stay confidential for very long once he starts getting passed around between police agencies. I'm sure you understand what I mean when I say that."

"I'm not asking your informant to testify in open court. I'm not asking him to go on the six o'clock news. I just want to interview him, ask him a few questions."

Bailey snatched a pencil off the desk. He drummed. "He'll never agree to be interviewed. He's told me that more than once. He won't talk to anyone but me."

"When he tells me that in person, I guess I'll have to be satisfied," Carr said. "I'll be able to put in my report that he looked me in the eye and refused to be interviewed. My headquarters couldn't dispute that."

Carr watched Bailey's jugular vein. It pulsed rapidly.

"My word should be good enough." Bailey fiddled with his collar.

"You know the brass. Particularly Washington, D.C., brass. They need to have things proven to them."

"Even if the informant agreed to meet with you, I know my captain would never go for it. He's from the old school. You know, informants are precious; better to hand up dead old mom than a good snitch."

"I'd like to talk with your captain."

"Talk to him?"

"That's right. I want to talk to him right now."

Bailey shrugged. "No problem. I'll go see if he's in." He stood up and left the room.

Carr turned to Delsey Piper, who started to nervously rearrange things in a desk drawer. "How do you like working in the Detective Bureau?" he asked.

She shut the drawer. "It's super," she said. "Really super."

Bailey stepped from the hallway into Captain Cleaver's office. Cleaver sat at his desk. On his desk was a jar of Vaseline and a pocket-sized mirror. He unscrewed the top of the Vaseline jar and moistened the tip of a finger with the lubricant. Looking in the mirror, he dabbed it carefully on his sunburned nose.

"Carr is here," Bailey said. "He's pushing to meet my informant. I told him no, but he wouldn't buy it. He wants to talk to you."

Cleaver did not look up from the mirrow. He dabbed again. "Who *is* the informant?"

"He makes lots of recoveries for us. As a matter of fact, you have two grand coming from a jewelry recovery he made for us a few days ago. California Life and Casualty will have the cash for us any day."

"Two grand?" he said to the mirror. "My nose is burned to a crisp." He looked up. "Send him in."

Bailey stepped back into the Detective Bureau and motioned to Carr. Carr followed him into Cleaver's office. Bailey made introductions. As he shook hands, Carr thought Cleaver's hand felt greasy.

"We don't reveal our informants," Cleaver said. "That's my policy and the policy of this department. I'm going to back up Bailey's refusal to let you talk with the informant. Is that what you were going to ask me about?"

Carr looked at the jar of Vaseline. He flexed his palm. "Are you aware you've grease on your hand?"

Cleaver looked embarrassed. He pointed to his face. "Sunburned nose. I was just applying some—"

"Thanks for your time," Carr interrupted. He turned and strode out of the room. Bailey followed him down the hall to the stairway.

"I'm sure you can see where I'm coming from. I'm just following orders. So I hope there are no hard feelings."

"How long have you worked the burglary table here?" Carr asked.

Travis Bailey furrowed his brow. "Quite a while."

"Funny that you never ran across Lee Sheboygan. You'd think a good cat burglar like him would have come to your attention."

"Every cat burglar in L.A. takes at least one shot at Beverly Hills at one time or another. After a while it's hard to keep the names straight."

"Are you saying that you may have known him by another name?"

"No. I said I don't recall having any contact with the man. If you've got something to say, Carr, why don't you come right out and say it."

Carr lit another cigarette. He blew smoke on Bailey. "How about lunch?" he said with a smile.

Travis Bailey looked taken aback. "Yeah, I guess so. I'll get my coat." As he entered the door to the Detective Bureau, Carr opened the stairwell door. He took the steps to the parking lot, climbed in his sedan and drove to the Field Office.

Having traversed the hallway, stairwell and the downstairs parking lot looking for Carr, Bailey returned to the bureau. He shrugged off his coat and flung it on his desk angrily.

"What's the matter with you?" Delsey Piper asked.

"I have something I want you to do," he said, glaring at her for the dumb question.

In the Field Office mail room, Carr checked his message box. There was a message from Cedars of Lebanon Hospital. He called the number from his desk.

A woman answered. "Nursing station thirteen."

"This is Agent Carr."

"You still want us to notify you when visitors come to see Mr. Kelly?"

"Yes."

"A lady detective just called. She said she'd be over in an hour to visit Mr. Kelly. I told her it was okay. Just thought I'd let you know about it."

"Thanks a lot," Carr said. He rushed out of the office.

Carr sat in a vacant hospital room adjoining Jack Kelly's. He had wedged the door to Kelly's room open a few inches, and shoved a serving cart against it so it couldn't be opened. The door to Kelly's room creaked. The sound of footsteps.

"Jack Kelly?"

"That's me."

"I'm Delsey Piper, Beverly Hills P.D. If you feel up to it, I'd like to ask you a few questions about the shooting incident. I've been assigned to do the shooting analysis report for our department. It's sort of a follow-up we do anytime an officer uses his weapon."

"Would you mind cranking me up a foot or so with that thing at the end of the bed?"

A metal cranking sound. "How's that?" she asked.

"Better."

"Well, why don't you just tell me what happened?" She laughed nervously.

"I don't remember a damn thing," Kelly said. "Not a thing. I can hardly remember going over to Hartmann's house. The doctor tells me that this is common with people who get shot. The mind just blocks out the whole incident."

"You mean you can't remember even one single thing about how the shooting took place?"

"It's a complete blank spot in my mind."

"Wow," she said. "How weird." Neither spoke for a moment. "Do you think you'll be able to remember what happened if I come back in a day or two?"

"Hard to say. The doc said it could come back at any time, or maybe never."

"Ultraweird. Sort of like the Twilight Zone." A giggle. "Well, I guess I'll be going."

"Would you crank the bed down again for me?"

She complied with the request and Kelly thanked her.

"I hope you get well really, really soon," she said. The door opened and closed.

Carr waited awhile. Finally, he shoved the serving cart away from the door and went into the room.

"Do you think she's in with him?" Kelly said.

Carr shrugged. "Would you let her in on anything?"

"Hell no. I wonder why he sent her over here?"

"Because he's hearing footsteps."

Bailey unlocked the front door of his apartment. He stepped into the living room and closed the door behind him.

Unbuttoning her blouse, Delsey Piper stood in the

bedroom doorway. "He didn't remember anything." The blouse came open.

Bailey aproached her. "What do you mean he *couldn't remember anything?*"

She took off the blouse and tossed it on the floor. "Just what I said. He doesn't remember anything. The doctor told him it's like shock or something. He may never remember what happened."

"Who else was there?"

She gave him a confused look.

"Who else was in the hospital room when you spoke with him?" Bailey enunciated each word sarcastically.

"No one. What are you so uptight about?"

"I just want to know exactly what he said."

She unsnapped her brassiere and tossed it. "I asked him to tell me about what happened at Hartmann's house. He said he couldn't remember . . . just plain couldn't remember. That was about it." Her tits jiggled as she massaged a red bra mark on her shoulder.

"Carr is a sneaky son-of-a-bitch. A rotten, underhanded snake."

"What makes you say that?"

"I know him. He's trying to get me in trouble because of what happened to his partner."

"Do you think he *told* Kelly to act as if he can't remember what happened?"

Without answering, Bailey went over to a liquor cabinet. He poured whiskey into a glass, sipped.

"You didn't answer my question," Delsey said as she followed him into the living room. She unzipped her skirt, let it drop to her ankles. She kicked it back into the bedroom.

"Can't you pick up your things?" Bailey said angrily.

"Is there some reason why you can't keep your clothes off the fucking floor?"

Hands on hips, she stared at him for a moment. "I think you need to let off some steam." She strutted back into the bedroom. Moments later, she returned to the living room holding an amyl-nitrate capsule between her thumb and index finger. With a coy smile she held it up as if it were a nugget of gold. She pulled off her panties. Having moved over to him, she shoved a hand down his trousers and massaged his cock. He felt himself becoming erect and reached between her legs. Teasingly, she stepped away from him and dropped to the floor. She lay on her back and spread her legs, massaging her pussy.

As he stared at the generous mound of hair between her legs, he tore off his clothing. His cock throbbed. He dropped to the floor and, without preliminaries of any kind, mounted her. They screwed fiercely. Delsey Piper moaned and made staccato yelps. "Tell me when," she whispered. "Tell me when, tell me when, tell me when . . ."

"Now!" he said as he felt the first surge of orgasm.

Deftly, she broke the capsule and shoved it under his nose; almond fumes. He inhaled deeply. The almond-smelling drug caused his heart and blood to race. His orgasm doubled, tripled. He moaned and squirmed in pleasure. Delsey Piper dug her fingernails into his buttocks as if to wring him dry.

Finally, he was spent. He rolled off her and drew deep breaths. His heartbeat returned to normal.

Delsey kissed him on the cheek and said something about wanting to go out to dinner.

Ignoring her, he breathed deeply a few more times, crawled to his feet and staggered to the bathroom. He showered for at least a half hour, taking special care to clean his fingernails, feet and ears. He washed his hair until it was squeaky clean. When he finally turned off the shower, the phone was ringing. He heard Delsey answer it. "It's Bones," she said, stepping into the bathroom.

"Tell him I'll call him back."

"He says it's important."

Travis Bailey slung a towel over his shoulders and went to the phone. "I told you not to call me at home."

"Amanda would like to speak with you," Bones said. "She would like you to come over right now so she could speak to you."

"Are you at your place?"

"Yes."

"Is she going along with the program?"

"No, not at all."

"Tell him to get his ass over here right now," Amanda Kennedy said. She sounded as if she were close to the phone.

"She says she'd like you to come over—"

"I heard her. Don't let her leave until I get there. Do you understand that?"

"Sure," Chagra said. The phone clicked.

Bailey returned to the bathroom, where he dried off completely. Moving to the bedroom closet, he dressed slowly as he thought about what Amanda Kennedy had told him when he interviewed her at the Women's Jail. He relived his confrontation with Carr. Dressed in slacks and a sport shirt, he combed his hair for a long time. He shoved a snub-nosed revolver, which he always carried off duty, in the waistband of his trousers.

"I want to go out to dinner," Delsey said when he came out of the bedroom. She remained lying on the floor where he'd left her.

Wordlessly he stuffed his car keys into a pants pocket and headed out the door.

Answering the knock, Bones Chagra let Bailey into his apartment. Amanda Kennedy sat on the sofa with her hands folded across her chest. The walls of the spacious apartment were covered with barroom photographs of Chagra in his bartender's outfit, posturing with smiling movie and television stars. In the corner of the room was a metal, chairlike device with two padded bicycle seats facing each other at different elevations. A plastic vibrator rested on one of the seats.

Bailey moved casually to the sofa and took a seat.

Amanda Kennedy stared straight ahead. "Are you aware that he brought me here against my will?" she asked. "When he picked me up at the jail, I asked him to take me home. He refused and drove straight over here. You're a policeman. Isn't taking someone against their will a crime? Isn't it called kidnapping?"

Bailey frowned at Chagra. "I apologize," he said. "Bones isn't the most diplomatic person in the world. Could we just chat for a few minutes before I drive you home?"

"There's nothing to chat about. I told him the same thing I'll tell you. If my case is not dismissed . . . and I mean *dismissed,* not just fixed to probation, you people are in trouble. I don't know what happened to Lee Sheboygan but I have a pretty good idea. We were friends and he told me all about you." She turned to Bones. "And you."

"How do I know what you're telling me is true?" Bailey said.

"Lee told me that you and some guy that's a stage hypnotist gave him the addresses and that he and Bones did the rest. He said that some of the biggest jewelers in Beverly Hills bought the stolen diamonds and gold and that the paintings went to two art galleries on La Cienega Boulevard. Now do you believe me?"

Bailey felt a tingling sensation in the tips of his fingers. "I believe you," he said, forcing a wry smile.

"And?"

"And I've got the right contacts at the courthouse. Your case is as good as washed."

"And what exactly do you mean by *washed?*"

"You won't have to go to court. You won't have to go back to jail. Your bad experience is ended."

"How do I know you're not just saying that to pacify me?"

"I can show you the paperwork tomorrow, if you like. I have a friend in the District Attorney's office. I did a little checking and found out that the owner of the necklace Lee gave you passed away a few weeks ago. Therefore, there's no victim to testify. It was easier than I thought. You have my personal word that the case will be dismissed. You'll never hear another word about it."

Breathing a sigh of relief, Amanda Kennedy leaned back on the sofa. "Thank God," she said to the ceiling, then sat up again. "I was worried to death. All I could think about in there was serving time for something I didn't do. Something I had nothing to do with. All I did was accept a gift."

"It's over now," Bailey said. "Can't we have a drink?"

"I can use something more than a drink." The remark was obviously more than in jest.

Like a dutiful waiter, Bones winked and rushed into the kitchen.

"The night they booked me, the matrons searched me,

fingerprinted me and shoved me in a cell. It happened so fast I didn't know what hit me. All of a sudden, I'm sitting in this jail cell. It was unreal. I mean unreal. It wasn't as if I was doing dope or something and got caught selling to the man. I was sitting in a jail cell simply because I had been given a necklace. Unreal."

Bones returned from the kitchen carrying a pocket-sized mirror and a small glass vial of white powder. He set the mirror down on the coffee table in front of Amanda. Having unscrewed the top off the vial, he tapped out a small line of cocaine onto the mirror. From his shirt pocket, he removed a red cocktail straw and handed it to her. "This'll make you feel better."

Blankly, she glanced at the two men. Then she leaned over the table and touched one end of the straw to the cocaine and the other end to her right nostril. She inhaled through her nose as she moved the straw along the line of coke, dropped the straw and leaned back. With her eyes closed, as if in ecstasy, she inhaled deeply a few times.

Bones stared at her tits while Bailey stepped to the bar. He mixed a strong drink and a weak one.

Amanda Kennedy opened her eyes.

"How is it?" Chagra asked.

"Lovely. Really lovely."

Bailey handed her the strong drink.

"I hope you don't think I was trying to be unreasonable about this thing," she said, taking a sip, "but I have to look out for myself."

"No hard feelings." Bailey hefted his glass and they both drank. Her eyes looked dope-hazy.

Bones went over to a wall unit, where he flipped some switches. Soft music filled the room.

"Mellow," she said. "This is the first mellow feeling I've had since they arrested me. Uptight City. That's what they should call jail. Uptight City. I couldn't sleep a wink. The lights were on all the time. It was like a fucking movie. Unreal." She took a big sip of the drink. "Ummmm."

Bones Chagra sat down next to her. "Really."

Amanda glanced at her blouse and gave it a little tug. "Totally wrinked."

"You still look great," Chagra whispered.

Travis Bailey walked to a wall phone in the kitchen. He lifted the receiver and dialed. Delsey Piper answered. "If anyone calls for me tonight, just say I'm in the shower and I'll call them back. Then leave the phone off the hook."

"What's going on?"

"An informant thing," he said, lowering his voice.

"Will you be home tonight?"

"It depends."

"You never give definite answers."

He hung up the receiver and returned to the living room.

Chagra and Amanda Kennedy had left the sofa. The bedroom door was only partially shut, and he could hear Amanda giggling. The cocaine and paraphernalia were gone from the coffee table. He turned on the television, looking for some diversion. For the next hour or so he stared at a courtroom drama starring an actor who he knew had once been arrested for molesting a twelve-year-old girl. As the screen credits were shown, Bones Chagra came out of the bedroom. He was naked.

"You want some?" he said, pointing a thumb at the bedroom door.

Travis Bailey shook his head. "It's getting late."

Bones nodded and returned to the bedroom.

Bailey stared at a quiz show in which the contestants

jumped up and down. The audience applauded intermittently.

Chagra came out of the bedroom again, this time with his arm around a staggering Amanda Kennedy. Sloppily, she tucked in her blouse.

Bailey stood up.

"How about another little drink?" Chagra asked her.

"I think I'd better go," she said, slurring her words. "You still here?" she said as she noticed Bailey.

"Just leaving," he heard himself saying. "Can I give you a lift?"

Chagra stared at Bailey as if he wanted to say something.

Amanda pulled Chagra by the arm. "Why don't you give me a ride home?" she said drunkenly.

"Uh, my car's in the shop."

Travis Bailey walked to the front door and opened it. "My radio car is downstairs."

Amanda giggled as Bones tried to keep her from losing her balance. "I guess I can't walk home."

Bailey stepped out the door and followed a hallway to a stairwell leading to the ground-floor carport. Chagra followed him, keeping his arm around Amanda Kennedy's shoulder in order to steady her gait.

In the carport, he unlocked the passenger door of his sedan and swung the door open. As Chagra led her out of the stairwell, Bailey looked around carefully. There was no one else in the carport. The street was deserted. He went over to the driver's side and climbed in, watching as Chagra led Amanda Kennedy to the passenger side and helped her in. Having said something about giving her a call sometime, he shut the car door. Without looking back, he hurried back through the stairwell door.

Amanda Kennedy leaned back in the seat. "Unreal," she said sleepily.

Travis Bailey started the engine. Driving out of the carport onto a street lined with apartment houses and luxury cars, he waited until he reached the corner to turn on the headlights.

"My ex used to write scripts about this sort of thing. I was a sounding board for his crazy ideas. His best script was about this man who would send poison pen letters by carrier pigeon. They were going to make it into a TV movie but this peanut butter company that was the sponsor didn't approve of the script . . ."

Bailey nodded. They drove along Westwood Boulevard past some newly built restaurants and shops that were designed with synthetic wood and brick to look European. Sandwiched between a candy store and French bakery was a gun shop with a three-dimensional bullet affixed to the front door.

"How many other people know about the things Lee Sheboygan told you about?" Bailey said as he turned a corner.

She sat up and rubbed her eyes. "I've never told a soul, if that's what you mean. I believe in not getting involved. If there's anything I've learned since coming to L.A., it's *do not get involved*. Lee and I met around the swimming pool after he moved in. He seemed lonely and he was very open about having served time in prison. I thought that was refreshing, that someone would be open enough to tell a perfect stranger about the mistakes he'd made in life. He told me about how awful it was in prison. He was a very different person. I could relate to him, share secrets with him. We just seemed to click. The right vibes were just there and all of a sudden we were getting down together and telling each other our innermost secrets. We were really communicating. The cocaine helped, of course."

"Was anyone else there when Lee was . . . sharing his secrets?" Bailey said, keeping his eyes on the road.

"Of course not."

They passed a Polynesian restaurant that Bailey knew as a hangout for movie stars. Situated on a corner lot in front of a large parking lot, the restaurant's entrance was covered with banana plants and other Pacific foliage. A walkway leading to the front door was lined with brightly colored island flowers that had been the subject of more than one California Living article in the Sunday paper. Like an oasis, palm trees leaned from the corners of the building toward a flora-filled atrium in its center. Bailey remembered answering a burglar alarm call at the restaurant one night when he was working a radio car. As he shined his flashlight into the kitchen area, wharf-sized rats had scurried out from under the sinks and work counters.

"Why didn't you come in the bedroom tonight?" Amanda said. She smiled pertly.

He shrugged.

"I'm very open about sex. The only thing that turns me off is doing it with another woman. A complete turnoff. You don't like to talk about sex, do you?"

He stared at the road.

"Some people are like that." She pointed to the right. "You should have turned there to go to my place."

"Would you mind if I made a quick stop? I need to drop off a copy of a report right up the street. It'll just take a sec."

"Sure," she said blankly.

A block later they passed a large furniture store that Bailey knew marked the Beverly Hills city limits.

Illuminated by mobile spotlights, an enormous helium-filled clown holding a sign that read Close-Out Sale floated above its roof.

Bailey slowed down. He turned right and pulled down the alley behind the deserted pizza house where he used to meet Sheboygan. He maneuvered the sedan under a canopy and turned off the engine. His heart raced. The tips of his fingers tingled.

"This place isn't open," she said. "Why are you stopping here?"

Travis Bailey pointed out the passenger window. "Who's that?"

Amanda Kennedy turned her head. Swiftly, he swung his right arm around her neck and wedged her throat in the crook of his arm. Using his left arm as a lever, he squeezed with all his might. Her fingers scratched his forearm as he pulled her toward him. Her hair was in his face. She made frantic guttural sounds and her fingernails dug deeper into his arm. She kicked desperately. Her feet wedged against the passenger door. In a violent paroxysm, she pushed off the door. His head slammed against the driver's window and they slipped down onto the seat. He maintained his grip and squeezed harder. Finally, her lips made a bubble-blowing sound and her body relaxed completely. She felt heavier. He readjusted his grip on her neck and maintained steady pressure for a long time. Out the passenger window he could see the inflated clown. It stared at him.

The headlights of a car illuminated the windows.

"No," he muttered aloud without releasing pressure on the woman's neck. He held his breath as the automobile drove past without slowing down. He felt wetness and realized he was soaked with Amanda Kennedy's urine. He wanted to push himself free of the contamination, but forced himself to hold on. He had to make sure she was dead. Exhausted, he released his hold. He shoved her body off him. Taking care not to make any unnecessary noise, he opened the driver's door and went to the trunk of the sedan. The air was cool and because of a slight breeze he felt a sensation of coolness on his urine-soaked trousers. He had the urge to strip off the wet clothing. He opened the trunk and removed a plastic tarp from an evidence kit. Quickly, he spread the tarp in the trunk.

At the passenger door, he looked both ways down the alley, then dragged and pulled Amanda's body off the front seat. Staggering, he carried it to the trunk, dropped the body inside and closed the trunk carefully. After a few deep breaths, he returned to the driver's seat, started the car and drove out of the alley. In a few minutes he was heading east on the San Bernardino Freeway, which, because of the hour, was clear. He opened the windows because of the odor on the front seat.

After traveling ten miles or so from the city limits of L.A., he swung off the freeway and headed north on surface streets, past an endless blur of one-story commercial buildings and stucco homes that could have been anywhere in Southern California. Finally, he made his way up a steep grade toward the San Gabriel Mountains. At the top of the grade the road took a sharp right turn and Bailey found himself on a two-lane mountain road that hugged the chaparral-covered mountain area as it crept slowly to a higher elevation. Below him on the right side was a steep cliff that provided an unhindered view of the city lights below. At the first turnoff he stopped and parked the car.

Bailey climbed out and walked to the edge of the cliff. Below, there was only inky blackness. He headed back to the car, unlocked the trunk and flipped it open. As the trunk light came on her hand reached out for him. Startled, he jumped back, jerked his revolver from his waistband and pointed it. The sleeve of Amanda Kennedy's blouse had caught on a portion of the trunk lock, lifting her hand with the trunk lid. She was dead. As he shoved his gun back in its holster, he realized his hand was shaking. He lifted the body by the arms and pulled it out of the trunk. He lost his grip and it fell to the gravel head first. Heart racing, he hoisted the body to the edge of the cliff and slung it over, then rushed back to the car and slammed the trunk shut. He flew to the front seat, started the engine and made a U-turn.

He drove down the hill slowly and listened to the squeaking of his brakes. Retracing his route, he traveled south to the freeway and headed east. In a gas station in downtown Los Angeles, he washed the front seat carefully with wet paper towels.

By the time he reached his apartment, he had stopped shaking.

Chapter 11

THE ANCIENT courtroom was a museum of symbols, high ceilings, marble, rich wood and leather. Above the judge's bench was a large American-eagle plaque, fashioned of brass and wood. As usual, the air conditioner was on too high. Carr's hands felt cold.

Carr thought that everyone—Judge Malcolm with his crooked toupee, the court clerk who stuffed counterfeit money into see-through evidence envelopes as if on an assembly line and Sally Malone, the court reporter—looked bored. Everyone, that is, except the defendant, who sat on the witness stand. A tall black man, he alternated between touching the witness-stand microphone (which made it hum) and cracking his knuckles. He wore white trousers and a purple, long-sleeved shirt. Come to think of it, Carr thought to himself, it was the same outrageous outfit he wore the night he and Kelly chased him into a backyard clothesline.

"I thought it was narcotics in the briefcase," the black man said with his head turned toward the judge. "I threw the briefcase and runned away because I didn't wanna get caught carrying no dope. A man asked me to pick up a load of dope for him and that's what I did. I went to the apartment and a lady handed me this briefcase. When I was walking away from the place, these two federal men came up on me. I threw the briefcase on the ground because I thought for sure it was filled with heroin."

The defense lawyer, a wiry young man with a bristling black moustache and unmanageable hair, removed his thick glasses and wiped the lenses on his necktie. He put them back on. "I have no more questions for the defendant, Your Honor."

"If you have nothing, Mr. Green, then the defendant may step down," Judge Malcolm said.

The man ambled off the witness stand. As he passed by the prosecution table, he glared at Carr.

Carr only looked at Sally Malone and smiled. She stenotyped as the judge announced a recess. Everyone in the courtroom stood up and, like a pharaoh, the judge exited the courtroom through a special door.

The defense attorney slid his swivel chair to the prosecution table in order to confer with the assistant United States attorney, a man who, by appearance, could have been his slightly older brother.

Carr went over to Sally.

"He has all his clients say the same thing," Sally whispered. "They always claim they thought they were carrying narcotics instead of counterfeit money."

"I know. And with good old Mushhead Malcolm, it works."

"Nick called while you were testifying. He wants you to meet him at the Olympic Auditorium tonight. He's refereeing. I guess that means that I get stood up again, right?"

"Unless you like wrestling matches," Carr said amiably.

"No thanks."

There was the sound of a buzzer. The court clerk said, "All rise." The judge came in his door and went to the bench.

The defense attorney called Carr to the witness stand and swore him in.

"Agent Carr," he said, "you previously testified that you watched the defendant enter the front door of the address in question and, watching through the window, you saw a woman remove money from a refrigerator and hand it to the defendant. Then you saw him remove some money from his pocket and give it to her. Is that right?"

"That's right."

"What denomination were the bills?" the defense attorney asked.

"I don't know. I was too far away to tell."

"But you could tell it was money?"

"It was money."

"Could you tell whether it was counterfeit or genuine money?" Green said.

"I was too far away to tell, but an informant had told me that a woman was selling counterfeit money at the address. After the man entered the door I saw her give him a large amount of money and he gave her a smaller amount of money in exchange. To me, that meant that a counterfeiting transaction had probably taken place."

"Your Honor," Green said, "the answer was not responsive. I ask that the answer be stricken from the record."

"So stricken," the judge said.

"Agent Carr," Green continued, "when the defendant

departed the residence carrying a briefcase and you approached him, what did you say?"

"I identified myself as a federal officer and informed the defendant I wanted to speak with him."

"I take it when you approached him, the briefcase was closed. You could not see what was in it, is that right?"

"That's right."

"So in actual fact, as you approached the defendant, you had no idea what he had in that briefcase. Isn't that right?"

"I didn't know for sure, but I would have bet a paycheck or two that it was counterfeit money."

The lawyer looked beseechingly to the judge.

"Mr. Carr, I'm going to have to ask you to limit your answers," the judge said. "Please don't make any more conclusions."

"And when the defendant threw the briefcase on the ground and ran away from you, you and your partner chased him," Mr. Green said. "Is that right?"

"Yes."

"You gave chase immediately, without stopping to see what was inside the briefcase. Is that right?"

"Right."

"So, therefore, when you were chasing him down the street you *still* didn't know what was in the briefcase. For all you knew at that point, it *could* have been heroin or anything else for that matter. Isn't that right?"

"I thought the briefcase contained counterfeit money," Carr said.

"As a matter of fact, isn't it true that you can't really be sure that the briefcase that you recovered from the street after you apprehended my client was the same briefcase you saw him leave the apartment with?"

"I guess someone could have switched briefcases by

the time we returned," Carr said. "I once saw a Charlie Chan movie where it happened." He smiled.

"Please move on, Mr. Green," the judge said. "I'm getting tired of this line of questioning."

"If it please the court, Your Honor, the defense rests," said Green.

"Mr. Carr, you may step down," the judge said, shuffling some papers. "The defense motion to suppress evidence in this case is based on the defense's contention that the prosecution has failed to show evidence of specific intent on the part of the defendant. Possession of counterfeit Federal Reserve notes, which is a violation of United States Code Title Eighteen Section four-seven-two, and the offense charged in this case, requires that *specific* intent on the part of the defendant be shown. The statute requires that the government prove beyond a reasonable doubt that the defendant possessed the counterfeit money with the *intent to defraud*. The court finds that a reasonable doubt exists as to whether the defendant then and there well knew that he was in possession of *counterfeit money* as opposed to any other type of contraband at the time of his arrest. This case is dismissed and the defendant's bond is exonerated."

The defendant smirked at Carr as Attorney Green congratulated him.

Later, the courtroom was clear except for Carr and Sally Malone. She arranged her notes in a briefcase. "All Green's clients have the same story. They all say they thought it was narcotics rather than counterfeit money in the package or box or briefcase. Malcolm always falls for it every time. It makes me sick."

"How about lunch?"

"I know you're angry. You're angry about losing the case, but as usual, you won't express your feelings."

"If I was really angry I would have lied and said I saw him fill the briefcase with the money when he was inside the apartment. That would have convicted him."

Her jaw fell open. She gave him a slap on the hand. "*Charlie,*" she said in mock disapproval.

"And if Judge Malcolm would have found him guilty, he would have sentenced him to straight probation anyway. The whole system is perverted and Mushhead Malcolm is one of the chief perverts. Just the sight of that ex-ambulance-chasing shyster sitting on the bench makes me think of retirement."

"See, you are angry," Sally said.

Charles Carr parked his sedan in a pay lot behind the Olympic auditorium. The rear of the three-story cement structure bore an enormous faded mural of boxers facing each other with dukes up. A security guard in a blue uniform stood beside a graffiti-covered door.

Carr showed his gold Treasury badge. The officer unlocked the door and let him in. Inside the ancient arena, which had the odor of dank cement, cigar smoke and hot dogs cooking in oil, most of the seats were filled. The crowd noise was deafening. In the middle of a regulation-sized ring was a shiny, circus-style steel cage. From each of its four corners, steel cable stretched to a hook extending from the ceiling.

An anxious crowd filtered between seats and refreshment stands. It was mainly made up of shabbily dressed people of retirement age, Mexicans wearing cowboy hats and shirts, black teenagers with funny hats, fat women and men casually dressed in old T-shirts and Levi's. At ringside was a group of raucous college-age men and women wearing USC sweat shirts. A paper plane constructed from newspaper floated down from the balcony and landed on the cage, which drew a murmur of appreciation.

Carr made his way way through the crowd and along a corridor to a locker room. He showed his badge to another security guard. The guard nodded and opened the door. Carr wound around banks of rusty lockers. He found Prince Nikola of Serbia standing in front of an open locker in the corner, pulling a referee's shirt over his head. "That sunnabitch Bones is tending bar at place in Beverly Hills. It's called the Blue Peach," Nick said on spotting Carr, ". . . a private club for movie people. Costs lots of money for membership. You know, one of those clubs all the big-shot phonies join because all the other big-shot phonies belong. Next year same sunnabitch that owns it closes up and opens under different name. Everybody pays new membership fee." Nick looked at his wristwatch. "I have only cupla minutes before first match." He tucked in his shirt.

"Does Bones have anything going on the side?"

"They tell me he still has the crap game." Nick sat down on a bench and pulled black wrestling shoes from a locker. He tugged one on. "But he keeps it away from where he works. He does conventions, bank openings, yacht parties . . . wherever the big shots go." He yanked on the other shoe and laced it up. "He's supposed to have a game at a bank opening this week. Some savings and loan in Beverly Hills . . . grand opening. If you go there you catch him easy."

"I appreciate the help, Nick," Carr said. He pointed his thumb in the direction of the ring. "Why the cage in the ring?"

"Tonight is grudge match," Nick said. "GI Joe against the Masked Phantom . . . no holds barred." He chuckled. "The cage was GI Joe's idea: *a fight to the death* . . . wonderful idea. The auditorium is complete sellout. You should stay and see the match. GI Joe is a nice Hungarian boy from Pittsburgh. I teach him everything, including Boston Crab."

A muscle-bound young man wearing olive drab wrestling trunks and an army fatigue jacket with corporal stripes lumbered over from behind a locker. Nick introduced him to Carr.

"I gotta ask ya something," GI Joe said to Nick in a discreet tone. He glanced suspiciously at Carr.

"Charlie is my friend," Nick said to the young man.

GI Joe nodded.

"Could you go over it once more for me," he said. He had a worried look.

"Which part?"

"The ending."

Nick stood up, put an arm around the wrestler's shoulder and spoke fervently in his ear. "Cage is lowered back into ring. I unlock door. You and Phantom wrestle out of door. I pull you apart from Phantom and walk you towards a corner. Phantom sneaks up and gives you judo chop. Go to your knees and do slow burn. Then you get mad and chase him around the cage. On the third circle around, you grab him by the mask. He goes down and you pin him with the Boston Crab. I give the *one*, *two*, *three*, and you are the winner. Got it?"

GI Joe rubbed his chin. "I hope so."

"Not to worry."

An intercom on the wall came alive.

"Ladies and gentlemen, welcome to the grudge match of the century," said a ring announcer with a tenor voice.

GI Joe headed out the locker room door, followed by a beefy wrestler wearing an executioner-style mask.

Nick shook hands with Carr and trotted out after the wrestlers.

Carr followed the wrestlers along the corridor to the arena. The crowd roared as they climbed into the ring. GI Joe tossed tiny American-flag lapel buttons at the crowd while the bull-like Masked Phantom stretched on the rope and growled. After introductions and referee instructions, the wrestlers climbed into the cage. Slowly the cage was hoisted above ring level. As the wrestlers made contact, the cage tipped from side to side. The crowd booed and cheered.

Carr left through the back door.

On the way to his apartment, he stopped at a supermarket to purchase the ingredients for chili and beans, one of the four or five simple meals he knew how to prepare. As he roamed the aisles in the market, his mind was on what Jack Kelly facetiously called *strategy*. Should he attempt to interview Bones the bartender? . . . Or was it too soon? He mused over the details of the shooting incident for the thousandth time. At the checkout counter, he shook himself out of his trance, paid for the groceries and drove to his apartment.

In his kitchen, Carr sautéed onions, then unwrapped a pound of hamburger meat and tossed it in the pan. As the meat sizzled, he wondered how much Amanda Kennedy really knew. By the time he added salt, tomatoes and flour, he decided that she probably knew a hell of a lot.

Having forgotten to get the chili, he searched frantically through the cupboards. "Damn," he said out loud. He was out of chili. He stirred the colorless mixture until it was cooked, said the hell with it and scooped it onto a plate. Having doused the mess with catsup, he took a bite. It tasted awful. He tossed the concoction into the sink. To allay hunger, he drank two glasses of water before he went to bed.

Carr got up twice in the night, unable to sleep.

The next morning he ate a double breakfast at a coffee shop on Santa Monica Boulevard and headed for the Field Office. There, he spent the day filling out On-the-Job injury forms for Jack Kelly, Daily Report forms (which he invariably managed to postpone until the end of the month when they were due), case status reports (he always checked the box marked *Investigation Continued—No New Leads* because he knew it avoided more useless paperwork in the long run).

As he sat at his desk and plodded through the fruitless tasks, he heard whistling in the hallway. Carr recognized the sound as he would the sound of a garbage truck passing by at three in the morning. He smelled pipe smoke.

Norbert Waeves stepped into Carr's office. Pipe jutting, he made a mighty puff and pulled the pipe from his lips as if it were a thermometer. He licked his lips. "Doing some paperwork I see."

Carr continued writing.

"Kelly's going to need a statement signed by a doctor stating that his injuries were caused by a gunshot. Without the statement, headquarters won't approve his temporary sick pay—new regulation. Three copies and one for the office file." He made a pipe puff.

Carr nodded and kept working. He felt like yanking the pipe out of No Waves's mouth and breaking it in half.

"Seen the new ammo headquarters sent us?" No Waves asked.

Carr shook his head without looking up.

"It's some supervelocity stuff," he said, ". . . real *stopping power.*" He made a punch gesture, then left.

Carr could hear him whistling "Stout Hearted Men" down the hallway.

By late afternoon, Carr had completed the paperwork. He paper-clipped the sheaf of papers and tossed them into a typing pool basket.

He phoned the Beverly Hills Chamber of Commerce and learned that First Fidelity Bank of Beverly Hills was holding a bank grand-opening party at 8:00 P.M. Carr wrote down the address.

It was dark.

Charles Carr pulled into an underground garage at the bank building and parked. He took an elevator to the ground floor. A young brunette wearing a strapless red chiffon dress sat at a reception table in front of the glass doors of the bank. "Good evening, sir," she said. "Welcome to First Fidelity of Beverly Hills. May I have your name?"

"Charles Carr."

She checked the guest list. "I'm sorry, sir, but I don't seem to have your name on the guest list."

Carr pulled his Treasury badge out of his pocket. He flashed it at the woman and shoved it back in his pocket. "I'm a federal bank examiner. The president of the bank invited me this afternoon."

"Uh, certainly," the woman said. She handed him a bank brochure and motioned him to the doors. Inside the plushly carpeted lobby, a crowd of well-dressed older men and mostly younger women milled about. In the middle of the crowd was a champagne fountain, a portable bar with two bartenders and an hors d'oeuvre table decorated with ice carvings and bouquets of flowers. As Carr roamed through the crowd, he heard bits and pieces of conversation: purchasing property, taxes, oil stocks, limited partnerships.

Crossing over to the opposite end of the lobby, he almost bumped into Bones Chagra. He was dressed in a blue double-breasted blazer with a Yale emblem, gray trousers and a maroon striped tie. Carr pictured his mug shot photograph. Chagra chatted with two young women wearing cocktail dresses. They looked like models.

Carr strolled to the hors d'oeuvre table and had a snack. He watched Chagra move through the crowd introducing himself and chatting amiably. The women followed him and helped with the conversation.

After an hour or so the crowd noise became louder. Two middle-aged men toting cocktails went with Chagra to a corner of the lobby, with Chagra's women following like quail. The crap game began. Carr joined the crowd that gathered to watch it.

Soon there were at least twenty people watching the game. Chagra lost for a while, and other members of the crowd joined the game. Lots of cash exchanged hands. Chagra's women slipped away from the crowd one at a time, leaving through the front doors. Chagra began to win. The bets increased. Chagra continued to win. Though Carr stared at Chagra's hands on every roll, he was unable to see the dice switch.

As the game started to break up, Chagra's blazer pockets were filled with cash.

Carr spotted a private office near the lobby doors. He opened the door and saw that it was unoccupied.

Chagra patted people on the back as he headed toward the door. As he walked past, Carr tapped him on the shoulder. "I'd like to speak with you for a moment if you don't mind," Carr said, showing him his badge. He motioned to the office.

Chagra gave a look of incredulity. "What's this all about?"

"Leon Sheboygan."

"I'm in a kind of a hurry," Chagra said, swallowing.

"So am I." Carr opened the door of the office. They stared at each other for a moment, until Chagra stepped inside. Carr followed him in and closed the door. The room was handsomely furnished with an oversized walnut desk, a conference table and sofa that looked like a page from an interior decorator's magazine.

"Who told you I was here tonight?" Chagra said.

"When was the last time you saw Lee Sheboygan?"

"I've never heard the name before in my life."

"You lived with him."

Chagra folded his arms across his chest. "I don't know what you're talking about. And I'll tell you something else, Mr. Gumshoe, I don't appreciate being followed around like this. It's very embarrassing."

"I bet you'd really be embarrassed if I yanked those loaded dice out of your pocket right now and showed 'em to all those suckers you just fleeced."

"I don't know what you're talking about."

"Lee Sheboygan is dead. Answering a few questions about a dead man isn't going to make you a snitch. If you'll answer a few simple questions for me, I'll guarantee that what you tell me will go no further. I'm working on an important investigation, and it looks like you're the only person that can help me."

Bones Chagra reached into his blazer and pulled out a package of cigarettes. He hung a cigarette on his lower lip and flamed it with a lighter. "Questions bore me," he said nonchalantly. He blew smoke and coughed.

"Did you share an apartment with Sheboygan up until a few weeks ago?"

Bones Chagra shook his head. He looked at his cigarette as if it had somehow just appeared in his hand by magic.

"I've already verified you lived there. I've spoken with the other residents at the apartment house."

"Come to think of it, I did live there for a little while."

"How was Sheboygan making a living?"

"I never asked him about personal matters."

"Who did Sheboygan hang around with?"

"He was a loner."

"When did you last see him?"

"I don't remember."

"Did Sheboygan tell you about the burglaries he was committing?"

"Your questions are starting to bore me," Chagra said. He blew smoke in Carr's face.

Carr stared at him for a moment. He reached into his suit coat pocket and pulled out a pack of cigarettes, gave the pack a little tap before removing one. "May I use your lighter?" Carr asked, placing the cigarette between his lips.

Grudgingly, Chagra dug the lighter out of his pocket and handed it to Carr. Carr lit the cigarette, held out the lighter to Chagra. He reached out to accept it. Carr flamed the lighter on the palm of Chagra's hand.

"Ouch!" he said, jumping backward. He kissed the burn.

"Are you still bored?"

Chagra stared at his burned hand. Suddenly he made a fist, swung at Carr and missed. Carr counterpunched and drove his fist into Chagra's stomach. Chagra slammed backward against the desk and slipped to the floor. Eyes wide and mouth open, he struggled to catch his breath.

Carr stood over him. "My partner is in the hospital, you goddamn creep. If you play dumb with me I'm going to show you some tricks that'll help wise you up."

Carr straightened his necktie, walked to the door. Without glancing back, he opened it and left.

Chapter 12

THERE WAS the smell of expensive perfume. The seats in the private projection room were filled with Mrs. Wallace's friends, most of whom were members of the Women's Club. All the women were attired in the latest Rodeo Drive fashions—dresses with thin belts or baggy pants and blouses.

Emil Kreuzer stood with his back to the projection screen. Charlene, the hitchhiker, lay on the floor in front of him with her head resting on a pillow. She wore a stylish blue jump suit he'd bought for her. Her eyes were closed and she breathed deeply. As Kreutzer spoke, he was careful to make eye contact around the room, a technique he'd learned in a Terminal Island public-speaking class. As his eyes roamed the flock of rich bitches, he noticed at least five four-carat diamond rings. In fact, a statuesque matron sipping coffee at the end of the first row had a diamond ring that he estimated at at least *six* carats. He gave her special eye contact. ". . . and as you can see," he continued, "Charlene has slipped very easily, very comfortably, into a deep and restful hypontic trance. Before Charlene came to me she suffered from insomnia and had an abnormal fear of heights. Even standing at a second-story window or riding a horse would cause dizziness, then eventually nausea and vomiting due to anxiety. Even two or three rungs on a stepladder would cause her to become light-headed. Her parents, who are both medical doctors whom I met at a conference at the Mayo Clinic, had tried every form of medical and psychological therapy to help Charlene. Nothing worked. After I was allowed to examine her, I came to the conclusion that she was an excellent candidate for rebirthing therapy.

A Mexican maid dressed in a white uniform came into the room with a coffee pot. Mrs. Wallace motioned her away and the maid scurried out of the room.

"And now, if I may, I'd like to ask everyone to be particularly quiet as I lead Charlene back to the beginning of her life, a journey that she and I often take for its therapeutic and cleansing effect." He knelt next to Charlene. Some of the women moved closer to get a better view. "If you feel comfortable and very, very relaxed and at ease, Charlene, I'd like you to give me a slight nod of the head."

Charlene nodded.

"And now slowly, as one would travel in a safe boat across a lake whose water is as calm and pleasant as mirrored glass, I want you to travel back to your fifth birthday. When you have made that trip backward through time, I'd like you to give me another nod."

Charlene continued to breathe deeply for what must have been a full minute. She gave another nod.

"Hello, birthday girl," Kreuzer said. "What do you see around you? You may respond verbally without coming out of your comfortable state of relaxation."

Charlene's lips moved a few times. "Birthday party," she said in a barely audible voice. "Mommy has the cake and the candles."

"What a wonderful happy day!" Kreuzer lowered his voice. "Should we move closer to warmth and total security?"

Charlene nodded before he finished the question.

Using a series of similar suggestions, he directed her backward in time to her first birthday. As he did so, Charlene turned on her side. She put her thumb in her mouth and curled into a fetal position. Some of the women gasped in amazement.

As he directed Charlene farther back in time by reeling off months, her body curled tighter. ". . . and finally we have returned to the womb." Gentle, Kreuzer pulled Charlene's thumb from her mouth. "How do you feel?"

Her lips moved. "Wet . . . warm . . ." she mumbled, ". . . and my tummy has something on it."

Kreuzer looked up at the audience. "As you can see, Charlene has now regressed all the way back to the womb, to the beginnings of her life. The feeling on her stomach is the umbilical cord. How do you feel, Charlene?"

After more lip movement, Charlene said, "I want to stay here."

More gasps from the audience.

"I know you'd like to stay longer," Kreuzer said, "but we must come into the world. We must be born." Charlene nodded. As he directed her out of the womb, she thrashed about. "What are you feeling at this moment?" Kreuzer asked gently.

"Something pushing down on me." there was fear in her voice. "I want to come out faster, but I'm too big . . . more pushing down . . . when I push with my feet it hurts me. I think I'm stuck." Her arms had moved to her sides. "I can hear her. My mom is crying. Push . . . push . . . push. Something hard around my head . . . jaw hurts . . . hurts bad . . . pulling me . . . pulling . . . pulling . . . I hear loud talk . . . push, push. Everything is tight and I can't move my arms . . ." Suddenly, Charlene burst into an infant-like cry. She thrashed furiously. Finally, she stopped. Her thumb found its way to her mouth.

"Welcome to the world," Kreuzer said. He patted her hand. Carefully, he gave gentle commands and she progressed forward in time through her birthdays. Finally, they were at the present. He snapped his fingers three times and she opened her eyes. He helped her to her feet. The women applauded, then burst into animated conversation.

Kreuzer raised his hands and the crowd quieted down. "It took Charlene and I five sessions until we discovered the root of her problems. She had been a forceps delivery, as I'm sure many of you were able to surmise. Moments after she was born, the doctor dropped her on the floor of the delivery room."

The women murmured.

"Once Charlene and I were able to determine this, we were able to completely eliminate her fear of heights and her insomnia and the other problems she had were taken care of. She is happier today than she has ever been in her entire life." He looked at her. "Isn't that right, young lady?"

Charlene nodded.

"Rebirthing is the wave of the future in personal development," Kreuzer said, giving his best smile. "This concludes my demonstration. If anyone is interested in rebirthing therapy, I've left some of my cards on the table near the door. Thank you." He made a slight bow as the women applauded.

Outside the house, Kreuzer climbed in the driver's seat of his Mercedes-Benz and started the engine. Charlene leaned back in the passenger seat. "Sometimes I feel like laughing when I'm doing it."

"You did a wonderful job today," Kreuzer said. "You have tremendous acting ability."

"You really think so?"

"I mean that with all my heart."

Charlene giggled.

A few minutes later they were back at his apartment.

Travis Bailey sat in a sedan parked across the street from the apartment house. He nodded as Kreuzer swung the Mercedes-Benz into the driveway.

Kreuzer turned off the engine and handed the key to Charlene. "You go on in. I have to talk with that man over there." She took the key and climbed out of the car. Kreuzer looked around carefully before he strolled over to Bailey's car. He opened the passenger door and got in.

Without a greeting Bailey started the engine, pulled out from the curb and headed north toward Sunset Boulevard. "Carr is causing problems," he said. "He paid Bones a visit."

"Damn." Kreuzer felt like he'd been kicked in the stomach.

"Bones shined him on."

"Carr does that sort of thing. I told you, the man is a snake. He squeezes people to get a reaction." He ran his hands through his hair. "But he has nothing. He has zero. And Bones is solid. The cops offered him a pass five years ago in exchange for testimony in the Athletic Club gambling thing. He kept his mouth shut and got two years when he could have walked. The man is solid."

Nothing was said for a while. They cruised along Sunset Boulevard past modern office buildings, billboards with motion picture advertisements and crowded sidewalk cafes. On the road in front of them a bus emitted a billow of black exhaust, like an urban crop duster.

"What about Lee's girl friend?" Kreuzer said. "The one you were worried about?"

"She's no longer a worry." Bailey turned south on La Brea Avenue.

"How can you be sure?"

"She went for a hike up in the mountains."

"I thought she was in jail."

"She was," Bailey said. "Bones bailed her out and she took a trip. I made the arrangements myself."

Kreuzer turned and stared at him for a long moment. He leaned back in the seat.

Bailey slowed down as they passed the Pascoe Military Academy. A group of cadets marched across the playground.

"That's where I went to school," he said. "I was one of the few who graduated without turning queer."

"Are you telling me that Amanda Kennedy is no longer a cause for concern?" Kreuzer swallowed twice.

Bailey picked up speed again. "That's what I'm telling you."

"We'll have to keep tabs on Bones," Kreuzer said. "I trust him implicitly, but we'll still have to keep an eye on him."

"I intend to." Maintaining the speed limit, he completed the circuitous trip back to Kreuzer's apartment. He pulled to the curb and parked, but left the engine running.

"I'll have some more addresses for you in the next few days," Kreuzer said. "My appointment book is full."

"I'll be in touch."

Carr sat on the edge of the hospital bed as Jack Kelly, wearing nothing but an open-at-the-back hospital smock, walked slowly around the room. Kelly needed a shave and his hair was matted on one side. Though his voice was weak, he spoke in animated fashion about the shooting. Because of his wound he didn't move his left arm. "Sheboygan sees Bailey jump from behind the bar with a riot gun. He says, *'No,'* as if to say, *'No. Please don't blow me away.'* Then Bailey blasts him out of his socks. It doesn't make sense. If Sheboygan was prowling with a gun in his hand, why would he say, *'No'*? Hell, you'd think he'd've either fired his revolver at Bailey or dropped it and given up. He wouldn't have stood there red-handed and said, *'No.'* The whole thing doesn't make sense."

Carr lit a cigarette. He climbed off the bed and looked around for an ashtray. There was none. He tossed the match into a waste can and moved to the window next to Kelly. Outside in the parking lot, a beefy nurse hiked her uniform skirt and climbed on a motorcycle, gunned the motor and drove off. "What if Bailey knew Sheboygan?" he said. "What if they were in on something together? What if the burglary was a setup?"

"Then he *had* to shoot him. And he had to make damn sure he was dead. And if I was in the way that was just too fuggin' bad. He *had* to shoot."

Carr took a drag off the cigarette and blew smoke out

the window. "That's the way I read what happened. He did it because he had to. There was no other way out for him. That's why he gave Sheboygan a second blast when he was down. He had to make damn sure he was dead."

"Why? Why did he want to kill a burglar?"

Carr shrugged.

Neither man spoke as they stood looking out the window. Kelly, having tired, made his way back into bed, groaned and sighed in the effort. "I'm through, Charlie. I'm gonna retire. The doctor told me that the wound is serious enough that I could retire on a forty percent disability. I could get another job and I'd be making as much as I am right now. I made my decision when the wife brought my boys in to see me. Little Johnny said, 'Who shot you, daddy?' Right then and there I decided to retire. If I would have died, Rose would've had to sell the house to pay the bills. It's a hell of a thing to think about."

"You'll be bored in a week."

"I'm tired of cracking heads. I'm tired of explaining evidence to a bunch of pot-smoking hippies who masquerade as assistant United States attorneys. I'm tired of working on weekends and holidays. I'm tired of watching Judge Malcolm give three-time losers probation. I'm tired of having pencil-pushing dummies like No Waves tell me what to do . . . and I'm tired of eating hamburgers on the run. I'm not just saying this."

"Maybe you'll feel differently when you get well."

"Get well? The more I think about turning in my badge, the better I feel. Maybe I'll get a job as an insurance adjustor or a real estate salesman. I'll get paid for taking people to lunch, shooting the bull. Jobs like that provide a company car. Ever think of how much money you could save with a free car and gas? Or maybe

I'll take a job as a football coach. For years my brother has begged me to start up a football program at All Saints. With a disability check, I could afford to do it."

Carr continued to stare out the window. Beyond the parking lot and across the street, a group of Chicano teenagers dressed in the L.A. street gang uniform of long-sleeved shirts buttoned to the collar and high-wasted khaki trousers strutted about in front of a mom-and-pop store.

"He knew I was in the line of fire when he pulled the trigger," Kelly said.

"I think you're right."

A short time later Carr steered out of the parking lot past the mom-and-pop store, thinking again of what Kelly had told him. The car radio crackled with a message for him to meet Detective Higgins at the Sierra Madre ranger station. He pulled to the curb and looked up the address in a Southern California street guide that he found in the glove compartment. The freeway trip west and north into the San Gabriel Mountains took him forty-five minutes.

After parking his sedan in a small clearing near a helicopter pad surrounded by four-wheeled ranger vehicles and police cars, Carr headed to the front door of the ranger station, a diminutive building nestled at the side of a mountain road across from a precipice. The view encompassed most of the suburban San Gabriel Valley. Because the altitude was slightly below the smog layer, the view of the suburbs was as hazy as a midday poison-air view from a freeway overpass.

Inside the station Carr showed his badge to a uniformed ranger sitting in front of radio equipment. The ranger pointed Carr down a hallway to a squad room filled with men wearing green jump suits, sipping coffee. The walls were covered with terrain maps. Higgins sat at a desk across the room in front of a tape player. He motioned Carr over.

Without saying anything, Higgins reached into a manila envelope and pulled out a Polaroid photograph that he tossed across the table to Carr. Carr studied it for a moment. It was a photograph of the body of a woman dressed in slacks and a blouse. Though there was no blood, the left side of her face was caved in. Her clothing was covered with dirt and mud.

"Amanda Kennedy?" Carr asked.

"Doesn't look much like her, does it?"

"I thought she was in the Women's Jail."

"I just got off the phone with the jail watch commander," Higgins said. "She bailed out last night at nine P.M. The next thing that occurs happens about midnight. Some Girl Scouts are camped about a mile from here at the base of a cliff near a stream. The lady scoutmaster just left here . . ." Higgins turned on the tape player.

". . . so we had five pup tents and the one larger tent for the adults," a female voice said. "Since it was the last night in camp, we'd allowed the girls to stay up a little late. They were all acting out skits and just being silly. They all had a great time. Oh yes, and we roasted marshmallows. Can you imagine a Girl Scout camp without roasting marshmallows?"

"What happened after you went to bed?" Higgins said.

"We went to bed about eleven-thirty. There was the usual horseplay for a half hour or so. One of the girls had a squirt gun and they were fiddling around keeping each other awake. That's when it happened."

There was a silence on the tape. Finally, Higgins said, "I'd like you to repeat what you told the rangers. That's why I turned the tape on."

"Oh, sure," the woman said. "So we were lying there in our tents and there was this thud sound. My first thought was that the kids were playing one of their practical jokes. It's sort of a camp ritual that the kids play jokes on the scoutmasters. Last year they put a frog in the—"

"Did you leave your tent to investigate the cause of the *thud* sound?" Higgins interrupted.

"Oh, yes. The sound was so loud, we all rushed out of the tent. At first we didn't see anything. We looked around the campsite using our flashlights, but we didn't see a thing. While we were doing this, I walked behind our tent. I'll never forget what I saw. Never."

"What did you see?"

"A body . . . though at first I wasn't sure what it was. Then as I stood there I realized it was a body. The body of a woman. I screamed. I screamed so loud I woke up the whole camp. The kids rushed out of their tents to see. One of the girls fainted and another one got sick to her stomach. We thought about administering first aid to her, but one of the adults in our group is a nurse. She said there was no need . . . that the person was dead."

"Did you hear anything before you heard the thud?"

"No . . . nothing . . . we were just lying there in our tents waiting for the kids to pull their nightly practical jokes. The body must have been thrown off the cliff above us. Or maybe it was dropped out of an airplane. There is no other way for it to have ended up there. It's the most horrible thing I've ever seen. Once I saw a horrible car accident, but this was much worse."

* * *

Higgins turned off the tape player.

Carr lit a cigarette. "How did they identify the body?"

"She had a jail property receipt on her. The rangers called the Women's Jail and identified her. Then the jail phoned the burglary detective who'd booked her. He phoned me. I got here just before the coroner took the body away. There was very little bleeding. I think she was dead before she got the boost off the cliff. Don't be fooled by the fact that her head was caved in. It looked to me like it probably happened during the fall."

Carr shook his head. "Did the property receipt have a—"

"The time stamp shows that she bailed out last night at nine-fifteen." Higgins stood up and stretched.

Carr took a deep drag on his cigarette, flicked an ash. "What do you think?"

"I think she knew a secret."

"Me too." Carr picked up the telephone and dialed the Women's Jail. He learned that Amanda Kennedy's bond had been posted by a bail bondsman named Cecil DeMille. Carr wrote down the bondsman's address as the jail clerk read it off the bail release form. Higgins looked over his shoulder as he wrote.

"He's a receiver of stolen property," Higgins said after he'd hung up. "Burglars who want out on bail trade diamonds and furs for his signature on a bail bond. He never touches the swag himself . . . has it delivered to a hotel room and one of his stooges picks it up and fences it. He's been arrested a couple of times, but he hires good lawyers. They postpone the case until witnesses disappear or the case winds up with a friendly judge."

"Let's pay him a visit." The two men got up and left, quickly making the trip back down the San Gabriel Mountains.

Chapter 13

THE WEST Los Angeles neighborhood was a jumble of stucco apartment houses that needed painting, small commercial buildings and car lots. The streets were congested with both parked cars and moving traffic. Everyone was coming or going, heading to or from the nearby freeway. Down the street was an empty lot that Carr knew was once a movie studio.

Higgins parked the unmarked police sedan at the curb in front of a tiny office building with a large sign on the roof that resembled a movie marquee. It read:

Bail Bonds—24 hours
directed by
Cecil DeMille
A cast of thousands to
serve you 24 hours per day.

"We'll have to play it by ear," Higgins said as they got out of the car and approached the door of the building. Inside, a young blonde woman wearing a knit dress sat at a reception desk in front of an inner-office door, talking on the phone. "May I help you?" she asked, setting the receiver down.

Higgins flashed his badge. "Is Cecil DeMille in?"

"No," she said as she pressed a doorbell-style button attached to the side of her desk. "He's gone for the day. Is there anything I can do for you?"

Higgins glared at the woman while she sat fidgeting nervously. Suddenly he stepped past her to the inner office and opened the door.

"Just what may I ask are you doing?" she said angrily, standing up.

Carr followed Higgins into the inner office, where a fortyish, overweight man with a Fu Manchu moustache sat behind a desk. His elbony hair was full at the collar and he wore a golf shirt that accentuated his fatty pectoral muscles. Higgins showed the man his badge as the blonde woman rushed in behind them.

"I couldn't stop them," she said apologetically. "They just walked right in."

Without expression, Cecil DeMille folded his arms across his chest and stared at the two cops for a moment. "Close the door and leave us alone," he said. The secretary backed out of the office closing the door behind her.

"I just want to hear what is so important that you would walk right into someone's office," DeMille said. "After I hear it, I'll decide whether or not I throw both of you out the way you came in. And just so we get things straight right off the bat, I want you to know that I'm a law school graduate. I know I have the legal right to throw you fuckers out of here right now. You're not dealing with some dumb ex-con that's sweating getting his parole violated."

"We want to know who bailed out Amanda Kennedy," Higgins said.

"Who the hell is Amanda Kennedy?"

"Your name is on her bail release form," Higgins said. "She was released from the Women's Jail last night around nine."

"I bail out lots of people every night. The name doesn't ring a bell."

"She was murdered shortly after she was released," Higgins continued. "Does that ring a bell?"

"What happens to people after I get them out of jail is something I have no control over." He picked up a ballpoint pen and clicked it a few times.

The men looked at each other without speaking while Cecil DeMille continued to click his pen.

"We just received a tip from an informant that you were involved in the woman's murder," Higgins said. "We stopped by to see if you could clear the matter up for us."

DeMille set the pen on the desk. "Bullshit."

"I'll ask you again," Higgins said. "Who retained you to post bail for Amanda Kennedy?"

"Like I said, I post bail for a lot of people every night. I have no recollection of the name you asked me about."

"Would you mind checking you records?" Higgins said. "I'm sure you have records . . ."

"I'm tied up with some other things today. Why don't you check back with me sometime next week?" DeMille flashed a mock smile.

"Since you're a lawyer, I guess you're familiar with the term *probable cause?*" Higgins said, his tone becoming slightly impatient.

"Of course."

"Then you'll understand that since you were the last

person to see Amanda Kennedy alive, that I have probable cause to arrest you for her murder."

DeMille stood up and pointed to the door, his flabby chest jiggling. "Get out of my office," he said angrily. "No one threatens me in my office. I mean it. *Get the fuck out of here*."

Higgins reached under his coat and unfastened a pair of handcuffs from his belt. "You'll be going with us, fat boy. You're under arrest for murder. Put your hands on top of your head," he said, moving toward him.

"You people are gonna regret this. I'm gonna sue for false arrest." He backed away. "This is an illegal arrest. I have a right to resist."

Higgins stepped closer, wrapping the cuffs around his right fist like brass knuckles. Carr went over to the door and locked it. In a fighting stance, Higgins moved closer to DeMille. "Come on, clown, you still wanna resist?"

DeMille looked frantic as he backed up until he was against the wall. "I don't know who the guy was who bailed her out," he said. "It was the first time I'd ever seen him."

"What was his name?" Carr said.

"He was a friend of a friend." DeMille's eyes were wide and focused on Higgins, who dropped his guard but remained standing directly in front of DeMille, twirling the handcuffs. "I don't know his real name. I swear to God."

"What name *do* you know him by?" Carr said.

"Just a nickname." DeMille kept his eyes on Higgins.

"Bondsmen don't post bonds for people they don't know," Carr said.

Cecil DeMille's eyes darted briefly from Higgins to Carr. With a catlike motion, Higgins snatched DeMille's wrist and twisted. DeMille groaned as he went to his knees and a handcuff was snapped on the wrist. He yanked the bondsman's other arm behind him and snapped on the other handcuff.

"His name is Bones," DeMille said. "That's all I know. I met him at a crap game one night about a year ago."

Higgins grabbed DeMille's collar. He jerked him to his feet, then roughly pushed him down into his desk chair. "Where's the file?" Higgins said.

"Will you let me go if I tell you?"

"Maybe," Carr said.

DeMille nodded toward a gray metal filing cabinet. "Top drawer."

Carr went over to the cabinet, opened the drawer and dug out a manila file folder with the word *Bones* scribbled on its tab. Carr opened the folder. Inside was a pink copy of a bail bond information form with Amanda Kennedy's name, date of birth and jail booking number typed on preprinted lines. In the section marked *Collateral*, the word *Bones* had been printed. There was nothing else on the form. Carr closed the folder and tossed it back in the drawer.

"What did he tell you when he asked you to bail her out?" Carr said.

DeMille squirmed in the chair, glanced up at Higgins. "If you take off the cuffs I'll tell you the story," he said in a defeated tone.

Carr and Higgins looked at each other. Higgins dug around in his pocket for a moment, then pulled out a small key ring. He motioned to DeMille, who stood up and turned around. Higgins removed the cuffs.

"Bones calls me up and asks me to bail this broad out of jail," he said softly while rubbing his wrists. "He says he's doing it as a favor to a friend. I said okay because I owed him a favor." He sat down in his chair.

"Why did you owe him the favor?" Carr said.

"Because I owed him some money. He sold me a set of silver and I still owed him some money for it."

"Where's the set of silver?" Carr said.

DeMille threw his hands up in exasperation, then dropped them back into his lap. "What does that have to do with the broad who got murdered?"

As if he were bored, Carr pushed back a sleeve and glanced at his wristwatch. Higgins spun the handcuffs on his index finger.

"The stuff's in the trunk of my car. It's been there for months. Bones told me the silver belonged to his aunt, who wanted to sell it and—"

"Let's see it," Carr interrupted.

"You want to *see* it?" DeMille stood up and headed out the door. Carr and Higgins followed him past the reception area and out the front door, where he turned right and followed the sidewalk to a small parking lot adjoining the building. Parked in the lot was a pink Cadillac with black leather upholstery. *DeMille Bail Bonds* was painted in black on the driver's door in large italic script letters. DeMille reached into his pocket, pulled out a key and unlocked the trunk. He pointed to one of five or six cardboard boxes. Carr reached into the box, pulled out a sterling silver dinner plate and examined it. An engraved *W* was on the bottom of the plate.

"If it's hot, it's a complete surprise to me," DeMille said. "He told me it belonged to his—"

"When you bailed her out, was anyone else there?" Carr interrupted.

"Huh?"

"At the jail to pick her up?"

"No. In fact, I didn't even wait for her to come out of the lockup. I just posted the bond with the jail clerk and went about my business. I was busy as hell that day. I just posted the bond and went on my way. Even when bail is posted, it takes an hour or so for the jail to process a prisoner out of the system. I never wait once I post a bond."

Carr massaged the edge of the plate. "So you bailed her out strictly as a favor and you weren't around when they let her out of jail. Is that what you're telling us?"

Cecil DeMille tugged his ear for a moment. "Okay, Bones was with me when I bailed her out," he said sheepishly. "He was still waiting there for her to come out when I left."

"Do you have Bones's address?" Carr said.

"No. If he wants to get in touch, he calls me."

Higgins gestured toward the office. DeMille reached out to take the plate, but Carr shook his head. "You're going to keep it?" he said. Carr nodded.

Back in DeMille's office Carr picked up a card index off DeMille's desk. He looked up a telephone number and address for Bones, took out a note pad and copied the information. He shoved the note pad back in his coat pocket.

"I guess I forgot that I had his number," DeMille said nervously.

The two men turned to leave.

"What about the plate?"

Carr tucked it under his arm. "What about it?"

"If it turns up stolen, you can have it. He told me it came from his aunt. He said she—"

"Thanks," Carr said as he opened the door. Higgins followed him out of the office.

* * *

That night at Ling's, Carr and Higgins hashed over the case as they sat at the bar.

"DeMille didn't tell us everything," Higgins said. He threw back a shot glass of whiskey and grimaced. Roughly, he wiped his mouth with a bar napkin.

"I agree."

"So maybe we should pay him another visit."

Ling filled Higgins's shot glass and dropped fresh ice in Carr's scotch and water.

"For all we know, he might have killed her," Higgins said, "or at least helped Bones do the job. For that matter, maybe he knows Bailey . . . hell, it could be any number of things." He turned his bar stool to face Carr. "I say we bag his ass for murder and let him sit in the county jail for a couple of days. It'll loosen him up . . . and if it doesn't, we haven't lost anything."

"I want to trace the silver plate first. I've got a hunch."

"So you find out it's stolen? That and ten cents will buy you a cup of coffee."

"Maybe I can tie it to an M.O."

Higgins downed another shot, wiped his mouth again. "Then again, maybe you can't. And you'll have wasted your time when we could have been getting somewhere on this investigation. I say we stop the cat-and-mouse bullshit and turn on the pressure."

"I think we need to surveil Bones for a few days."

"Great idea," Higgins said sarcastically. "But who the hell are we gonna get to do it? He knows you, and I can't do it alone. It takes at least six cars for a decent surveillance. Where are we gonna come up with five bodies? If I ask my lieutenant for manpower I'll have to fill him in on the caper. If I do that, he'll call the captain and so on up the line. The whole damn department daisy chain will know about it. And if just one officer along the way says no I'll be out of business . . . the cat will be out of the bag and the brass will be in an uproar because they weren't notified from day one. I'll be up shit creek and we'll still be short five bodies."

Carr twirled his drink on the bar. "If I tell No Waves, he'll notify the Chief of Police in Beverly Hills because the Treasury Manual of Operations requires notification to other agencies in an internal investigation. The Chief would probably notify Bailey's pal Cleaver, and the cat would still be out of the bag."

"We could make up another reason why we want to follow Bones. We could say it's because he's associated with Tony Dio or something."

Carr shook his head. "It'll never work. The men on surveillance would figure out we were pulling a fast one."

Higgins nodded in agreement. "Then how do we do it?"

Carr lit a cigarette. "We play *Who Do You Trust*." He unfolded a bar napkin and pulled out a pen.

"Ernie Kun would help," Higgins said. "He once told me he hated Bailey . . . some deal about Bailey shaking down one of his informants a couple of years ago."

Carr wrote Kun's name on the napkin. "B. B. Martin and Bob Tomsic from the Field Office will help. They can take heat . . . and Larry Sheafe."

"Ed Henderson owes me a favor," Higgins said. "Put his name down."

Having compiled a list of names, Carr handed Ling a dollar bill and asked for a dollar's worth of dimes. Ling scooped dimes from the cash register and dropped them in Carr's hand.

For the next half hour, Carr and Higgins alternated placing phone calls from the pay booth just outside the front door. Within an hour Carr had placed a check mark beside all five names.

"If this thing comes apart we'll all burn and the guys we've brought in will have us to blame," Higgins said.

"Think positive," Carr said, turning to him. Neither he nor Higgins smiled.

As he wound carefully in and out of the westbound Santa Monica Freeway traffic, Carr half listened to a radio talk show host interview the tenor-voiced governor of California. "It's like the song goes," the governor said, ". . . *'The Times They Are A-Changin'* . . . and the title of that song has a lot of meaning for Californians . . ."

Carr turned it off and thought of Sally for a while. Because he was sleepy, he had both front windows rolled down. The smog was gone for the day, allowing him to breathe deeply a few times. Because he was close to Santa Monica, there was a hint of salt air. Carr turned off the next exit and pulled into the first service station with a telephone booth. He dialed Sally's number and listened as the phone rang about ten times. He hung up. After filling the sedan's gas tank with regular and buying a newspaper from a vending machine, he steered back onto the freeway.

A few minutes later he was in his apartment. He took off his suit coat and tossed it on the sofa, kicked off his shoes and plopped down with the newspaper. He read the front page and the editorial pages (they were all he ever read), stood up and went to the sink. He tossed the newspaper in a trash can. Because the sink was brimming with dirty dishes he opened the cupboard and searched for dishwashing detergent. He remembered he was out. "Damn," he said out loud.

The doorbell rang.

It was Sally, dressed in a blue jogging outfit with a matching sweatband. Her hair was soaked with perspiration and she was out of breath. She pecked his cheek with a kiss as she brushed past him.

"I called you a while ago," he said.

"Sure you did," she replied sarcastically. She stared at the messy kitchen. "And I'm sure you were just getting ready to wash those dirty dishes." She sat down on the sofa and leaned back. Her eyes closed.

"Why are you out jogging at eleven P.M.?" he said.

"Because I need the exercise." She didn't open her eyes.

"You're taking a chance at this time of night."

"I can't live my life worrying about such things," she said, this time looking at him. "I was going to ask why you haven't called me. But if I did, you would tell me you've been busy. Then I would get angry. So I won't ask."

"Would you like a drink?"

She shook her head. "Are you aware you're still wearing your gun?"

Carr looked at his side. Hastily he unclipped the inside-the-belt holster and went into the bedroom, opened a dresser drawer and shoved the gun in it. He closed the drawer and returned to the living room. Sally stood in the middle of the room with her hands clasped together behind her neck, doing torso-twisting exercises. He pulled her into his arms and kissed her. When she didn't respond he moved away, letting his hands rest lightly on her shoulders.

"Our relationship has been a sexual one right from the beginning," she said. "We get along in bed. I sometimes wonder if there is anything . . . I mean *anything* beyond sex between you and me. Even when you tell me you love me I'm not sure that you really mean it."

"I mean it," he said softly.

She pushed his arms away. "I have to do my hair and nails tonight. I've got to go. It's late and I have an early-morning deposition. She jogged to the door and opened it. Having blown him a kiss, she jogged down the steps and into the darkness.

Carr shut the door and locked it. He thought of his first date with Sally. They had gone to a jazz club in Studio City . . . was it nine or ten years ago?"

After a search, he found a container of liquid hand soap under the sink in the bathroom. Using it as a substitute for dishwashing detergent, he washed and dried the pile of dishes and glasses in the sink, then put them away.

The telephone rang. It was Sally.

"You're having second thoughts about marrying me, aren't you?" she said.

He didn't answer.

"I know you are," she said, her voice cracking. "I can tell."

The phone clicked.

Chapter 14

AFTER A wrong turn or two in the hilly residential area of Beverly Hills, Carr noticed a curbside sign that spelled out Beverly Hills Revolver Club in delicate type. He turned right and followed a driveway that led up a slight elevation to the club's parking lot. In the corner of the lot was a small building with a canopied entrance. He parked his sedan and got out. The view from the lot was of the Santa Monica Freeway, which guarded the southern perimeter of Beverly Hills like a moat.

On the other side of the freeway was a bank of gray apartment houses that Carr recognized as one of the many L.A. neighborhoods populated by Mexicans who had fled their cardboard houses in Tijuana for the high life of loud mufflers and garment district piecework. All things considered, Carr thought to himself, even cramped quarters in a run-down apartment house with a greenish-tinted swimming pool was better than cardboard city.

He entered a lobby and showed his badge to a red-haired receptionist with a bouffant hairdo. She wore a tan safari blouse. He told her what he wanted.

"Artie can probably help you," she said as if she were interested. "He's on the range right now." She pointed to a glass door. "You can wait for him inside if you like."

Carr thanked her and went over to the glass door. She pressed a button. The lock clicked and Carr went inside, making his way down a hallway to a glass-enclosed viewing area behind an indoor firing range with four firing positions.

Three middle-aged women stood at positions on the firing line holding loaded revolvers. They each wore ear protectors and jogging outfits. Artie, the rangemaster, a flyweight-sized man with a safari jacket similar to the receptionist's, checked the ladies' weapons and stepped back. Using a microphone, he gave firing instructions. Target lights came on and the targets (man-sized gorillas pointing guns) faced front. The women fired, turning the targets sideways. Without conversation, the women reloaded. At the end of the firing set, Artie retrieved the women's targets and gave shooting advice. The women chattered and giggled with one another on the way out.

Carr left the booth and strolled onto the firing line. He showed Artie his badge.

"I could tell you were a cop," Artie said, offering a jockey-sized hand. They shook hands, and Artie made a salesman's grin.

"I recovered a thirty-two revolver during the course of an investigation," Carr said. "It's registered to you."

"No lie? Where'd you find it?"

"It was used during the commission of a burglary."

"I have nine or ten thirty-twos registered to me . . . or to the Revolver Club I should say. We used them on the firing line. They're small. The ladies love 'em. Purse size. Personally, I like automatics. I fired a new style Beretta last week that was a dream." He made his hand into a gun. "Bap bap bap bap. People in this town are scared shitless. Muggings, burglaries. The scum bags from Watts drive through like marauders ripping off whatever or whomever they see. They thrive on weakness. Everybody thought I was crazy to open a gun club in Beverly Hills. They said the rich folks would never go for it. Well, I've made enough money in the last year to open another one in San Marino. Wealthy people believe in self-preservation. Have no doubt. Did ya see the women who just walked out of here?"

Carr nodded.

"Anyone who tries to rob one of them is a goner. They're not great shots, but they know how to pull the trigger. Fuck with any of those grandmas, and they'll scatter your brains." He laughed.

"How did you lose the thirty-two?" Carr asked.

Artie shrugged, bent down and picked up a few expended shells off the floor. "Don't really know."

"When did you first notice that the gun was missing?"

"Hard to say," Artie said as he reached for a light switch, turning off the target lights. Carr followed him out of the range area and down the hallway to an office. The wood-paneled walls were covered with shooting certificates. Trophies decorated the top of a desk. Artie motioned Carr to a chair as he sat down behind the desk in a swivel chair that made him look even shorter than he was. "Ever had to shoot anybody?" he said.

"Yes. How do you keep track of the guns you have here?"

"What's this all about?"

"A burglar ended up with one of your guns," Carr said impatiently. "I'm here to find out how he got it."

Artie stood up, closed the door and returned to the desk.

"What if I was to tell you I didn't know what happened to it?"

Carr said nothing, waiting for him to continue.

"I had it in my car one night," he said. "I was barhopping . . . I must have hit every place on the West Side of town. I got arrested for drunk driving about two in the morning. I bailed out that night. It wasn't until two or three days later that I realized the gun was missing. Yes, I know it's illegal to carry a loaded gun around in one's car. My answer to that is that I'd rather be safe than sorry. I'd rather be tried by twelve than carried by six. I'm ready to kill to protect myself and I don't care who knows it."

"Where? . . ."

Artie raised his hands and shook his head at the same time. "I have no idea where I lost it. It could have been stolen from my car at any one of eight or ten bars we hit that night. I had it in the glove compartment."

"Where were you arrested?"

"Right here in the city. On La Cienega. I was driving south on La Cienega. I'm pretty sure it was south. I was bombed, man. Three sheets to the wind. Soused. My girl friend was with me. She said I drank twenty grasshoppers during the course of the evening. If you so much as showed me a bottle of crème de menthe right now, I'd throw up right on this desk. Since it happened I drink only vodka on the rocks. You wanna know why? It's because I hate vodka. I drink less. For me it's the answer."

"What happened to your car after you were arrested?" Carr said.

"The police impounded it I guess. My girl friend

picked it up for me the next day. The hangover was so bad I couldn't get out of—"

"Do you have a copy of the impound receipt?"

Artie pulled open the center drawer of the desk and rummaged through a mound of papers. "My lady friend stops by now and then to help me with the paperwork around here. Great gal. Just divorced from Trent Beckwith, the producer. She bought me a Rolex for my birthday . . . here it is." He pulled a blue receipt from the drawer and handed it to Carr. It was a receipt from a police contract tow service.

"May I keep this?"

"Sure," Artie said.

Charles Carr stood up to leave.

"You should stop by sometimes when you have time to fire. I like to have cops around."

"Thanks," Carr said, moving to the door.

"The women around here all have lots of bucks. Lots of bucks and lots of time on their hands."

Carr opened the door, paused briefly. "Why didn't you report the gun missing?"

"I was embarrassed to tell the police I couldn't remember where I'd been that night."

"Thanks again," Carr said. He walked out the door.

It was Saturday morning.

Three weeks had passed since Jack Kelly had been shot. With the single exception of Carr's trip to Las Vegas with Sally, he hadn't taken a day off. As he parked at the curb in front of the auto impound yard, Carr realized that for the last few days he'd been waking up tired and staying that way all day . . . and he'd been drinking more than usual. He rubbed his eyes and got out of the sedan.

He walked past an open chain link gate into a lot filled with cars. A doorless shack that served as an office was next to the gate. Most of them were luxury cars; a few were smashed up, including a purple Maserati that looked like it had been crushed with a steamroller. All the vehicles bore grease-penciled numbers on the windshields.

Carr showed his badge to a puffy-eyed heavy woman whose feet rested on a grease-covered table in the shack. She wore a dingy mechanic's shirt and trousers and a smudged baseball hat that covered her closely cropped gray hair. She was reading race results.

"What can I do ya for?" she said in a nasal voice that reminded Carr of male comedians who imitated women.

Carr handed her an impound receipt. "I'm tracing a gun," he said. "The man whom the gun is registered to told me that he was arrested for drunk driving a couple of months ago, about a mile from here. The Beverly Hills Police booked him and impounded his car. He says the gun was missing from the trunk of his car when he checked it out of this lot."

"Did he make out a theft report?" she asked.

"He didn't report the gun missing because he didn't notice it was gone until a week or so after he'd bailed out and picked up his car. He figured making a theft report wouldn't help him get the gun back."

"People say things like that all the time," the woman said. As she spoke Car noticed snuff between her lower lip and gum. She examined the impound receipt.

"May I see your copy of the impound receipt?" Carr said.

"It'll be the same as this copy except for the arresting officer's signature." The woman slung her feet off the table and got up, moving over to a cardboard box in the corner of the shack. Squatting down, she flipped through folders full of receipts. A short time later she stood up holding a blue copy of an impound receipt, handed it to Carr and returned to her chair.

Carr held the paper to the light of the grease-covered window. The signature line on the bottom of the printed form read:

D. Piper
Serial ™7 1439
Beverly Hills P.D.

Carr handed the receipt back to the woman. "Thanks," he said.

"Sure." The woman turned a page of the newspaper. "Everyone in this town claims to have valuables stolen from their car. Usually it's cameras . . . five- and six-hundred-dollar cameras." She looked up. "Can you imagine people that can afford to drive thirty- and forty-thousand-dollar cars chiseling an insurance company for five hundred bucks?"

"Yes."

The woman shook her head, turned another page.

Carr returned to his sedan and wrote the name D. Piper in his notebook. He put a question mark after the name and drove off.

It took him less than half an hour to drive to Jack Kelly's tract-style home in Orange County. As usual, he made a wrong turn or two on identical cul-de-sacs before he found it . . . even the curbside mailboxes in front of the newly built stucco row houses were the same. He parked and, because it was still early, headed straight for the garage, hoisting its heavy door. The lawn mower was in the corner where he'd left it a week earlier. He rolled it along the driveway and onto the lawn, first mowing a strip of grass along the sidewalk.

Rose Kelly waved at him from the front window, then hurried out the front door. She wore a blue housecoat. "There's no need to do that," she said. "Jack's coming home from the hospital today. He gave me strict orders not to let you mow the lawn. He said he was perfectly well enough to do it himself. You know how he is."

Carr nodded and mowed another strip of turf.

"Breakfast will be ready when you're done," she said before returning to the house.

"No thanks, Rose," Carr called after her, though he was starving. "I'm in a hurry."

About an hour later Carr washed his hands at the kitchen sink before he sat down at the kitchen table in front of a platter of four eggs and what must have been half a pound of bacon. "I won't be able to eat all this."

"I'm so used to cooking for Jack . . ." she said as she washed out a frying pan. "I'm so excited about Jack coming home . . . and the boys . . . I'm glad they had a soccer game this morning. They'd be tearing the house apart in anticipation."

Carr smiled. He made it through half of the eggs and a sizable portion of the bacon.

Rose Kelly bustled around the kitchen, turning things on and off on the stove. She washed out another pan at the sink. "Jack told me that he's going to retire," she said. "Did he tell you?"

"He mentioned something about it."

Rose Kelly refilled his coffee cup. She returned the coffee pot to the stove and stood facing it. "He's doing it for us."

"What do you think of the idea?"

She turned towards him. "I think it's a great idea

. . . if it's what Jack really wants. I'd love to have him home at a decent hour every night. But I know Jack. He's not suited very well for other kinds of work. He's too . . . I don't know what the word is . . . aggressive. He won't be happy doing anything else. I know that."

Carr sipped coffee. "Will you tell him that?"

"God spared Jack's life. The doctor said that he was lucky to have survived. I don't think the Lord saved him to spend the rest of his life just taking it easy. I don't think that." She stirred something on the stove for a while. "But on the other hand, I'm not going to encourage him to stay in law enforcement if he doesn't want to."

"I think he wants to stay."

Rose came to the table with the coffee pot again. "I'll stand by Jack no matter what he wants to do." She tried to fill Carr's cup, but he held his hand over it. "I'm so glad he's coming home," she said, returning the pot to the stove.

"Gotta run." Carr carried his plate and coffee cup to the sink. "Thanks a million for the breakfast."

"I just want to have my husband." Her voice was almost pleading, but not with Carr. "And my boys need their father. I don't care about anything else. Perhaps that's selfish of me, but I just don't care about crime and crooks and the things I hear you and Jack talk about when you play cards. It all ends up for naught. My husband has been in the hospital for three weeks and nothing has changed. The crooks are still there. The lawyers are still getting rich. I'm still alone nights and weekends." She paused, looking down at her hands. "I guess I shouldn't be so negative."

"Tell Jack I'll be giving him a call," Carr said with a nod. He opened the door and went out.

Rose Kelly followed him to the door and thanked him profusely for mowing the lawn, then waved as he trotted down the driveway.

Though the Chez Doucette was the latest West Side "in" spot, there were few customers as Travis Bailey and Delsey Piper sat having lunch.

The walls of the French restaurant were floor-to-ceiling murals of people (both men and women diners had similar faces) sitting at tables in a French restaurant. As Bailey listened to Delsey drone on about her *Playboy* photo deal, he wondered why Bones Chagra had left a message for him at the office. He glanced at his watch again.

"The layout is called *Officers of the Raw,*" Delsey said. "The photographer wants to do a shot of me standing in front of a police car with nothing on but my Sam Browne and my hat. The other one is with my tits hanging out of the driver's window as I point my gun at the camera. The photographer is a real pro. He has every shot planned out. The photos will have a caption about me being the daughter of Rex Piper the movie star. The whole thing sounds great . . . really *super*. And if the Department tries to fire me, just think of the free publicity I'll get! I talked to daddy about it and he thinks it's a fantastic idea. Like he says, to break into show business, *ya gotta use what ya has*. One of the kids I went to high school with got a movie contract by starring in a fag porno flick. He was dressed up like a sailor. Now he plays the part of the guy who lives next door in "The Riley Family." His name used to be Barry Chernowitz but he changed it to Barry McDonald. The casting director for the program was named McDonald and he thought that he would get more attention if he—"

"Gotta make a phone call," Bailey said abruptly. He left the table, found a pay telephone in the rest room and dialed Bones Chagra's home number. Bones answered. "Been trying to call all day," Bailey said. "What's up?"

"L.A.P.D. leaned on DeMille real heavy like. He—"

"I don't want to talk on the phone," Bailey said. "Meet me at Chez Doucette."

"I'm on my way to work."

"So be late for fucking work." He hung up the phone and returned to the table. A hairsprayed young waiter with a New York accent was serving Chateaubriand. He opened a bottle of wine and poured, then rushed off.

Bailey sipped the wine as he sat staring at his plate.

"You've been so preoccupied for the last few days," Delsey said.

"Is your father in town?" he said, ignoring her remark.

"He gets back today from the desert. He had a part in a remake of *Beau Geste*. They're doing it as sort of a black comedy . . . a low-budget thing, but he says it's very creative. They filmed on the sand dunes on the way to Las Vegas. He's costarring with the guy who's the host of that game show where the little birds pop out of the box with the answers. I can never remember his name." She broke a French roll in half and pulled a piece from its soft center. She popped it into her mouth and chewed daintily.

"I want you to go see your father," Bailey said. "Have him phone the mayor and tell him about the opening for a commander in Traffic Services Division. Mention Cleaver's name."

"Why should you care about doing a favor for that do-nothing, Cleaver."

"Think about it for a minute."

"Oh," she said. "I see what you're getting at. You'd be in line for Cleaver's job. You'd be in charge of the Detective Bureau."

"And you'd be my number-one detective. I'd be able to soft-soap any heat that would come down when your photos come out in the magazine."

"The rest of the detectives are going to really hate me."

"So what else is new?"

"I really hate all of the macho bullshit that goes along with police work. It's a real *turnoff* . . . a superturn-off." She slipped an oversized chunk of beef into her mouth, chewed and washed it down with a swig of Beaujolais.

As they finished eating, Bailey saw Bones Chagra at the entrance of the restaurant. Without saying anything he left the table and joined him. At Bailey's suggestion, they went outside.

"Who was it?" Bailey said.

"Higgins from L.A.P.D. homicide and a Fed named Carr."

"What did they ask him about?"

"They squeezed him for who hired him to post the bond," Chagra said. "He said they weren't just fishing around. It was like they knew something."

"Where did they book him?"

"They didn't book him. They talked to him at his office."

"What did he say he told them?"

"He said he didn't tell 'em shit."

"He told them something or he would have been booked." Suspiciously, he surveyed the busy street.

"DeMille's got too much to lose by hanging me up. He does a grand a week with us."

"I don't like the way you handled this. You should have used someone else to go to the bondsman. You would have kept yourself one-removed."

"You're the cop," Bones said. "You're the Sherlock Holmes. If that's what you wanted me to do you should have said so."

Bailey looked Chagra in the eye. "From now on you and I don't meet," he said. "Don't call me unless you call from a pay phone. I'll do the same."

"So they find out I had the broad bailed out. It's not against the law to bail someone out."

Bailey grabbed Chagra's collar with both hands. *"You think too much,"* he hissed. *"Like your pal Lee."*

Bailey slammed Chagra backward into the synthetic-brick wall of the restaurant. As Chagra rubbed the back of his head, Bailey turned and stared at the traffic on La Cienega. A sedan driven by a black man wearing a snap-brim hat drove slowly by. Bailey stared at the car. It continued north toward Sunset Boulevard and turned right

"I'm sorry, Travis. I wasn't trying to be wise. I really wasn't."

"Call me tomorrow," Bailey said as he started toward Sunset.

Chagra hurried away.

Bailey returned to the table and sat down. "We're leaving," he said as Delsey took a bite.

"Right now?"

Bailey motioned for the waiter, paid the bill in cash and then slipped him a twenty-dollar bill.

"Oh, thank you, Mr. Bailey," the waiter said. "You're very kind."

"Is there a back way out of here?"

"Is everything all right?"

"My friend is involved in a divorce," he explained. "A private eye is following her."

The waiter led them through the kitchen and out the back door. Bailey surveyed the parking lot. Seeing nothing suspicious, he walked to his car with Delsey tagging behind. They quickly got in, and Bailey drove out over a low curb onto a side street rather than use the normal exit. He made three U-turns to see if he was being followed, then headed west on Sunset Boulevard toward his apartment.

"Would you please tell me what's going on?" Delsey asked for the third time.

"The Tony Dio mob might be following me," he said. "Bones just told me he heard a rumble. They want to get back at me because I killed Sheboygan."

Delsey looked puzzled. "That doesn't make sense."

"Nothing makes any sense in police work."

"What are you going to do?" She poked him gently. "Really," she said when he didn't answer, "what are you going to do?"

"Let them make their move," he said without taking his eyes off the road. "I'm going to let them make the next move."

The Sheriff's Department Records Bureau had the musty smell of a library. As if on a track, female clerks and Sheriff's cadets moved about between tall shelves containing manila files. There was the muffled sound of rock music coming from a radio on a windowsill.

Carr watched the computer screen as Della Trane

tapped keys. She had greeted him with friendly talk and made no mention of their last date. Her hair was pulled back into a handsome chignon and her khaki uniform was starched and neatly pressed. She wore an even layer of makeup and her lipstick was generously and meticulously applied. Carr thought she looked more attractive than he'd seen her in years.

"One more time," she said without taking her eyes off the computer screen. "You want all burglary reports with silver listed as stolen property for the last ninety days?" She turned and gave him a quizzical glance.

"With victims whose addresses are listed in Beverly Hills," Carr said.

She tapped the keys for a moment. BevH printed out on the screen in green electronic letters.

"Anything else?"

Carr shook his head.

Della Trane punched a key. The teleprinter raced. She stood up and stretched, arching her back. Her profile was striking. Carr offered her a cigarette, which she accepted. He gave her a light and lit one himself.

"I hope things worked out with your friend," she said.

Before he could answer, she turned to the teleprinter and adjusted the paper and handed it to him. "The funny part is, that wasn't the first . . . not even the *second* time that has happened to me. And I don't even go out that much. That's the funny part. I don't have that many dates. It's like if a piece of plaster was to fall from the ceiling at any given moment in time, it would probably fall directly on my head." They both chuckled.

Carr examined the computer printout. There were at least twenty-five names and addresses on the list. He folded it and stuffed it in his coat pocket.

"I have forty-five minutes for lunch," Della said, glancing at her wristwatch.

"Olvera Street okay?"

Nodding in agreement, she slipped her arm in his as they strolled out of the building and down Spring Street to a Mexican restaurant sandwiched between some Olvera Street tourist gift shops. A young waiter wearing a serape showed them to a table on the patio.

During a quick lunch of tacos and chile rellenos, Della drank three margaritas.

Afterward, Carr walked her back to the Hall of Justice and headed to the Field Office. To avoid No Waves, he entered through the back door.

At his desk, he circled six names on the list that started with *W*, dug a telephone book out of a filing cabinet and thumbed through for the names. As he expected, the names, like the names of most affluent people, were not listed. Having lit a cigarette, he dialed the number of the Pacific Telephone Company Security Office. The woman who answered asked for his agency code number. He read a seven-digit number that was scribbled on his desk's ink blotter.

"Lemme have the name," the woman said as if she were half asleep.

"I have six of them," Carr said.

"I can only take two names at a time. Rules."

Since he knew there was no use arguing, he gave her two of the names. She flipped pages and read off two phone numbers. The phone clicked. After two more calls (she made him repeat his agency code number each time), he had compiled a list of six unlisted phone numbers.

He dialed one of the numbers. A man answered.

"Is this Mr. Waterford?" Carr said.

"Speaking."

"I'm Special Agent Carr, U.S. Treasury Department. I'm calling about the burglary."

"Which one?"

"The one that occurred within the last three months."

"Treasury Department?" Waterford said. "Does this have something to do with my income tax?"

"No, sir. I just need to know if your silver that was stolen in the burglary had a *W* engraved on each plate."

"No," the man said. "There was nothing engraved on it. What's this all about?"

"Just a routine crime survey."

"Another way to waste the taxpayer's money."

"Thank you for your time—"

The phone clicked, Carr set the receiver down. He drew a line through Waterford's name and address, then dialed the next number on the list.

Chapter 15

CARR SAT on a sofa. He wanted to smoke but he couldn't decide whether the crystal upturned hand on the coffee table in front of him was an ashtray. Gertrude Wallace sat across from him in a thronelike chair. She examined the silver plate.

"Yes," she said. "It's ours. It's *definitely* ours. Our jeweler engraved them. I must call my husband and tell him . . . Where are the other pieces? Will we get them back?"

"Yes," Carr said, "but it may take some time."

"I hope it's by the end of the month. We have an important dinner planned. My husband and I have invited the Danish and the Swedish consuls and a whole group of studio people. You see, my husband's last movie was filmed on location in Denmark and Sweden—"

"Do you suspect anyone of having committed the burglary?" He gave the glass hand another inquisitive glance.

"It's an ashtray if you'd like to smoke."

"Thanks." Carr lit a cigarette and dropped the match in his hand.

"I used to smoke but I quit. I've never felt better in my whole life."

Carr acknowledged her remark with a smile.

"We thought the maid had stolen our things," she went on, "and Detective Bailey pointed out to us that domestics are often involved in burglaries. We fired her the day after it happened. She made a big fuss."

"Was there anything she did that caused you to suspect her?"

"She was in need of money to get her mother across the border. She'd been working next door at the Redfords on her days off in order to save money. I guess the temptation finally became too much for her."

Carr puffed. He turned his head away from Gertrude Wallace and blew out smoke.

"It's funny," she said. "I smoked for many years, but I can sit here and watch you smoke and I haven't the slightest urge. Not the slightest."

"Thinking back to a month or so before the burglary occurred . . . other than close friends and relatives, who visited your home?"

Gertrude Wallace touched the palm of her hand to her cheek. She sat that way for a moment. "Come to think of it," she said finally, "I had just hired a new man to clean the pool. But I'd used him before, off and on, and never had any problems . . . and there was a group of ladies from the Cancer Foundation. I showed them all through the house. Certainly it couldn't have been them."

"I agree," Carr said. "Was there anyone else?"

"Just my therapist. He's the one who cured me of my smoking. He's a psychiatrist."

"How long have you known him?"

"Just for a few weeks, but he was recommended to me by a close friend. He's very well thought of . . . the highest recommendations. He's highly respected in his field."

"I see. Had you ever met Detective Bailey before the burglary?"

She shook her head. "We've never been burglarized before."

Carr stood up. He took a final puff and carefully mashed the cigarette into the delicate ashtray. Having slipped a business card out of his shirt pocket, he handed it to her. "If you remember anything else," he said, "I'd appreciate a call."

"Certainly." She rose and followed him to the door.

"You're at the right age to quit smoking," she told Carr as he opened the door. "Mature people have more self-discipline. Dr. Kreuzer told me some of his best patients were—"

"What did you say his name is?" Carr interrupted. He felt his heart race.

"Kreuzer," she said. "Dr. Emil Kreuzer. He's a hypnotherapist. He's been a savior to me . . . a real savior. I used to smoke until I had a sore throat."

"How could I get in touch with him?" Carr tried to avoid sounding too eager. Could Emil Kreuzer have been released from prison already?

"Just a moment." Gertrude Wallace returned to the living room.

As Carr stood in the hallway he remembered being told by a veteran T-man more than twenty years ago to never be surprised when investigation after investigation ended up focusing on the same crooks. As the old trooper told him, "*There are only so many bad guys in* town. So when a case gets tough, check your old arrest cards."

Gertrude Wallace quickly returned and handed Carr a business card with Kreuzer's name and a Wilshire Boulevard office address. Carr slipped it in his shirt pocket.

"I must warn you though," she said pleasantly, "he's always booked up weeks in advance, but he's worth the wait."

Carr stepped off the elevator in the office building. He wandered down a hallway to a pair of high polished wooden doors bearing brass letters that read Probe Incorporated—Doctor E. Kreuzer.

Carr opened the door and stepped into a reception area furnished with leather sofas. A young girl who looked to be high school age sat at the reception desk. She hurriedly shoved the paperback book (nurse hugging handsome man on the cover) she was reading into a desk drawer.

"Do you have an appointment?" she asked, as she'd obviously been trained to do.

Carr shook his head and showed her his badge. She looked up at him in awe. "Wow."

"I'd like to see Doctor Kreuzer for a moment," Carr said.

"Is that like the FBI?"

Carr nodded. The girl hurried into another room. On a wall behind one of the sofas Carr noticed a framed photograph of Emil Kreuzer shaking hands with the president of the United States. He could tell by the slight blurring of the hands that the photo was a composite fake.

Moments later Emil Kreuzer followed the girl out of the room. He approached Carr.

"Remember me?" Carr said with a disarming smile.

Kreuzer smiled back. "Of course."

As they shook hands, Carr noticed a flicker in the con man's carotid artery. His palm was sweaty.

Kreuzer ushered him into another office and closed the door. There was a large desk and a black leather Danish-modern sofa and a matching pillow. The walls were decorated with hypnotist's spirals and framed diplomas. Kreuzer offered him a chair.

"How's business?" Carr said, sitting down in front of a large desk.

"Emotion still rules reason," Kreuzer said. He laughed nervously.

"Seen any of your old friends since you've been out?"

"As a matter of fact I haven't. And I'm not just saying that. I've broken all the old ties. I guess it's because of my age. Doing a deuce or a trey in the joint didn't seem like much of a jolt when I was thirty, but it seems like one *hell* of a lot at this stage of life. Believe it or not, I've cleaned up my act."

"I could tell by that photograph of you and the president in the other room."

"Just because the picture is a phony doesn't mean that I am. I use that as a psychological tool to gain my clients' trust for the purpose of hypnosis. The photo, being in their subconscious, helps them to relax and go into a trance. The photograph violates no law. If I'm asked about it, I always tell the truth." He drummed his fingers on the desk.

"Mrs. Wallace told me that you cured her of her smoking habit."

"Wallace?"

"She lives on Coventry Circle in Beverly Hills." Carr stood up and walked to the window. On the street below he observed the crowds of people, many who seemed to be alone, as they roamed about and window-shopped in the exclusive business district. Few carried packages.

"Of course," Kreuzer said. "Mrs. Wallace. Her husband is the director."

"Her home was burglarized." Carr continued to stare at Wilshire Boulevard. Finally, he returned to his seat.

Kreuzer had stopped drumming his fingers.

"I appreciate the help you gave me on that case a few years ago," Carr said. "I really mean that."

"I have no compunction about ratting on someone when it benefits me in the long run. I've been around too long to be stupid enough to ride a beef for someone else. I'm a realist. I pride myself in being able to say that. On the other hand, I'm far from being what you people call a *police buff*. I'm not into cooperating with the Feds or the cops in order to earn a merit badge. You know that. You should know that very well."

Charles Carr took a fresh package of cigarettes from his coat pocket and opened it. Kreuzer shoved an ashtray toward him on the desk. Carr crumpled the wrapper and dropped it into the ashtray. "I don't want to cause problems for you," he said, pausing to light a cigarette.

Kreuzer made a wry grin. "What kind of problems are we talking about?"

"Conspiracy to commit burglary. He who sets up a burg is guilty of conspiracy."

"That's a very difficult crime to prove," Kreuzer said. "If someone hit me with that kind of beef, I think I'd probably go on trial and let the chips fall where they may. Conspiracy is hard to prove, particularly if the other conspirators are stand-up guys. Without one or two good witnesses who'll testify about the whole thing, there's no way to get a conviction."

There was a pause before Carr spoke again. "I wish you'd have given me a call about all this. It would have been a lot simpler if you'd have given me a call. We could have worked something out . . . found a way to keep you off the witness stand, but still made the case. I know how you hate to testify against people. I can't say that I blame you. There's always an element of risk."

"I don't like these kinds of conversations," Kreuzer said. "I prefer to be up-front about things. If you've come here to accuse me of something, then go ahead and accuse me. If you're going to arrest me, then have at it. Otherwise, we're wasting each other's time. We're sitting here in my office jerking each other off while my patients are lined up outside."

"You're got guts, Emil. I've always admired that," Charlie Carr said. "You're not afraid of the dark."

"Fuck all this bullshit." Kreuzer obstinately folded his arms across his chest.

Carr stood up again, walked to the wall behind Kreuzer and examined a diploma from a university he'd never heard of. Emil Kreuzer remained seated with his arms crossed.

"This is the last chance you'll get," Carr said to the phony diploma. "If I walk out of this room right now without your help, I'm going to work twenty-four hours a day at putting you back in the joint. I'll stir up things at the Federal Parole Office, interview your patients. I'll Teletype your name and address to every police agency in the U.S. I'll frame you if I have to. I'll do whatever I have to to ship you back. If you want to be Mr Big in this thing that's fine with me. I'll close my case the day you process in at Terminal Island. It wouldn't be the first time I've had to settle for missing some of the players in a case."

Emil Kreuzer sat without moving for what must have been a full minute.

Carr checked the other diplomas on the wall. He moved toward the door.

Kreuzer rubbed his temples. "I want to ask you a hypothetical question," he said.

Carr nodded.

"Would you rat on a policeman? If you were someone who'd been around the horn a time or two, who knew how the system worked . . . murderers getting bail, defense attorneys hired just to find out who the informant is, million-dollar dope dealers sentenced to probation . . . would you actually take the witness stand and testify against a *policeman?*"

Carr shook his head. "Probably not."

"Then how the hell can you come in here and ask *me* to?"

"You wouldn't have to testify."

"I've heard that before. But when the case gets right down to the nuts and bolts, I'd have to testify."

"You have my word you won't have to testify."

The men stared at each other for a moment.

"What *would* I have to do?" Kreuzer said.

"Do you deal directly with Bailey?"

"Yes. We're still speaking hypothetically, of course."

"Of course. Then, hypothetically, I might ask you to wear a microphone and meet with him to talk about some things."

Kreuzer shook his head. "I won't wear a wire. I know that means I'd have to take the witness stand. The only reason for a recorded conversation is to play it for a jury. I will never wear a wire. I'd rather go back to prison than wear a wire."

"We might be able to work around that."

"How?"

"I'll figure a way."

"I'm sure you will." Kreuzer rubbed his temples again. "If you had a plan that would keep me out of the soup . . . I mean *completely* out of the motherfucking soup *all together,* I might go along with it. Not that I *will* go along with it, but just that I will give consideration to any plan you have. I want to help. I think you can see that, but on the other hand, you have to appreciate my position."

"I'll be in touch," Carr said. He opened the door, then paused. "Did Bailey kill her himself?" he turned to face Kreuzer again.

"You're talking about murder now. Violence is something I've never been involved in. Nor do I intend to. You can check my record. You'll see that I have never even been questioned about any heavy-handed shit. It's against my nature. I really mean that."

"I'm not asking you who made it happen," Carr said. "I already know that. I just want to know if he did it himself or contracted it out."

"Off the record, you'd probably be safe in assuming the former rather than the latter." He stared at the palms of his hands. "I want to cooperate. I'm sure you can see that. It's just that this isn't your average drop-a-dime-on-a-pal operation. You're asking me to rat on someone who carries a gun *legally.* He could walk in here right now and blow my brains out. He'd beat the rap in court. He'd just say I reached for a gun."

"I guess I could do the same thing," Carr said.

"That's not funny."

"I'll be in touch." Carr opened the door and walked out.

* * *

Though it was 8:30 P.M., the summer heat had not diminished. The weather was par for the course for Los Angeles—anyplace else it would be a portent of a summer storm—but rather than distant thunder, there was only the hum of air conditioners.

In the small patio at the rear of the house, Charlie Carr sat at a wooden table with Kelly and Higgins. They were dressed similarly: short-sleeved white shirts, loosened neckties. Kelly wore a T-shirt and Bermuda shorts. The table was littered with beer bottles. Kelly's young sons, armed with toy swords and squirt guns, chased each other in and out of the backyard.

Carr finished recounting his meeting with Emil Kreuzer. He picked up his beer and finished it.

"He could double-cross us," Higgins said. "He could go straight to Bailey."

"He *will* double-cross us," Kelly said. "One way or the other he'll double-cross us. When we used him as an informant in the Larry Phillips case, he played both ends against the middle. That's the kind of an asshole he is."

"But I don't think he'll double-cross us yet," Carr said. "I think he'll wait to see how the land lies. He'll wait to get more information from us before he sets his course. Right now there are too many unknowns for him. He doesn't know enough about what kind of a case we have at this point because I didn't tell him."

"There's no predicting a confidence man," Higgins said.

"Anything can happen," Kelly said.

Carr drank more beer. As if on cue, the others drank from their bottles.

"The surveillance isn't doing us any good," Higgins said. "Bones hasn't been going anywhere except the supermarket and to work at the Blue Peach. Women drop by his apartment now and then and he usually takes one home with him every night from the Blue Peach. He likes skinny broads with short hair. We've been on him twenty-four hours a day for four days and that's all we've come up with: skinny broads with short hair. I mean really short hair. My wife says it's the latest movie-star style."

"Sounds more like Bones is having auditions," Kelly muttered.

A sedan drove into the driveway and parked. Because of the hat, Carr could tell it was B. B. Martin.

Martin climbed out of the car. His sleeves were rolled up and though his trousers hung below his ample paunch, his gunbelt stretched neatly across his midsection. From the belt hung a patrolman's holster that held a six-inch revolver. He walked over to the table, thumbed his hat back on his head and sat down.

Jack Kelly opened another beer and handed it to Martin. Martin drank fully three-fourths of the bottle. He set the bottle on the table and wiped his mouth with the back of his hand. "Something funny happened tonight," he said. "On his way to the Blue Peach, Bones stops off at a French restaurant on La Cienega. I set up down the street where I can keep an eye on the front door. He's in there about ten or fifteen minutes. Then he steps out the front door with another guy. I was too far away to tell who it was, so I do a drive-by. Bones and this other dude are standing on the sidewalk in front of the place. As I'm crusing past, the other cat is definitely giving me the eagle eye. I just keep my eyes on the road all the way up to Sunset. Then I turn off and circle back to the restaurant. When I got there, Bones was gone."

"What did the man look like?" Carr asked.

"He looked like Travis Bailey, but I can't say for sure. I was too far away." Martin finished the rest of his beer with one swig.

Kelly popped open another bottle and set it in front of him.

"I checked the parking lot," Martin said as he fondled the fresh beer. "Bailey's car wasn't there, but he had time to leave by the time I returned. So I went to a pay phone and dialed the restaurant. I asked the maître d' if Mr. Bailey was still there. He says, 'No, he just—' then catches hisself and says that there was no Mr. Bailey in tonight. It sounded fishy, so I head over to the valet parking lot at the place. I buzz the attendant and he tells me that he notes the license number of every car he parks on the valet parking ticket stub. I look through the evening's ticket stubs. The license number of Bailey's car was written on one of them."

"It was him," Carr said.

"I think he made me," Martin said. "He stared right at me as I went by."

"Now what the hell are we going to do?" Higgins said.

Carr stood up, shoved his hands in his pockets. As the other men bantered, he strolled to the front of the house. Dusk was changing to dark; the streetlights came on. As he stood in front of the house, he again went over the facts in his mind. Gradually the plan took shape and he knew exactly what he was going to do.

Carr walked to the backyard and sat down again. He pulled a pen and some three-by-five cards from his shirt pocket, then wrote "PRESS RELEASE" on one of the cards. After some scratch-outs, he completed the following paragraphs:

Federal Agents have been following leads in what is beileved to be a foiled Mafia-style contract murder of a prominent Beverly Hills banking official. Preliminary investigation has shown that Jerome Hartmann, president of the Beverly Hills-based Bank of Commerce-Pacific was the proposed target of an organized crime hit man. A federal informant in Chicago has recently told federal authorities that the July sixth break-in at Hartmann's Beverly Hills residence may have been instigated by organized crime figures who stood to gain from eliminating Hartmann as a witness in a counterfeiting case in which Hartmann was a potential government witness. A shoot-out at Hartmann's residence resulted in the death of convicted burglar Leon Sheboygan and the wounding of U.S. Treasury Agent John Kelly.

Sources within the U.S. Treasury Department, which is investigating the case, have stated that a major organized crime figure in the Los Angeles area may be called before the federal grand jury in the near future. "Progress has been made in narrowing down the motive for the attempt on Hartmann's life," one veteran Treasury agent said. "Since Mr. Sheboygan is deceased, it is doubtful whether we will ever know the complete story. This is not the first time that Le Cosa Nostra has tried to thwart an ongoing investigation."

Since it was dark, Carr read the press release out loud to the others.

"That should help Bailey sleep a little better," Higgins said.

"He may not buy it," Kelly said.

"Who'll cover for us on the Chicago angle?" B. B. Martin opened another bottle of beer.

"Bob Tomsic was just transferred there," Carr said. "He'll back up the informant story if it ever comes down to it."

Martin nodded.

"And there should be no problem getting No Waves to issue the release," Carr said, smirking.

"Problems?" Kelly said. "He'll call a press conference at the drop of a hat."

"What comes after the phony press release?" Higgins said.

Carr pulled his chair closer to the table. As he explained his plan, the others sat in silence. After he had finished his explanation, more beers were opened.

"It's complicated," Higgins said.

"There's a lot of unknowns," Martin said, drinking down another half bottle of beer.

Carr looked at Kelly.

"Lots of things can go wrong," Kelly said. He bit his lip.

"If they do, we'll make repairs along the way," Carr said. "I say we're in a corner and there's no other way to fight our way out of it."

Everyone nodded in agreement. After finishing their beers, Higgins and Martin left, and Kelly asked Carr to join him for a walk.

For the next hour or so, they strolled the darkened suburban streets. Children sped about on bicycles with reflectors. From some of the homes they walked past, they could hear television dialogue, commercials, Hollywood-style gunshots, screeching tires, shouted commands, music.

They talked about some of the cases they had worked

on together earlier in their careers. Finally, as they turned a corner and headed back toward Kelly's house, they ran out of conversation. The two men continued up the street to Carr's sedan, which was parked in front of the house. He pulled car keys from his pocket.

"I really think I'm gonna do it," Kelly said as he gazed in the direction of his home. "I'm not one hundred percent positive, but I've been doing a lot of thinking since this thing happened and I'm thinking seriously about taking the disability retirement."

Carr didn't respond. He unlocked the car and climbed into the driver's seat, started the engine.

"Well, why don't you say something?" Kelly said.

"If you want to get your charge by watching TV from now on, that's up to you, Jack," Carr said.

"The whole job is nothing but a goddamn game."

"True."

"If you had a wife and kids, you'd think differently."

"Maybe I would." He winked at Kelly and drove off.

Chapter 16

IT TOOK Charles Carr twenty minutes to reach Jerome Hartmann's home in Beverly Hills. He pulled into the circular driveway and parked near the front door. The lights were out in the house. Nevertheless, Carr got out and rang the doorbell. After a long wait, he heard footsteps inside. The peephole opened and closed. The outside light came on and the door lock was unfastened.

Jerome Hartmann opened the door. He was wearing a blue terry-cloth robe and leather slippers.

"Sorry to stop by so late," Carr said. "But I want to take you up on your offer to help."

"Come in, Mr. Carr," Hartmann said, stepping aside. He ran his hands through his hair.

"That's not necessary, this will only take a minute. I need the use of a furnished house in Beverly Hills for a few days. I'd like to have the house by tomorrow afternoon. Can you help me?"

Hartmann rubbed his chin. "Greg Peckham and his family are in Cannes the next week or so. I'm sure if I phoned him he'd give me permission . . . may I ask what you need the house for?"

"I can't tell you all the details right now, but it involves the people who tried to kill you. If we can use the house for a few days we might be able to catch them."

Hartmann nodded. "Call me tomorrow at the bank. I'll have it all arranged."

"Sorry to have disturbed you."

Jerome Hartmann shut the door.

The Beverly Hills Detective Bureau was busier than usual.

There had been an armed robbery at one of the Rodeo Drive jewelry stores and the office was buzzing with activity. Detectives filled out reports as they interviewed the witnesses: a well-dressed young woman, a middle-aged jeweler who still looked pale, a turbaned man wearing a tailor-made suit. Because it was almost time for shift change, uniformed officers roamed in and out of the office, stalling their return to patrol duties.

Travis Bailey stood in the corner of the room sharpening his pencils in an electric sharpener. As he checked each point, he wiped the excess lead on a tissue, then tossed the tissue in the wastebasket. After honing exactly fifteen pencils, he wrapped them with a rubber band and returned to his desk. He opened a drawer and placed the sheaf of pencils in its proper place, then closed the drawer.

"Hold the line," Delsey Piper said, and pressed the hold button on her telephone. "Line three." She looked at Bailey.

Bailey picked up the receiver on his desk.

"It's me," Emil Kreuzer said.

"Where are you calling from?" Bailey's tone was less than friendly.

"In a phone booth of course. We need to get together."

"I can't get away today."

"Could you make time for the score of a lifetime? I mean *of a lifetime?*"

Bailey looked around the room. "I might be able to get away for a few minutes," he said casually. "Meet me at the department store." He hung up the receiver.

He looked at Delsey, still at her desk. "We have to go see an informant."

Bailey checked an unmarked sedan out of the motor pool and drove a few blocks to an exclusive, five-story department store. He drove into the underground garage and parked. "You wait here," he said.

"Can't I go with you? You keep telling me you'll let me meet some of your informants, and then you never do."

"Next time."

"That's what you always say."

Bailey climbed out of the car and entered the store through a bank of glass doors. Inside, he made his way through a cosmetics department staffed with immaculately groomed women of all ages and a circular platform featuring a display of male and female mannequins wearing see-through plastic coats and black leather tights. He took an elevator to the fourth floor, then wound through the fur department to a restaurant furnished with small white tables and cane-backed chairs. They were surrounded by trellises wrapped with artificial greenery.

Emil Kreuzer was the only male customer. He waved Bailey over. A waitress dressed in a puffed-sleeve uniform came to the table and took Bailey's order for coffee.

"I hope this is important," Bailey said after the waitress had left.

"I'll run it down to you and you tell me what you think. Yesterday I did my hypno thing on this movie star's wife—"

"Name?"

"Fay Peckham, wife of Greg Peckham."

"Go ahead."

"After I do the hypno thing I have conversation with the bitch. Somehow or another we got on the topic of gold coins. She tells me she and good ol' Greg are collectors; that they have lots of U.S. gold coins, numismatic pieces worth lots of bucks. I do the *'I-happen-to-be-a-coin-collector-myself'* act and after a while she gets up and goes in the den. A minute later she comes back out with a tray of Krugerrands and Austrian Coronas. She tells me that her husband has been collecting for the past ten years and has his collection insured for *three hundred thousand*. The dumb bitch trusts me."

"How do you know the whole collection is in his house?"

"If you'll let me finish, I'll tell you."

Bailey nodded.

"While I'm sitting there jawing with the bitch, the doorbell rings. She goes to the front door While she's signing for a package or something, I zip into the den. What do I see? A wall safe! The woman is so dumb she actually left the safe open. I got a glimpse of something beautiful. I'm talking about *trays* of gold coins. I almost came in my pants."

"You're telling me you *saw* the coins?"

"I saw them. And when I asked her about her next appointment, she told me all about her trip to Cannes. They'll be gone a week starting today. The safe is one of those little ones. Just have your man take an axe. He can chop the safe out of the wall and take it with him."

The waitress came to the table, served the coffee and hurried off.

Bailey tasted the coffee. "This may not be the best time to put Bones to work," he said. "Things have heated up lately."

"I take it you've read the newspaper?" Kreuzer sipped coffee. "It sounds to me like the Feds are chasing their tail in Chicago."

"Anyone can plant a newspaper story. As a matter of fact, it's the kind of thing that Carr would do."

"It's one of the best scores I have ever seen. It's not like taking ten percent on furs and silver. This is gold. Cash to cash. But, of course, it's whatever you think. You're the *expert,* so to speak." Kreuzer chuckled, then stirred his coffee with a tiny spoon.

"How did you meet the woman?"

"A coffee klatch referral. She attended one of my hypnosis demonstrations." Kreuzer drank almost the entire cup of coffee and looked into the cup. Placing it to his lips again, he threw his head back and drained it. As he did so, Bailey noticed that Kreuzer had thick fingers. A diamond pinky ring he wore was half hidden in flesh.

"Alarms?"

Kreuzer shook his head. He pulled a white card from his pocket and handed it to Bailey.

Bailey read it. It was Peckham's address. "Dogs?"

"No dogs."

"It sounds too easy," Bailey said. "I don't like things that sound too easy."

"Of course, it's not like *we're* tiptoeing in the house. And with gold coins, we don't have to worry about talking to a fence. They're untraceable. Any coin store in the world would be happy to buy them with no questions asked. Three hundred grand is a lot of bucks. A *load* of bucks."

"I'll think about it."

Bailey finished his coffee and Kreuzer paid the bill. "Whatever you think," Kreuzer said amiably as they strolled past mannequins wearing sable and chinchilla coats. They reached the bank of elevators and Kreuzer pressed the down button. A vacant elevator arrived; they stepped on and pressed different floors. Nothing was said as they descended.

"I hope you go for it," Kreuzer said when the elevator stopped at the ground floor. "I really do. I have a real good feeling about it."

"We'll see." Bailey stepped off the elevator into the underground garage and made his way to the unmarked police car. Delsey Piper was leaning back against the headrest with her eyes closed.

Bailey got into the car and started the engine. He backed out of the parking space and steered toward the street exit.

"What did your informant have to say?" she asked without opening her eyes.

"Routine info. Someone's planning a burglary in Beverly Hills. He'll find out more and get back to me in a few days . . . blah blah blah."

"What are we going to do about it?"

"There's not much we can do about it."

"I wish you'd stop keeping me in the dark."

He reached out and pulled her close to him. He ran his hand up her skirt and she giggled.

"And now I guess we're headed for the apartment?" she said coquettishly.

He shook his head. "The golf course," he said with a wry grin.

"If anyone ever catches us up there we're going to be in trouble."

"But no one ever will."

"You like to do it up there because of the risk."

"Maybe." Bailey slipped his hand inside her panties and massaged her pussy. Delsey spread her legs and he felt wetness.

He stepped on the accelerator and zoomed out of the garage.

Charles Carr waited in his sedan. He was parked on Wilshire Boulevard a block east of the department store. He watched Emil Kreuzer leave the main entrance of the department store and walk across the intersection. Following Carr's instructions, he walked down a side street to his Mercedes-Benz, got in and drove off.

Carr started the engine and followed him as he made a few turns in the Beverly Hills business district. At a signal light in front of a store with a display window full of oriental rugs, Carr sounded his horn.

Emil Kreuzer pulled across the intersection and parked at the curb.

Carr pulled up behind him. Kreuzer got out of his car and looked around fearfully. He trotted to Carr's sedan and climbed in the passenger side.

"I gave him the rundown just like you told me," Kreuzer said.

Carr lit a cigarette, tossed the match out the window. "Did he go for it?"

"Hard to say. He didn't jump on it like a free piece of

ass, but on the other hand, he didn't say no. He took the address."

"How did he act today as compared to other times when you've given him a rundown on a score?"

"Pretty much the same. He's not the kind of guy to come right out and tell you exactly when he's going to have a place hit. He's a noncommital person. That's the best way to describe him. Cagey and noncommital." Kreuzer smiled. "He's somewhat like you."

A Rolls-Royce pulled in front of them and parked. A middle-aged man wearing a tennis outfit got out of the car and went into the oriental rug store.

"If this thing goes the way you want it to, I'm home free, right?" Kreuzer said. "Immunity from prosecution, like you promised?"

Carr nodded. "If it goes the way I want it to."

"And I won't have to testify?"

"And you won't have to testify."

"What if something goes wrong and Bailey figures out I set him up?"

"Then he'll probably kill you."

"That's not very funny."

Carr drove straight to his apartment after meeting with Kreuzer and telephoned Higgins.

"I put out the bait," he said.

"When?"

"Just now."

"Then I guess we have to set up. Do I need to bring anything?"

"Bring a shotgun and a couple of flashlights. I have the transmitter," Carr said. "I'll meet you at the West Hollywood Sheriff's Station in an hour."

"I'll be there."

After they hung up Carr dialed Sally Malone's number.

"I just walked in the door," she said.

"I'm going to be tied up for a few days. I wanted to let you know—"

"We need to talk," she interrupted. "Can you come over for a few minutes?"

"I'm on my way to a stakeout. I don't really have time right now."

"Will you do this for me? Will you please come over for just a few minutes? I want to talk with you in person."

"We'll just end up in an argument."

"Are you telling me that your job is more important, more important *overall* than our relationship?"

Carr's eyes closed in frustration.

"All I'm asking for is five minutes."

"I'll be by." Carr set the receiver down.

Hurriedly, he tossed shaving items, shirts and underwear into a briefcase. It barely closed. He locked the windows and front door before leaving, then drove the few short blocks to Sally's apartment. As he knocked on the door, he realized he was out of breath.

"It's open," she called out.

Carr went in. Sally sat at a dinette table. She offered him a drink; he declined politely.

"I know you don't have much time," she said, "so I'm just going to say what I've been thinking for the last week and let the chips fall where they may."

Carr sat down at the table.

"I've felt strongly about you for years and unless I'm wrong I think you feel the same way about me. Maybe we love each other and maybe we don't. I'm really not sure that our relationship isn't some form of mutually destructive behavior. The thought has been on my mind for the past few days and I wanted to share it with you. If you think I'm crazy, please say so."

"I don't think you're crazy."

"But just the way you're looking at me right now I can tell that you haven't the slightest idea of what I'm trying to say." Sally looked at her hands.

Carr stifled the desire to check the time. "I really have to go," he said. "As soon as the stakeout is over we can get together and talk. Maybe I'll take some time off."

"Nothing will have changed. You'll still be the same Charlie Carr. Your job will still be more important than anything else in your life. You'll still prefer the company of sociopathic informants and alcoholic policemen over me. As soon as your precious stakeout is over, there'll be another and then another and another. Please don't go to work tonight. Please call in sick or do whatever you have to do. Please don't walk out of here and leave me sitting at this table."

Carr stood up. He pushed the chair back to the table. "You called me over here to argue," he said on his way out the door.

"Don't be surprised if I never call you again," she called after him, her voice cracking. "I mean that."

Carr met Higgins in the parking lot of the West Hollywood Sheriff's Station. After a brief discussion, they drove to Hartmann's bank and picked up the key to Peckham's house. They made a quick stop at a delicatessen on Hillcrest and bought lunch meat and bread. By the time they made the short drive to Peckham's hillside home it was dusk. As Hartmann had described, there was a locked mailbox on a post at the entrance to a descending driveway.

Carr made the sharp turn and proceeded down the

driveway past an elevated tennis court on the right. The house itself was a sprawling one-story structure balanced on hillside struts. It had a four-car garage. Higgins climbed out of the sedan and used a key to unlock the garage. Carr steered into an empty space between a Rolls-Royce and a Maserati and parked.

They carried shotguns, radio transmitters and the sack of groceries into the house. The living room was an expanse of deep black carpeting leading to a semicircle of glass windows covered by sheer curtains. Outside the windows was a plank-floored patio that looked down onto Beverly Hills and West Los Angeles.

Higgins followed Carr through the huge master bedroom and into a study with floor-to-ceiling bookcases. The facing wall, behind a mahogany desk, was covered with photographs of the square-jawed Greg Peckham in scenes from various movies. The most imposing photograph was a color shot of Pekcham costumed in pirate's knickers, gold earring and a colorful puff-sleeved shirt as he stood on the prow of a sailing vessel. He wore lipstick and heavy makeup.

Higgins stared at the photo. "Can you imagine wearing a costume like that all day to earn a living? All actors must be queers."

"Could be." Carr stepped out of the study and made his way down a hallway lined with oil paintings of Peckham in various flattering poses. The other bedrooms off the hallway were decorated in strikingly different motifs. The walls of one room were covered with zebra skins.

After surveying the entire house, they returned to the living room.

Carr picked up a shotgun, pulled shells from his coat

pocket and thumbed them into the magazine. "How would *you* break in?" he said.

"It's a toss-up between either kicking in the front door or coming around the side of the house. But I don't think he'll hit the windows. They look fairly secure."

"The front door looks like the weak spot to me."

Without discussion, they took positions catercorner from one another in the living room. As it grew dark inside the house the city below became alive with lights. In the distance the flashing red lights of airplanes descended slowly in an arc toward Los Angeles International Airport.

For once, Carr mused, the night was clear. He remembered being on guard duty in Korea. It had been foggy and pitch dark. He knew that if the enemy had approached his position, he would probably feel a bayonet before seeing it. Consequently, he stood as still as possible through his tour of guard duty, knowing that the enemy might be close enough to hear him.

Sitting across the room from one another in the darkness, Higgins and Carr bantered about the case. Around 10:00 P.M. they shared a meal of bologna and bread, which they ate under flashlight illumination at the kitchen table. After finishing their sandwiches, they returned to their posts.

"When you talked with Kreuzer," Higgins said from across the room, "did he sound confident that Bailey would take the bait?" It was the same question he had asked in a number of different ways through the course of the evening.

"He said Bailey reacted the same way he always does when he gave him an address for a score."

"We might end up sitting here all week."

"I was afraid if I told Kreuzer to say that the house

would be vacant for any shorter period it might sound like a setup."

"You're right," Higgins said. "It was the best way to do it. It's just sitting here not knowing whether he'll ever come. That's the hard part. The thought of wasting a week sitting here for nothing."

The conversation became even more banal after midnight.

During the morning hours they alternated taking catnaps. Finally, the sun came up.

Carr stretched. He phoned the Field Office and left a message for No Waves that he was on a stakeout at Tony Dio's home. Higgins called his captain and did the same. They took quick showers, changed underwear, ate more lunch meat and bread, made a joint command decision to make a pot of Greg Peckham's coffee. When it was brewed, they drank the entire pot. For a while they discussed whether it was worth taking the chance of separating long enough for one of them to drive to a store and pick up a morning newpaper. They decided against it.

They spent the rest of the day playing gin rummy. After dark, they continued playing by arranging a flashlight on the dining room table. Finally, at 11:00 P.M., Carr grinned and Higgins said he'd played enough cards to last him the rest of his life.

At Higgins's suggestion, they watched the eleven o'clock news on TV with the volume turned down. After the news, they found themselves meandering about the darkened house like prisoners in an exercise yard. Carr found himself standing on the patio again staring at the city lights. He thought of Sally, and of the case, and about how he would busy himself if he retired.

And the hours passed.

Eventually Carr returned to the living room, where he found Higgins lying on the sofa.

"Most burglars work during the day," Higgins said. "They ring the door bell. If no one's home, they shim the door and do their thing."

"That's what they say," Carr agreed. He remembered Higgins making the same comment the night before.

Suddenly, there was the sound of a car pulling into the driveway.

Carr grabbed the shotgun, ran to the kitchen window and peeked out. He saw the figure of a man climbing out of a sedan and cautiously approaching the front door. He carried an axe.

Higgins trotted down the hallway toward the den.

There was the sound of metal against metal at the front door. A snap. The door opened slowly.

Carr ducked behind the kitchen work counter.

A beam of a flashlight preceded the man as he passed through the front door. With the light leading his way, he walked through the living room and down the hallway. Carr stood up, tiptoed behind him.

As the man reached the door of the den, Carr flipped on the hallway light. Higgins, holding his pistol in a combat stance, stood in the doorway. "Surprise," he said.

Bones Chagra backed up in fright. His back touched the barrel of Carr's shotgun. He dropped his flashlight and axe and his hands flew over his head. "Please don't kill me," he cried. "Please don't kill me."

Higgins reholstered his revolver. He stepped from the doorway and slammed Chagra against the wall. After frisking him thoroughly, he grabbed him by the shirt collar and dragged him past Carr into the kitchen, where he shoved him violently into a chair. He yanked a pair of handcuffs off his belt and snapped one cuff on Chagra's right wrist and attached the other to a table leg.

Carr unloaded the shotgun and returned it to his sedan. Back in the kitchen he prepared coffee in an electric pot. He set the pot and three cups on the kitchen table. As he did this, he glanced at a wall clock.

It was 3:00 A.M.

Chapter 17

AT 8:00 A.M. they were still sitting around the kitchen table. The coffee pot was empty. Carr had filled an ashtray with cigarette butts.

"It's like I said," Chagra said in a fatigued manner. "I've been bullshitted before by the cops."

"That must be the fiftieth time you've said that," Higgins said as he rocked back on his chair. "Maybe more."

"You people can promise me anything you want and then go back on your word."

And you've said that fifty times too, Carr thought. He lit his last cigarette and crumpled the empty pack. "Let's look at this situation realistically," Carr said as he pulled his chair closer to the table. "We were waiting here for you. We knew you were coming. That means only one thing; someone set you up. Now, being the intelligent man that you are, you should know exctly how many people knew you were going to break in here tonight. One of those people handed you up. One of them dropped a dime on you. So who the hell are you trying to protect?"

"Me," Chagra said emphatically as he touched his thumb to his chest. "I'm just trying to protect myself. There's people involved in it who'd snuff me in a minute. I've lived through time in the joint before. And *living* is the important thing. I'm not going to talk. That's my final decision. You might as well take me downtown and book me and stop wasting your time." Chagra picked up his coffee cup with his unshackled hand. He tossed back the few cold drops in the bottom, grimaced and set the cup back down.

"If we take you downtown we're not going to book you for burglary," Carr said. "We're going to book you for murder."

Bones Chagra swallowed as he stared at the table.

"You were the last person to see Amanda Kennedy alive."

"I didn't kill her. I've got nothing to worry about."

"The day will come when you'll want to help us," Carr said. "We'll make a case on Bailey with or without you. When we arrest him, do you think he'll keep his mouth shut? He's a policeman. He knows the ropes when it comes to making a deal with the prosecution. My guess is that he would hand you up on a platter if it meant so much as one day less on his sentence. I'm going to give it to you straight one last time before we book you for accessory to murder, burglary and everything else we can think of: If you will give us Bailey, we will make your cooperation known to the District Attorney. We'll recommend that you be released on a personal recognizance bond. We will be on your side. If Bailey tries to cause you problems, we will provide you protection."

Chagra was quiet for a while, still staring at the table.

"I'll cooperate if I get immunity," he said finally. "That's the only way I'll do it. I want a free pass. I want to be able to get up and walk right out of here. For anything less than that, it's not worth the risk."

"Can't do it," Carr said. "It's out of the question."

"I know you can't. That's why I'm ready to go downtown right now. I'm ready to be booked. You people are wasting your breath."

The men looked at one another around the table.

"I say we throw a phone call in to the district attorney's office and see what they say," Higgins said.

"They'll never go for immunity," Carr said, "but I guess it can't hurt to give 'em a call."

"You tell the D.A. that I want it in writing," Chagra said. "I want it in writing that if I cooperate and do what you want to make a case on Bailey, that I will get complete immunity from all charges and you will let me go with no strings attached. Tell 'em I said that."

Higgins stood up and walked to a phone in the living room. He dialed information and asked for the number of the district attorney's office. He wrote the number down, then made another phone call. Without lowering his voice, he explained the case in detail. Having completed the call, he returned to the kitchen and took his seat. "A deputy district attorney will be here within the hour."

"I'm not trying to be an asshole about this," Bones said. "It's just that I've been screwed on deals before."

"We understand." Carr stood up from the table. Exhausted, he went over to the refrigerator and pulled out a carton of eggs. He set the carton on the work counter. "Two or three?"

"Are you talking to me?" Chagra said with a quizzical look.

"I'm going to make breakfast," Carr said. "How many eggs would you like?"

Chagra smiled. "You guys are all right."

"We're just doing a job," Higgins said. "Just a job."

After preparing enough eggs and toast for all of them Carr set the plates on the table. Higgins unshackled Chagra's hand from the table leg.

There was little conversation as they ate. When they finished, Carr refilled their coffee cups. As they sat drinking their coffee, the doorbell rang. Higgins left the table and opened the front door. He returned to the kitchen followed by Jack Kelly, who wore a blue suit and carried a briefcase. He set the briefcase on the kitchen table before he pulled out a chair and sat down.

Carr introduced himself. They shook hands.

Kelly turned to Chagra. "My name is Harry Weese," he said. "I'm a Los Angeles County deputy district attorney. Before we go any further I must warn you that you have the right to remain silent and anything you say to me could be used against you in a court of law. Do you understand that?"

"Do you have any identification to prove you work for the district attorney's office?" Chagra said.

Carr's stomach muscles tightened.

Without hesitation, Jack Kelly pulled out his wallet. He thumbed out a business card and handed it to Chagra, put his wallet back.

Chagra stared at the card for a moment. "Do you have anything else . . . an I.D. card or something?"

Kelly frowned. "A few minutes ago I was sitting in my office preparing for a very important trial. My supervisor walks in my office and tells me to drive to Beverly Hills to write out a prosecutory deal. I drive through peak rush-hour traffic. Here I am. And now you want to see my I.D.? Like who in the hell do you think I am? You called me. I didn't call you."

Chagra paused for a moment, looking at Kelly. "Never mind," he said sheepishly.

Carr's stomach muscles finally relaxed. "We were staked out here," he said. "We apprehended Mr. Chagra in the act of breaking into this house. Because we're more interested in the person who set up the burglary, we'd like to offer him a deal."

"Look, I don't like these do-a-deal-at-the-scene operations," Kelly said. "In general, I don't approve of them." He glanced at his wristwatch. "Excuse me." He stood up, walked over to the phone and dialed a number. "This is Weese," he said. "Tell the clerk in courtroom twenty-three I'll be a few minutes late. Thanks." He hung up the receiver and returned to the table.

"We want to give this man immunity because it was a policeman who set up the burglary," Carr said. "He can lead us to him."

"And I want it in writing," Chagra said. "That's the only way I'll do it."

"I have about fifteen minutes before I have to leave to be in court." Kelly opened his briefcase and took out a sheet of paper and a pen. He wrote "Grant of Immunity" across the top.

"You understand that this grant implies that you must cooperate fully with the investigation that these officers are conducting," Kelly said.

"Yes, sir."

Kelly spent a quarter of an hour preparing the phony document. Finally, he signed it and handed it to Carr. It read:

> In exchange for complete cooperation with Special Agent Charles Carr, U.S. Treasury Department,

and Detective Ralph Higgins, Los Angeles Police Department, the District Attorney of the County of Los Angeles agrees not to prosecute Robert Chagra for the burglary committed this date at the residence, 1678 King's Circle Road, Beverly Hills, California. Immunity herein granted applies to no other crime in this nor any other jurisdiction and implies no further immunity for crimes. Cooperation by Robert Chagra is defined for purposes of this limited grant of immunity as his (Chagra's) full, complete, and honest efforts in the gathering of evidence concerning other conspirators.

Harry K. Weese
Deputy District Attorney

Carr handed the document to Chagra. He moved his lips as he read. When he finished, he looked up at Kelly, who reached out for the sheet of paper.

"Don't I get to keep the agreement?" Chagra said, drawing it toward him.

"Sure," Kelly said. "But I suggest you allow me to take it back to the courthouse and file it in the immunity file. If a dispute ever developed between you and these officers, the original copy would be in possession of the Office of the District Attorney. It will be a matter of legal record."

Chagra stared at the agreement for a moment, then looked at Carr.

Kelly stood up to leave. Grudgingly, Bones Chagra handed the agreement to Kelly.

Without expression, he flipped open his briefcase and dropped the agreement inside. He shut the briefcase and, after making another comment about being late for a hearing, rushed out the door.

Carr had the urge to sigh but didn't. "How do you and Bailey usually get in touch after you make a score?" he said.

"He usually phones me."

"Where?"

"At my apartment. He gives me a number and tells me to go to a pay phone. I call him back. He asks me how everything went. I tell him."

"Then what?"

"Then he picks me up. We drive around in his car and discuss where to fence everything. But lately he doesn't want to meet in person. He said there's too much heat."

"This isn't going to be easy," Higgins said.

"Does he talk freely on the phone?" Carr said.

Chagra shook his head. "No way. On the phone it's just yes and no and how'd everything go? He doesn't trust anyone. He's a cop, man."

"And when you meet in person?" Higgins said.

Chagra nodded. "He talks pretty freely."

"Did he ever tell you how he killed Amanda Kennedy?"

Chagra shook his head as if to say of course not. "This is not something he would do. The man is a loner. He doesn't spring with a lot of talk. He does his own thing and never says too much. He's the kind of guy that, if there's a lull in the conversation, he'll just wait you out until you say the next thing. I know what you're thinking about."

"What are we thinking about?" Higgins said.

"You're thinking about having me wear a transmitter when I meet with him. You want to record what he says to me for evidence." He paused. "Am I right?"

"You're right," Carr said.

"Then what happens?"

"Then we arrest Bailey for the murders of Amanda Kennedy and Lee Sheboygan," Higgins said.

"I don't think I can do it," Chagra said. "I really and truly don't think I can do it. If I'm being taped I'm afraid my knees will shake or something. He'll know something is wrong. He wouldn't hesitate to kill me on the spot if he thought I was setting him up. He's told me he ain't going to the joint. No matter what. He means it. He's a cop. He knows he'd never survive."

"Do you feel particularly nervous right now?" Higgins said.

"Not particularly."

"What if I told you that we've been tape-recording every word you've said?"

Chagra glanced nervously at both men. "Then I'm nervous."

"That's my point," Higgins said. "When you wear the wire, just pretend that you're not. It's easy."

"Are you recording me right now?"

Higgins shook his head. "Nope."

Chagra scratched his head.

Carr stood up and started to move about the kitchen, straightening things up. Higgins gathered up the playing cards that were spread about on the coffee table in the living room.

"Where are we going now?" Chagra asked.

"To your apartment," Carr said.

"Sometimes he doesn't call the same day. It might be tomorrow . . . or even the next day."

"We have patience," Carr said.

"And you're really going to let me go when this is over?"

"Yes."

* * *

Half asleep, Travis Bailey stood in front of his bedroom mirror. He buttoned his white shirt and tucked it into his trousers. As he straightened the button line in the shirt to meet the zipper line of his trousers (the gig line, as it was called at Pascoe Military Academy), he mused, as he had while he showered and shaved, over the possible causes of his recent insomnia. As Delsey flitted back and forth between the bedroom and the bathroom ratting her hair, he realized that she was, without doubt, one of the causes. He was getting sick of her. He just could not bring himself to fuck her in the morning any longer.

She came out of the bathroom and joined him at the mirror. "I want to handle some forgery cases," she said. "When you get Cleaver's job, don't forget." She applied lipstick and leaned forward to check it in the mirror. "Did you hear what I said?"

He nodded and wished she would disappear.

After tying a perfect Windsor knot in his necktie, he fastened a holster onto his belt and slipped the belt through the belt loops on his trousers. He shoved his .38 into the holster, then put on a sport coat.

Bailey wordlessly headed out the front door. As he waited for Delsey Piper in his car, he wondered for the thousandth time what Carr knew. On the other hand, he mused, maybe the newspaper article about the Chicago informant meant that Carr was truly on the wrong track. Without thinking he started the engine. He rubbed his eyes for a while, yawned.

Delsey soon came out of the apartment and got in the passenger side. "Why didn't you wait for me?"

He ignored her and drove to the police department.

Bailey parked in the police lot and made his way up

the two flights of stairs to the Detective Bureau. Delsey followed.

"You've been acting really weird lately," she said.

He grunted.

During the next hour as he took routine phone calls, he drank three cups of coffee and started to feel better. Mollified for the moment, he went to the men's room and came back with a wet paper towel, which he used to wipe a coffee ring off the glass top of his desk. Though it was unnecessary, he cleansed the entire glass and used another towel to wipe it dry. He tossed the used paper towels into the waste can.

Bailey sat behind his desk again, picked up the receiver and dialed Bones Chagra's number.

Chapter 18

BONES CHAGRA's living room was overwhelmed by an artist's rendition of a reclining, pointy-breasted nude that had been painted on the inside of the white drapes.

Charles Carr pulled the drawstring and the nude separated at the waist. Midday sun filled the apartment. Chagra, who was lying on the sofa, covered his eyes with a forearm. Higgins sat at the kitchen table reading the paper.

The furniture in the spacious apartment was modern—white sofas with tube-shaped pillows, pendulous chrome floor lamps, a pink easy chair with an ottoman shaped like a heart. The walls were covered with color photographs of various sizes: Bones Chagra standing behind a bar with his arms around two blondes, Bones Chagra on the beach with his arm around a bikinied young brunette, Bones Chagra frolicking in a pool with three bare-breasted women. In one corner of the room was a pile of oversized pillows and a movie projector aimed at the wall.

Carr sat down in an easy chair.

"Are you clear about what you're supposed to say?" Carr said.

"What if he doesn't want to talk about it?"

"Then you *make* him talk about it," Carr said. "Argue with him, threaten him, do whatever you have to to make him open up. The only way we can make a case on him is to get him to talk about the murder on tape. If you don't get him to talk, your deal is off. We drive you down to the county jail and book you. It's as simple as that."

Chagra sat up, rubbed his eyes. "Let's say he *does* talk about the murder. Then what do I do?"

"Then you let him drive you back to your car."

"What if he gets suspicious and searches me? What if he finds the wire? *Then* what the fuck do I do?"

"We'll be able to hear everything that goes on," Carr said.

"I could get killed."

"And L.A. might have an earthquake today," Higgins said. He turned another page.

"I feel like a scotch and water," Chagra said. "Is it okay if I make myself a drink?"

"No," Carr said.

Chagra gave a sigh of disgust and lay back down on the sofa.

Suddenly the telephone rang. Chagra sat up as if he'd received an electrical shock. He reached for the phone sitting on the coffee table in front of him.

Carr made a "take-it-easy" motion with both hands. He hurried to the bedroom and placed his hand on the receiver of an extension. Stepping into the bedroom doorway, he nodded to Chagra. They lifted the receivers simultaneously.

"Was it there?" Bailey said.

"Even more than you said would be there." Chagra stared nervously at Carr.

"We'll get together tomorrow."

Carr shook his head violently. He mouthed the word *today.*

Chagra swallowed. "There's something we need to talk about."

"I'm listening."

"Somebody paid me a visit. They asked me about—"

"Not on the phone," Bailey interrupted.

"Can you come over?"

There was a silence. "I'll pick you up in front of the Blue Peach in an hour," Bailey said and hung up.

Carr set the phone down and stepped back into the living room.

Bones Chagra was wringing his hands. "He sounds more suspicious than usual."

Carr noticed that Chagra's face had lost color.

Higgins picked up a medium-sized black leather suitcase off the floor and set it on the sofa. He unsnapped the latches and flipped it open. It was filled with electronic equipment fitted into Styrofoam padding. He removed a miniature transmitter attached to a long wire and a small battery pack. "Take off your shirt, Bones," Higgins said as he examined the equipment.

Bones shook his head, backed away from the detective. "I don't think I can do it. I'm too nervous. He'll know something is wrong as soon as he looks at me. Besides, this whole thing turns my stomach. I've never ratted on anyone in my whole life."

Higgins and Carr exchanged worried glances.

"It's your choice," Carr said to Chagra. "If you want to do Bailey's time that's strictly up to you. But I'll tell you right now that if you back out on us, we'll interview Bailey right after we book you. And we'll tell him that you handed him up. We won't have enough evidence to arrest him, so he'll beat the rap. And you'll be in jail wearing a snitch jacket."

More wringing of hands. Chagra rubbed his temples as he stared blankly at the floor. In a show of disgust, Higgins shoved the transmitter and battery pack back into the suitcase. He slammed the lid shut and snapped the latches.

Chagra turned toward the window. "Okay," he said. "I'll go through with it."

As Higgins flipped open the briefcase again, Carr phoned the Field Office and asked for B. B. Martin. He gave surveillance instructions and told him to pick up Jack Kelly, then hung up.

Chagra took off his shirt. It took Higgins less than fifteen minutes to tape the four-inch battery pack to the small of Chagra's back. He looped the microphone wire around his left shoulder and taped it above his collarbone.

Chagra put his shirt back on. The microphone was invisible.

"I'm scared to death."

"We'll be close by," Carr said.

Higgins packed up the briefcase. "Just relax and pretend you're not wearing it."

"But I am, man. If he finds it he'll kill me. I know he'll kill me."

They barely made it to the meeting spot on time. Carr parked the government sedan around the corner from the Blue Peach and let Chagra out. He walked to the corner and turned right toward the nightclub.

"I have our boy in sight," Kelly said over the radio.

Carr clicked the transmit button twice to acknowledge receipt of the transmission.

"I can see him too," B. B. Martin said. The radio made a squelch sound.

Higgins sat in the passenger seat with the transmitter briefcase open on his lap. He adjusted the volume. There was the sound of footsteps and the rustling of clothes. "If Bailey doesn't admit to the murder on the tape, we're through. There's no way the district attorney will ever file a murder charge on him."

Carr didn't respond. He knew Higgins was right.

A few minutes later the radio buzzed. "We have an arrival," Kelly said.

Carr started the engine and put the car in gear.

"Bones is getting in the passenger side," Kelly said. "It's a white police sedan with no markings. He's taking off southbound . . . southbound and pulling up to a stoplight."

Carr stepped on the accelerator and raced to the corner. He proceeded slowly around the corner. As he made the right turn, Bailey's car was a block or so ahead.

Static buzzed from the transmitter. Higgins adjusted the dials frantically. More static. He plugged and unplugged the recording jack, flipped switches. More squelch sounds. "Come on, you son-of-a-bitch." He slapped the sides of the briefcase.

". . . half gold and half silver," they heard Bones Chagra saying. "I haven't even looked at the coins real close yet." Higgins turned up the volume.

"Where are they?" Bailey said.

"I've got the coins in a rental locker. But that's not what's important right now. Carr just paid me a visit. He was with some guy from L.A.P.D. Homicide. They asked me about Amanda. I think they know something."

"Tell me exactly what they said." Bailey's voice was calm, almost soothing.

As the transmitter volume became weaker, Carr stepped on the gas. Ahead, he saw Bailey's police car pull into a lane leading to a freeway on-ramp. The car entered the northbound freeway. A traffic light turned red and vehicles in both lanes stopped in front of Carr. He backed up and swerved around the tie-up in a parking lane. Cross-traffic sped by, blocking him from going through the red light. The voices on the transmitter faded to nothing. The Treasury radio barked with Martin's and Kelly's voices. They had lost sight of the police car.

Brakes from the oncoming traffic squealed as Carr slammed the accelerator to the floor and zoomed through the red light and onto the freeway.

Travis Bailey flicked the turn indicator and exited the freeway. He turned right on Santa Monica Boulevard and drove east for a mile or so. He made a left turn onto a manicured residential street and continued north toward Sunset Boulevard. He noticed that Chagra kept wringing his hands.

"So they asked me what I was doing the night Amanda Kennedy was killed," Chagra said. "I told them, 'How the hell do I know what I did on such and such a day? I don't keep a daily diary.' DeMille, the bondsman, gave them my name. He told them that I put up the money to bail Amanda out of jail. The rotten bastard copped out on me. So Carr says he wants me to come down to his office to make a statement. I said no, but I'm worried, Travis, really worried."

Travis Bailey said nothing. He made a left turn on Sunset Boulevard. A block later, he turned right onto a side street and then left into a steep driveway leading to the porticoed entrance to the Beverly Hills Hotel. He proceeded up the driveway and turned into the outdoor elevated parking lot, which faced the front of the hotel. A black limousine with smoked-glass windows was parked at the front door.

"I don't want you making any statements," Bailey said as he gazed at the panorama of million-dollar homes below.

"I have to tell 'em something," Chagra said. "If I just clam up they can get me for being an accessory. I bailed her out of jail and she ends up dead. They can arrest me."

"So let them arrest you. They'll never get the case filed. They don't have enough evidence."

Chagra's hands were shaking. He clasped them together. "That's easy enough for you to say. Nobody's knocking on *your* door."

"And if anybody does knock on my door, I'll know just who gave them my address," Bailey said. "You and Emil are the only ones who know I killed her."

Chagra licked her lips, cleared his throat. "What if they trace the bullets to your gun?"

"I didn't use my gun."

"How did you—"

'I squeezed her neck," Bailey said. "Which is exactly the same thing I'd do to both of you if I thought you were going to talk." He smiled coldly.

A sedan with two men drove out of a side street west of the hotel. Slowly, it entered the parking lot entrance. Another police-type sedan occupied by two men drove past the front of the hotel and drove in the parking lot's exit lane. The passenger in the car looked like Jack Kelly and the black man driving was the same man he'd seen drive past him as he stood in front of Chez Doucette.

The cars were moving toward him; a car horn sounded three times.

Frantically, Bones Chagra fumbled for the door handle.

Bailey grabbed him by the hair. Chagra yelped as his head was jerked backward. Bailey's left hand tore open the front of his shirt.

"They made me do it," Chagra cried.

Brakes squealing, the sedans blocked him in from behind; their doors swung open. Chagra pulled away from his grasp, flung the door open and vaulted out of the car. He ran and dove for cover behind Martin's car.

Travis Bailey pulled his gun. Checking the rearview mirror, he saw that men were shielded behind the doors of the sedan in the usual "felony-stop" police configuration.

"It's over," Carr shouted. "We have you on tape. Place your hands on the steering wheel."

Travis Bailey squeezed the butt of his revolver. He glanced down at it, then at the rooftops that started across Sunset Boulevard and extended south on wide streets to the Beverly Hills business district. The thought of bending over waiting for a swat in the Pascoe Military Academy commandant's office flashed through his mind, as did the memory of peeking out a dormitory window and watching his mother walk out the front gate of the Pascoe Military Academy. The wind had carried the smell of her cologne.

There was the sound of sirens in the distance.

He touched the barrel of the revolver to his temple.

"Don't do it!" Carr screamed.

Bailey pulled the trigger.

With the blast from the gunshot was the sound of breaking glass. As Bailey's head slammed against the driver's window, Carr dropped his .38 to his side, left the safety of the car door and crept slowly toward Bailey's sedan. As he reached the rear fender, he saw the bullet hole on the blood-sprayed driver's window. Bailey was slumped against the steering wheel. Carr holstered his weapon.

Jack Kelly walked to the passenger side of the car and peered in. "Holy Mother of Christ," he said. Carefully, he leaned in the passenger door, reached across the seat and touched Bailey's neck. He drew his hand away and backed away from the sedan. He looked at Carr and shook his head.

Higgins used the car radio to call for the coroner.

B. B. Martin handcuffed Chagra and shoved him in the backseat of his sedan. Having locked the car, he removed a rope from its trunk. By looping the rope around bumpers and door handles of the vehicles parked on either side of Bailey's sedan, he secured the crime scene. He got into his car, started the engine and drove over to where Higgins stood with Carr and Kelly.

Reaching behind him, Martin swung open the rear door. Higgins climbed in the backseat next to Chagra and shut the door. He leaned his head out the window to speak. "We'll book him in and see you back at the Field Office," he said. He sat back in the seat.

"You said you were going to let me go!" Chagra screamed.

Carr nodded. B. B. Martin put the sedan in gear and drove out of the parking lot.

During the next two or three hours, police and emergency vehicles sped in and out of the parking lot. Various police brass, including Captain Cleaver and the Beverly Hills Chief of Police, arrived and departed, as did Special Agent in Charge Norbert Waeves and the

Chief of Detectives of the Los Angeles Police Department. Delsey Piper broke into tears after seeing the body and was helped away from the scene by another policeman.

In the midst of the activity a doorman dressed in gray tails and an Austrian soldier's hat helped people in and out of Rolls-Royces and limousines. Carr noticed that some of the people arriving at the hotel pointed at the jumble of police cars. Others did not.

Coroner's deputies wearing olive drab overalls finally arrived and lifted Bailey's body onto a gurney, then covered it with a plastic sheet.

"I can't help but feel sorry for him in a certain way," Kelly said. He stared at the body as it was loaded roughly into the Coroner's station wagon. "Nothing is so bad that a man should take his own life."

"He might have beat the case in court," Carr said somberly. He continued to make notations in a small notebook.

A thirtyish man with suntanned features and a tailor-made suit approached from the direction of the hotel. He introduced himself as the resident hotel manager. Carr nodded and kept writing.

"May I ask how long you people plan to be here?" he said.

Carr stopped writing and looked up at the man.

"We're short parking spaces because of a studio party," he said.

Carr and Kelly both glared at the man. He turned and hurried back to the hotel.

Chapter 19

IT WAS after nine o'clock by the time Carr arrived at his apartment that night. He heard the phone ringing as he unlocked the front door. Hurrying inside, he picked up the receiver. It was Sally Malone.

"I thought you might like to join me for a late dinner," she said. "No big thing."

"Sure," he said, though he wasn't hungry because of what had happened earlier. At her suggestion, they agreed to meet at a small seafood restaurant on the Santa Monica Pier that was an equal walk from either of their apartments.

Knowing she would never arrive anywhere before him, he decided to wait for her outside at the entrance to the pier. She arrived a few minutes after him, wearing a new jogging outfit. They touched lips and headed toward the restaurant, a tiny weathered building situated in the middle of the pier next to a bait shop. Its only identification was a flaking sign over the door that read Seafood. Inside, the tables and small bar were filled. They stood at the bar while a young T-shirted bartender whose nose was covered with a layer of zinc oxide served them drinks.

Though Carr felt like downing the drink in one gulp, he settled for a healthy sip. "It looks like Jack's not going to retire after all," he said because he couldn't think of anything else to say at the moment.

"I'm happy for him if that's what he and Rose want."

The bartender pointed them to an open table in the corner. They took their drinks and sat down.

"May I ask you something?" Sally said.

"Sure."

She shook her head. "Never mind."

"Go ahead and ask."

"Would you have asked me to marry you that night if you hadn't been drinking?"

There was a pause while Carr sipped his drink. "I'm not sure," he said finally.

"Then I guess the trip was nothing more than a drunken fling."

"I didn't say that."

"You've never brought marriage up before or since."

Carr fidgeted in his seat as he tried to think of something to say. "Look," he said, "I asked you and I'm not going to back out on it. On the other hand, I don't think there's any real hurry at this point. No use rushing in—"

Sally gently reached over and put her hand over his mouth.

A few minutes later a lanky waitress who wore a T-shirt similar to the bartender's came and took their order of steamed clams and beer. The walk and the liquor had perked up Carr's appetite.

During the meal, Sally recounted what she'd learned from a recent health food seminar she'd attended (all meat contains cancer-causing substances) and gossiped about Judge Malcolm's wife. Carr wondered, as he had before, if he could bear listening to such drivel every night of the week. But as the evening wore on and he continued to drink, he came to the realization that he probably could. She was his friend as well as his lover, and, he reminded himself, nobody is perfect. Not even—he thought philosophically—Carr.

Later that evening they walked from the restaurant along the dimly lit pier, taking in the sound of their footsteps on the wooden walkway, waves slapping and swirling against pilings and, faintly, from the business district east of the beach, a siren.

And elderly couple riding bicycles with tiny lights attached to the handlebars whizzed by them and continued into the darkness as they followed a cement walkway along the strand toward Sally's place.

"I'm not an easy person to live with," he said, surprising himself.

"I'm not either. We'd probably end up hating one another."

The sound of the waves seemed to grow louder.

Suddenly Sally stopped and threw her arms around him. Oblivious to others who walked by, they held each other tightly. When they got chilly Carr put his jacket around her shoulders and they continued on to her apartment.

The next day at the Field Office, Carr used his notes to prepare a written report that stated, in effect, that he had been assisting Detective Higgins in an investigation of the Leon Sheboygan incident. Under the preprinted section marked Details of Investigation he wrote the following: "*See the official L.A.P.D. reports of Detective*

Higgins, Robbery-Homicide Division for investigative information. Case is in jurisdiction of L.A.P.D." As he was writing, the phone on his desk rang. He picked up the receiver. It was Higgins.

"How does this sound?" Higgins said. "Investigating Officer was assisting U.S. Treasury Agents. See Treasury files for further information."

"Sounds good."

"Catch ya later," Higgins said and hung up.

Jack Kelly trudged into the office. He looked tired and his necktie was askew. "The public defender is making a big issue about the trick we played on Bones Chagra—"

"No law against lying," Carr said.

"—and the Beverly Hills chief is screaming because we didn't notify him that we were working a case on one of his detectives."

"Figures."

"And the district attorney has assigned a team of investigators to look into the whole incident. They're interviewing Higgins now."

The intercom barked. It was No Waves. He wanted to see Carr in his office right away. Carr walked down the hall. Waeves was on the phone. Carr sat down in the chair he pointed to with his pipe.

"Yes," Waeves said in a lowered voice. He swiveled around his chair, so Carr could see the bald spot on the back of his head. "One case of the raspberry and one case of the strawberry. And of course you won't forget the law enforcement discount? Thank you." He swiveled around again and hung up the phone. "Three-zero-two-point-five," he said with one of his forced smiles.

Carr furrowed his brow as if he didn't understand what No Waves was talking about.

"Three-zero-two-point-five," No Waves repeated.

"The section in the Manual of Operations requiring special agents to promptly brief the special agent in charge of all ongoing investigation. I'm afraid you're in violation of this section because you failed to keep me apprised of what you were doing on the investigation. I'll have to write you up. I hate to do it, but I have to cover myself. Unfortunately, covering one's ass is part of the game." Another forced smile.

Carr said nothing.

"Well?" Waeves said. "Don't you have anything to say?"

Yes, thought Carr, *I'd like to say that you are a prick.*

The intercom on the desk buzzed. "A news reporter on line three," a secretary said.

No Waves picked up the receiver, listened for a moment. "That's correct," he said. "It was an ongoing organized crime investigation. I directed my men to stake out a number of locations and the plan was successful. My plan worked. We were able to draw out the Mr. Big in the operation, who, as it turned out, was a police detective . . ."

Carr stood up and walked out of the room.